MW01075685

BATTLE WITH FIRE

Also by K.F. Breene

BATTLE WITH FIRE

FIRE

By K.F. Breene

Copyright © 2021 by K.F. Breene

All rights reserved. The people, places, situations and craziness contained in this book are figments of the author's imagination and in no way reflect real or true events.

Contact info:

www.kfbreene.com

books@kfbreene.com

CHAPTER 1

"P<small>ENNY</small>, P<small>ENNY</small>, P<small>ENNY</small>, *Penny!*"

"Saying my name over and over is not going to help me steer this boat!" Penny shouted at me. She squinted through the glass of the captain's area...or cockpit or whatever it was called. Penny's boat jargon fell on deaf ears. One of her hands clutched the steering wheel and the other gripped the red knob marking the throttle.

My butt slammed against the fiberglass surface at the front—bow?—of the convertible fishing boat. The rough sandpaper stuff, intended for grip when standing to fish in still waters, rubbed against my leather-clad butt before I went airborne again. Jaw tight, I gripped the calf-high metal railing, not nearly high enough to keep me from whipping overboard and into the turgid waters of the gulf. Then again, I was pretty sure no one was supposed to sit up at the front while the boat was jamming through the waves.

"It's over there—right, Penny, *right!*"

"Starboard side," she yelled as a spray of water

splashed the glass windshield.

I blinked salt water out of my eyes before throwing up an air shield. Only it turned out water marred visibility on air just like it did with glass. I mean…I should've known, but who stopped to think about things like that when chasing a grotesque water sprite through rough waters?

"Starboard!" I watched as the jengu's wooly-haired head disappeared beneath the sparkling surface, the afternoon sun reflecting rays bright enough to blind me. "Go starboard!"

The engine roared and the boat swung right. My butt slammed into the fiberglass again as we took another wave. A slap of spray hit my air shield.

Water sprites were known for curing diseases and helping sick kids reach adulthood. Or so I'd heard. I didn't know if there was any truth to it—I only knew that the one we were after was a bit of a dick. He was supposedly haunting these waters with the intent to kill the merpeople during their mating ritual.

Yes, I did offer my services to the Magical Law Enforcement office so that I could spy on merpeople and figure out how they mated. Absolutely I did. I'd been wondering all this time, and this was my chance to hopefully answer that burning question. Bringing in the water sprite and finally claiming the crown of best agent over Garret, my dickface former colleague, would be pure bonus.

"You're going to lose him!" I yelled at Penny, the words ripped from my mouth by the lashing wind.

The being crested the waters straight ahead, thirty yards out.

I see it, Penny thought, adjusting our direction.

Who would've thought she could handle a fishing boat like this? I would've asked how she'd learned, but I was afraid she'd answer, and I'd be treated to a boring story of family bliss.

I chanced a look to the side and then behind. Garret and the captain trailed us by some distance, a lot more cautious than Penny on these rolling waters. Then again, they hadn't stolen money from their rich boyfriend and rented the fastest fishing boat they could find. Neither had Penny, of course, but she was always easy to lure into trouble. Two more boats came along behind them. We were safely in the lead and closing in fast on the water sprite.

"Okay, Penny, nice and easy." I peered out through the transparent spell Penny had devised, muffling our sound and rendering us mostly invisible. We could sneak up on this SOB even in the water. It was good to be friends with a natural mage.

The boat plowed through the waves, full steam ahead. Clearly she hadn't heard me.

"Penny!" I turned back so that she could see I was

talking to her. "*Nice and—*"

The boat's engine cut dramatically, and with it our forward trajectory.

"Holy—!" My ass slid across the rough sandpaper stuff. Leather on slick fiberglass squeaked as I sailed across the wet surface and to the point at the front. More sandpaper stuff tried to grab me, but I was going too fast. "Shit birds!"

My body hit the railing, rolled over, and I was falling.

The boat swung right, away from me, Penny seeing what was happening. My body crashed down into the water before I could think to hover. Dripping wet but in the air a moment later, I watched as Penny goosed the power until the prop at the back was a safe enough distance away.

Thank God for those family fishing trips or whatever had made her a fishing boat master.

The boat slowed once more, and she was hurrying out of the captain's area and edging closer to our quarry. I could feel the spell she was devising even from here. She was in go mode and obviously didn't plan to come back for me.

I'd saved her ass from the elves and a prison in the Underworld, and she was leaving me behind on a jengu fishing trip? The nerve of that woman.

I was so proud. It was annoying when she was too

nice.

Hovering higher, rolling fire over my body to burn off the residual water, I drifted toward the fishing boat.

Shapes moved within the ocean's depths to my left, two figures floating just below the surface.

My attention snapped like a rubber band, Penny and the jengu forgotten.

A wave rolled by, washing up to my waist. I created an air bubble around me and lowered into the water. The next wave rolled over my air bubble, not touching me. I had plenty of air to breathe, though I didn't need it.

Two merpeople floated five feet below the surface, lowering slightly as their fins swayed in sync. The mermaid smiled up at the merman, no regard for anything but him. She floated on her back beneath him, her hands clasped around his neck. His touch caressed her exposed breasts, occasionally pausing to remove her flowing golden hair from around her chest.

This was it. *This was it!* I was giddy with anticipation. Penny might be embarrassed by voyeurism, but I definitely was not.

I lowered a bit farther just in case stupid Garret came roaring by and his boat prop was deep enough in the water to puncture my air bubble and rip off my head.

The man's touch flowed down her sides now and

along her scaly hips, the light dimming. He leaned forward with a passionate kiss, pulling his groin area—which was all fin, from what I could see—away from hers—which was also all fin at the moment.

I drifted closer, wishing I could record this on my phone, but thankful at least for my fantastic vampiric memory, courtesy of my bond with Darius. I'd remember everything as vividly as if I'd taken footage.

The merman tensed, and I knew something was happening, but I couldn't see what. The couple was still kissing passionately, his hands on her hips, her arms around his neck.

Gritting my teeth, I lowered a little more, knowing I didn't have all day. Penny might take her new attitude to the bank and leave me out here. I wouldn't put it past her. She blamed me, for some reason, for the way she'd let loose in a demon sex club. Dirty birdie. Darius had filled me in. I could tell he found great humor in the whole thing.

The couple stopped in their watery descent, and then started floating upward again, apparently liking the feel of the water softly moving around them. I got it. Water banging was a good time.

The guy continued to tense, and then I saw it! From a slit in his front emerged his dick, shaped like normal but longer and with an engorged tip. It was basically coming out of the fly in his fin suit.

I'll be damned.

It curved upward at the root and kept growing, now on the *very large* side. If Darius was working with that thing, I'd pat him on the head and tell him he'd have to be a bottom, because no way.

Passion intensified between the couple, the kisses turning fervent, his fingertips going white as he gripped her hips. He lowered toward her, and this was it. It had to be. This was what I'd been waiting for. Merpeople banging. An as-yet-unsolved mystery.

I drifted closer, in rapt attention. Penny could leave me for all I cared, I would get this payoff, and I'd finally know what these folks got up to during their watery mating ritual, something they kept very close to the chest. I needed to know why!

His massive dick drifted closer to her, and he eased her up a little so they weren't totally lined up anymore. He pulled her closer, and his tip touched just below her fin-covered groin. It would be like poking a woman in the triangle at the top of her closed thighs.

Her moan was audible, even in the water. Clearly that was a sensitive spot.

Drifting ever closer, since they didn't seem to notice my presence, I watched in scientific fascination as his length pushed against her scales. Her scales dented but didn't part. He moved his hands a little higher on her hips, getting a better grip. I nodded with his efforts.

Make it happen, bro. You're almost there!

He moved up a little, but she spread her hands across his shoulders and pushed him back down. He'd had the right spot the first time. So what was the holdup?

Time ticked past. I hoped Penny didn't think I was drowning and crash down here looking to save me. She'd bust up the party, and I was on the precipice of this thing. I had to see it through! *They* had to see it through.

He pushed again, that massive member seeking entrance, but there was nowhere for it to go. The gal put her palms against his cheeks and increased the fervency of their kiss. She pushed her lower half against him, clearly willing him inside. Uh-oh. It kinda seemed like she was trying too hard. Trying for something that she knew likely wasn't going to happen. But why not? What was the problem?

He thrust forward, readjusted, and thrust again. She moved against him, like a woman trying to get wet so the man could slip in. His next thrust was wild, and she flinched, her hands moving from his cheeks to his shoulders, the classic "That hurts, and if you don't get the hint from my lightly pushing, I will buck you the fuck off."

Their lips came apart, and I could feel the disappointment emanating from them. His fingers relaxed, but he didn't let go, keeping his touch on her. They floated for a moment, his dick starting to retract, looking into each other's eyes. Sorrow shone brightly in her gaze, and frustration glittered in his.

Not a match, then. When merpeople mated, clearly it required more than attraction and the desire to bang. Interesting. I wondered how many of these trysts failed before they found their true mates. Did they date on shore and then try their hand at mating season? That would be a letdown if you loved someone in real life, but when you tried to fornicate in the deep sea, nothing happened.

The couple startled, their heads jerking my way. I drifted merely three feet away, staring intently.

Realizing I had been caught, I gave a thumbs-up. "Better luck next time," I yelled through my bubble, not sure if they could hear me. "It'll be okay. More merpeople in the sea, as they say. Question—do you guys just go looking for someone else right now, or is that it for the season?"

The guy's junk snapped the rest of the way into his fin pocket and he pushed the woman away. His meaty chest swung around, and suddenly I remembered that not everyone was like vampires. Some people weren't cool with voyeurism.

"Sorry!" I hovered my bubble backward and held up my hands. "Don't mind me. I was just passing by."

He rushed toward me, and I threw up an air wall, just as effective in water. He slammed into it, and I hightailed up to the surface.

Intruder, he thought, fighting against the air shield. *What is this thing that traps me?*

"Don't fight it. You don't want to add injury to insult in regards to your ego, know what I mean, bub?" I called through the water, still not sure if he could hear me. It didn't seem like it.

It struck me that they hadn't been thinking at all during their exchange. I would've known. That had to mean it was definitely something other than attraction, and they were acting on biology or something. So very interesting.

I wondered if shifters were like that? Vampires certainly weren't. I'd have to ask Roger, even though he definitely wouldn't want to answer. He got prickly whenever I pried into his sex life. Which I had been doing an awful lot since we'd brought our dragons to his secret residence. He had a couple of drawers full of women's lingerie, in two different rooms! He clearly brought a few special ladies over, maybe two at once, and had a good time of it. Would he give any details, though? *No!*

I crested the surface and kept rising, catching sight of Penny nearby on the back of our boat, her hands on her hips as she stared at Garret on the MLE captain's smaller fishing boat.

"Oh no," I murmured. He looked smug, and a smug Garret was the absolute worst thing in all the worlds, and that was saying something, given I'd been tortured by elves.

I pulled away the air bubble and sucked in a fresh gulp of crisp sea air as I lifted over the waves. Then, because I didn't want to cock-block Free Willy for too long, I released him from his air prison before I continued on toward Penny.

A splash was the only indication I had that something was amiss. Thick, wet arms wrapped around me from behind, dragging at me. I startled and turned, whipping the merman around behind me, clinging to my back as I hovered.

"Dude, you gotta let this go," I hollered, swinging around again. "Dang it, get off. This looks ridiculous."

"You are not permitted here," he ground out in rough, sexy tones. A spice of his magic coated my skin, prickling my nipples pleasantly. Heat wormed through my core, suddenly pounding.

"Oh wow, is that part of it too?" I gripped him with air so he couldn't get spooked and fall off. Still hovering, I drifted toward the boat, working at this next piece of the puzzle. Two birds, as it were. "You're making me horny even though you're mad at me. Do mermen make their women horny on land, too, or just in the water?"

"What are you?" he asked, looking down at the water he was now floating over. He kept his firm hold on me, though, jerking, trying to take me down into the depths with him. Courageous, this merman. Gallant, too. He was likely doing this to protect the woman who wouldn't, or couldn't, open her lady bits for him.

"Yeah, bad choice in accosting me. I'm Lucifer's daughter—a very big deal, I must say. I'd offer you a business card, or more proof, but he basically tried to trap me down there and force me to follow his will. Not a great father-daughter relationship, I'm afraid. I'm now wanted by two worlds in a very bad way. So…now we know about each other's lives. Tell me, do you blast that horny feeling to bring all the girls to the yard? Then you try to bang them and eventually find the right fit, right? Also, is your human cock that big?"

"Our mating is private." He ripped at me, his arms like thick bands of steel. His thoughts poured into my head. *What is holding me? What magic is this?* "It is only for our kind to witness."

"Except you're in public waters. Have you never heard the expression *get a room*? This is hardly my fault. Though I can understand wanting to keep it private, what with the rejection… Her body basically cock-blocked you. That's intense."

As we neared the boat, I chanced a look at his face,

something I hadn't paid much attention to when watching the almost-fornication earlier. Strong cheekbones, straight nose, defined jaw, and deep-set eyes with thick black lashes. Quite the looker. He could've graced the big screens.

"You can at least bang ladies topside, right? You surely have no problem there?" I asked.

Penny caught my progress out of the corner of her eye and turned, face red and screwed up in frustration. "Reagan, stop messing around with that merman. The captain says this is a shared kill, but I was the one who did all the work. I didn't ask for any help!"

"Let me free." He thrashed against my magic, his power ballooning out and eroding at my air. Not enough to break it, but enough to hint at the strength of his magic. Maybe that was why the woman had been so disappointed by the mismatch—he was probably a catch in the mer-world, what with his looks and his power level. "Let me down or I will send out a request for aid."

I huffed in annoyance. "*Fine.*" I released the air, so many questions left unanswered, and flung him away. He bent and arched at the last moment, diving into the water instead of flopping like I would've. In a moment, he was gone.

My feet touched down on the standing area at the back of the boat.

"What took you so long?" Penny demanded. "I

could've used your help."

"Any other time, I would be sorry, but boy have I got an earful for you!" I pushed my wet hair out of my face and stepped closer to the MLE captain's boat. The other boats drifted some distance away, waiting for instruction.

The jengu lay on the captain's boat without a net, its arms pale green and its lower half an enormous fin, similar to the merpeople. A thick mop of hair covered its face and what had to be sightless eyes.

"What happened?" I asked the captain, standing behind Garret with a clipboard.

"I'll tell you what happened—"

"I didn't ask you," I told Garret, spearing him with a glare. His mouth clicked shut, and his pinched, weaselly face glowered at me. They'd all heard what I truly was. Most of them had gawked but said nothing, the captain had nodded thoughtfully, and Garret had raised his chin and said, "That doesn't stop you from being second best."

Man, I hated Garret.

"I closed in on the jengu," Penny said as the captain stepped closer, his black rain suit slick and the expression on his aging face placid. Garret and I had fought over many a victory. He was no stranger to waiting until someone got punched in the face. "I worked a spell to ensnare it—no small feat, because the creature had some sort of ability to resist magic clinging to it."

The captain frowned, his brows lowering. "That isn't typical of these creatures."

"She's just compensating for shoddy spell work," Garret said.

"Shoddy spell work?" Penny screeched. She still wasn't totally right in the head since leaving the Underworld two months before. She was getting back to normal but not quite there yet. "I am a natural dual-mage of the highest order in the newly defined Mages' Guild—"

"A guild you control. Cheat to win, huh?" Garret smirked.

"Why, you little ape's dingleberry," she said.

"Okay, okay." I put a hand on her shoulder, trying desperately not to laugh. For once it wasn't me fighting with Garret, which was the only reason it was comical. "Captain?"

He looked down at the creature, his dark brown skin creased in concentration. "It looks like one of their kind, but its actions certainly don't fit their mold. I've never heard of them resisting mages' spells." He threaded his pencil behind his ear and put the backs of his hands on his hips. "We've brought in a few creatures with unexplained characteristics over the last few months, some with unexplained behavior and some far from home. This is just another occurrence in a growing list."

He frowned, and I knew that look—there was a puzzle to work out. In the past, I would have welcomed the weird. I would have sat back and waited for the jobs to roll in. Now, however, I knew what the bigger picture looked like. The war of the worlds. These strange occurrences might be related to that, but either way, a few rogue water sprites or whatever were the least of anyone's problems.

"Okay, so after you ensnared it?" I asked Penny.

"I—"

I gagged Garret with my magic. His eyes bugged out.

"Yeah. I can do that now," I told him. "Penny?"

"I left it floating there, spitting obscenities at me, as I turned the boat around."

"Why didn't you just kill it then?" I asked.

A vein throbbed in her locked jaw. She stared at me defiantly.

I hazarded a guess: "You felt bad?"

"I just wanted to make sure it was guilty," she responded.

I tore the gag off Garret so he could finish the story, because I knew full well what was coming. "What happened next?" I asked him.

"This is usually my job…" the captain said with a twinkle in his eye.

"Sure, fine." I waved him away. "Have at it."

He went back to his clipboard. "Nah. I don't have the ability to gag with air magic."

Garret's brow furrowed, and he glanced at the captain in outrage. I couldn't help but laugh.

He turned back to finish. "Seeing as she trapped the creature but couldn't kill it…"

Garret threw that smug smile Penny's way again. I had unraveled her invisibility spell when I left the boat, so he'd definitely known that she had it handled and was just getting the boat turned around. He'd wanted the prize.

Penny sputtered in indignation. I patted her shoulder to keep her from blowing up his boat. I liked the captain—I didn't want him to get caught in the crossfire.

Garret shrugged. "I naturally delivered the killing blow when the captain moved us within range and then hauled the beast up onto the boat. I did all the work, so I should—"

I lifted Garret with air and launched him over the side. He hit the water headfirst, his arms windmilling and his legs splayed. Hopefully he'd run into that merman from earlier.

"Captain, come on," I said, tilting my head. "You know that she had it covered."

"Honestly, I didn't see you on the boat and wondered if maybe you'd fallen overboard and she was looking for you," he replied. "By the time I knew what was what, Garret was hauling the creature onto our boat. I couldn't chance letting it get away."

"She fell overboard way back there!" Penny pointed behind her. "You must've seen that. Obviously I was leaving her to die."

The captain stared at her in disbelief, and I left my hand on her shoulder, fighting chuckles and losing.

"Captain, come on," I pleaded. "Penny closed in on the jengu, snared it, was about to do away with it, and Garret stole her prize. It's hers. You know it's hers."

He shook his head slowly and took a deep breath, glancing over his shoulder to where Garret was sputtering in the water.

"She didn't even retaliate." I pointed at Garret. "I did. She is totally by the book on this one."

The captain put up his hands helplessly. "It was a team kill, Reagan. My hands are tied. The kill goes to Garret, but Penny made it possible. Both of their names have to go in the books. They don't get anything special for it anymore—no bonuses or anything. We no longer have the budget for it. I'm not sure why it matters so much."

"It matters," Penny and I said together.

"It matters because he sucks," Penny added. She heaved out a sigh and turned toward the front of the boat. "Let's go, Reagan. I'm sick of these people."

"I thought she was the nice one," the captain called as she started the motor.

I threw him a wide smile. "I'm rubbing off on her."

"Poor thing," he yelled.

I waved as Penny expertly turned the boat and headed back for shore. I'd wait until the drive back to New Orleans to tell her what I'd seen. And then direct her to the bar, because after a run-in with Garret, a stiff drink was absolutely necessary.

Maybe I'd finally convince her to take her aggression out by chasing around a couple of shifters. There was no telling what post-Underworld Penny would do. Especially once she was on the battlefield in front of a host of non-friendlies.

Roger had gathered all the shifters that he could, and all the fae, and sent a demand to the elf king and queen that they step down. Obviously they didn't—who was he fooling? So now the whole outfit was resigned to doing as Charity's visions said they'd need to—stand between the two forces, stop them from killing each other, and reach some sort of compromise.

We were headed for bloodshed. Post-Underworld Penny would be just the ticket.

CHAPTER 2

L UCIFER'S BOOTS GROUND dirt between their soles and the sun-bleached, cracked sidewalk. Decrepit homes, shapes hunkering in the fading light, lined the right side of a narrow street, which played host to dented and scratched automobiles. A cemetery lurked on the left, devoid of tourists wandering around its walls.

A lone figure stood halfway down the block, opposite the pulse of his daughter, her demonic magic shining like a beacon in this dim world. He was on his way to her house in the Brink, a visit he'd spent the better part of two months planning. He wanted to get it right. There were...things to clear up. Things that would hopefully help them repair their relationship.

A door swung open in a pale green house, emitting a haggard sort of creature with too much padding around the middle and a face full of bristly white hair. It stopped on the front stoop, five steps up from the ground, and scowled at Lucifer passing by.

The look kindled rage in Lucifer's gut, banked one

moment and burning brightly the next. Magic seeped around him, fire licking his white button-up shirt and crackling through the air. He met that stare with his own, daring this creature to defend its territory. There were no masters in the Brink, not those silly were-humans, and certainly not the mortals. It was dog eat dog in this world, Lucifer knew well, and he was at the top of the food chain.

The man held Lucifer's stare for a solid beat, longer than any demon would dare. Longer than most mortals that Lucifer could remember, as well. Its—his—fuzzy white brows stitched together, and he huffed and glanced down the street. To Reagan's residence?

The human had plenty of reason to show fear—he must see that—but he didn't, and the reason was evident in that look. He thought someone bigger and badder would handle this territory breach.

A surge of pride wormed through Lucifer's gut. This was a rough neighborhood for humans. His daughter had clearly fought for her place, and she'd been recognized as owner of her domain. As a queen. Of course she had—it was a family right.

She belonged on the throne here just as she did on the throne he would soon offer her. He understood now why she hadn't wanted to forsake this place. It was a small kingdom, but it was hers all the same.

The creature—man—on the other side of the street

pushed back into the shadows as Lucifer neared. He lifted a square of power that brightened, blaring light onto a lined face and white hair. Were all these creatures old? Surely Reagan would've wanted a better challenge than that? Or was she protecting them from a greater foe…

Perplexed, he noticed the house reaching into the sky, taller and newer than its counterparts and expertly appointed. Ordinary flowers sat peacefully in little white boxes hanging off the railing, and the front yard was a carefully tended thatch of grass. Two polished wooden chairs sat on the porch, facing the cemetery opening, an interesting view for a dull day.

A man walked out of the house next to it, the residence a fading affair with chipping paint and ragged wood. Nails were trying to work their way out of the structure. The look on his dark brown face suggested such unspeakable menace that Lucifer had to laugh, delighted. His robust body, thick chest, and posture— hands hanging loosely at his sides—all suggested this human had some power strapped somewhere around his waist. He expected trouble and had no problem handling it with vicious resolve. Fantastic.

"Hello," Lucifer said, and offered a light bow. "What is your role here?"

The man tensed, and his eyes turned shrewd, as if he were working through an internal debate. His gaze swept Lucifer's person before flicking to what must be Reagan's residence.

"I ain't got no role with you fuckers," the man said, his voice deep and rough, as though someone had taken sandpaper to it. As though he had been screaming for all his life and no one had heard. What wonderful havoc he would create in the Underworld.

"Tell me, are you magical?" Lucifer asked.

"Fuck that shit." The man spat over the porch railing and onto the patch of dirt at the front of his house, dotted with weeds.

"How colorful." Lucifer continued on toward Reagan's house, and as he approached the steps, another presence caught his eye—a figure emerging from the bushes to the right of the porch. She approached him with a hunched posture, arms akimbo, a flurry of red hair around her head. Despite her strange hobble-walk, he recognized the grace behind her steps. "And a warrior fae. Quaint. It appears as though my daughter takes in strays."

"Your daughter, huh?" The woman straightened up, as though realizing her strange antics did not influence him. "You are a black hole to *Seers*. Did you know?"

"Yes. By design. I am the ultimate cheater, didn't *you* know? I can't very well have others spying on my plans, or the angels would always know what I was about. Scrying won't work, either. Your crystal ball will return only static. If I had known of your presence, it would've been the first thing I taught my daughter. I'll remedy that shortly."

"I do not advise that, not until the war is through."

The *Seer's* eyes filled with a gravity that made him pause with his foot on the first step.

"My goal is to keep Reagan alive," she said. "I must do everything in my power to help her…" The woman shook her hands above her head theatrically. "If she stays in the middle of the two factions at war, she will perish."

That stopped him short. He studied her for a moment, getting a read on her. There was no mistaking the mischievous glimmer in her pale eyes, the tiny smile playing about her lips, both seemingly unconscious. Very unlike the *Custodes*, for certain. But then, she was a *Seer*, not a warrior. She didn't belong exclusively to the fighting sect of their people, although she'd obviously been trapped with them before coming to the Brink. The warrior fae had been hiding in the Flush, he knew, until recently. A suffocating sort of place, Reagan had said. The *Custodes* could be suffocating creatures, so he believed it.

He checked out her odd choice of clothing—a clean, flowered apron over a dingy dress overlapping baggy purple sweats with holes in the knees. A foot-long broom handle stuck out of one of the pockets, the end filed down into a point, like a stake. A silent threat to the vampires, perhaps, who likely wouldn't take her seriously.

Her wild hair was ratty and unbrushed, and dirt marred her pale complexion. Her unkempt look had to be planned. She was going against the grain, as it were, of her very put-together *Custodes* counterparts.

Underneath all of that, though, he felt her frustration. Her plea for true freedom. Her wildness and her savagery. Her desire to play tricks and create mayhem. She had more to offer than what she'd been allowed to give, and she was begging someone to notice. Given the crow's-feet around her eyes and lines denting the skin around her mouth and on her forehead, she'd been waiting a long time.

"Do you come here often?" he asked, wanting a bit more information.

The violent man huffed, leaning on his railing, continuing to watch.

The fae didn't notice, her gaze glued to Lucifer. She knew he dealt in lies and tricks. Everyone did. She was trying to tread carefully.

It wouldn't matter, not unless his daughter interjected. Reagan was the only being to have thoroughly bamboozled him and lived to tell the tale.

"She is the favorite of the fates," said the fae, speaking more slowly than before. "I need to keep an eye on her."

He squinted an eye, and a smile stretched across his face. "Care to give a real answer?"

The man from across the street skulked closer, his hands in his pockets, watching the fae warily.

Ah. There was too big of an audience.

"How's this?" Lucifer sent a plume of fire at each of the watchers, shrouding them in hot air but not allowing the flames to touch their flesh. Reagan wouldn't take kindly to him infringing on her territory.

A squeal rent the air from the skulking man, and then he set off running, through the flame and toward the cemetery. Lucifer doused the fire from the man's head and clothes. He'd forgotten how prone to flight humans could be. The man's hair would suffer, but the flame probably hadn't touched skin for long enough to do more than give him a sunburn.

Lucifer tore the fire away from the violent man next door. Rather than run, he'd gone for the gun tucked into the back of his belt. Lucifer waved his hand and knocked the man's hand aside.

"The fire was not a threat. It was a request for privacy," he said.

"If you want privacy, ask for fucking privacy," the man responded. "If you want to get shot, try to light me on fire again."

"And you are not magical, correct?" Lucifer asked.

"Because it would be wonderful to have you come to the Under—"

"Don't even fucking say it." The man reached the gun around to his back, using the wide radius Lucifer was allowing him, and stuffed it into his belt. "Don't say another fucking word. Obviously you're busy..." He waved at the fae. "I don't want none of that. Handle your business." He jogged down the stairs and walked off in the opposite direction.

"He's not fond of knowing magic exists," the fae said with a grin.

Judging by her delight, she'd clearly taunted him in the past. Very mischievous, indeed.

"So. You've escaped the Flush," he said, monitoring her closely. "When this is all over, will you go back? Or will you stay here?"

"You asked if I come here often, and I do. As often as I am able, in fact. It isn't because this place is comfortable and crazy, though it is. It is because of the part I must play in all of this." She licked her lips. "My magic doesn't work like that of a normal *Seer*. I don't need cards or a crystal ball to use it. I don't need to study you or look into your eyes. If I am in tune with you, I *See* without trying. Without wanting to. I use hallucinogens and other mind alterants to crystalize my focus, or else I would be bombarded at times. Especially at a time where the future is so uncertain and there is so much at stake. My nemesis can step away from her trinkets and act normal, without feeling the pressures of her magic. I cannot."

She paused and pulled back her shoulders.

"I call the other *Seer* my nemesis for a reason. She is the light, and I am the dark. She is the one who must steer the shifters and the fae—the goody-goody crew. I am the one who needs to monitor Reagan, the princess of the Underworld." She cocked her head at him. "A title she can only claim if she lives, and that seems to be a very narrow outcome. There is something lurking in her future that I cannot quite grasp. It is her salvation, I know that much, and it is monumental. But it…"

She hissed and slowly curled her fingers into a fist.

"It is beyond me. All I see is death right now. A thousand ways she might die. More. My mind frays when I think of it. No amount of hallucinogens is helping. She is on a very shaky road, the drop on each side precipitous. I need…*more.* I need *Sight* on you."

He squinted at her, turning that over in his mind, when she continued.

"I'll also need to betray my faction in order to do my duty to them." She licked her lips. "I will be heavily policed. Maybe jailed, I don't know. I certainly won't be a favorite."

"And so you will need a place to go. A place that, you will be grateful to hear, can help with your *Seer* issues—your magic won't work in the Underworld. You'd go blind to the future."

"Yes." She sighed in relief.

He studied her for a moment. "You can't *See* me, so to speak, but…did you know I would come here?" he asked.

"I knew something big was going to happen in Reagan's life today. I made arrangements to make sure she wouldn't be home."

"Except…her demonic magic is pulsing in that house. If she is not there…"

"Oh yes, that." She waved it away. "She had Penny the mage rig up a spell with Reagan's blood to direct you here. She didn't want you to catch her out in the wild."

"Your idea…"

"Guilty. A good idea, nonetheless. I don't know where she is, though. I only know she will make a wonderful discovery, and it will likely be followed by drinking."

Clever, creating a spell like that. He hadn't known that could be done. It would explain the heightened feeling of it, something he'd thought could be attributed to Reagan's power level or maybe his attachment to her.

"You orchestrated that because you knew it would be me?"

"You're my only blind spot. I sensed Vlad was making an arrangement hours ago, securing the sort of power he would need to sweep through the Realm. The details were hazy, though, and I figured it was because *you* were involved."

"Yes. It seems it was not he who snuck into the Underworld. He had a traitor. I brought him that traitor, who had been left behind by some others, and found the viciousness with which he handled the situation to my liking."

"I know. I see his path with crystal clarity now. He is undermining Darius and a few of the dissenting elders as we speak, give or take ten minutes." She tilted her head up and looked at the sky. "The unicorns might be a problem for you. That is part of the deal he offered, but he cannot control the outcome. It will depend on the goodness of a certain heir."

Lucifer kept somewhat still, watching her. No one could've known they'd discussed the allegiance of the unicorns, given they'd done so while wrapped up in Lucifer's magic. Lucifer had come straight here—even if Vlad had spread the knowledge, and it would have hurt his cause to do so, it couldn't have traveled here so fast, especially not to this creature.

Her gaze came back to rest on him.

"We already knew you would work with Vlad, though, and the unicorns won't make or break you." Her stare was direct. "Reagan can, however. She can break you as no other heir could."

With her death, the *Seer* meant. He might be a blind spot for her, but she could still sense his attachment to his daughter. His hope for her. Insightful, this creature.

"She must be subtly directed," the *Seer* said. "You do want her to help destroy the elves' hold on the Realm, correct?"

He huffed a somewhat bitter laugh. "You will have a job manipulating her."

"I will not be manipulating her. I will be manipulating everyone around her. She is the most important piece of this battle. Reagan will finish the job that young Charity started when she brought about change. When she pushed the fae on this path. Reagan will be the one to initiate victory. I see spilled blood." She paused and furrowed her brow. "But that is it. I have no idea of an outcome. You must have a piece in this. You *must*. I just cannot *See* it."

Lucifer narrowed his eyes slightly. He wasn't following. He also wasn't sure how much sanity this creature was hanging on to.

"He is the only chance you have at keeping her on the right path," she continued. "Which is the only chance you have at keeping her in your life. And you are the only chance they have at having a family. Do you see? Everyone has a vested interest here, and to get to the end result we desire, we cannot follow the path of the righteous. We must follow the path of the villain."

She had to be talking about Durant, then. Reagan wouldn't want to sire children with anyone else. She'd made her attachment to the vampire abundantly clear.

"And...you will instruct him on which path to direct her to?" Lucifer asked.

"Of course not. She will guide him. You will need help from another."

His patience was starting to wear thin. "And who will that be?"

"A vampire who loves to straddle sides. One you would've caught had you not let Reagan go when she was escaping the Underworld. The villain to crown all villains. She is rooting for Reagan, as you are rooting for Reagan, but self-interest is her only motivation."

He stilled. That *was* useful information. She referred to the vampire who had left the Underworld shortly after Reagan's departure. The vampire had somehow moved through his kingdom undetected. He had hoped his daughter had another powerful ally, but apparently not.

This infestation would need to be dug out by the root. It was clear it would need to be him who did it. He had more skill than Reagan at dealing with meddling, dangerous creatures. More experience, at any rate.

"And what is in it for you?" he asked. "All this for a place to stay when it is all over? Mind you, your people will be able to find you in the Underworld, as Reagan would like to keep the borders open."

"They can find me if they want. I don't care. They'll walk in, but they'll limp out. I'd like to retire. I want that blindness you spoke of. But that's not why I do this. This is my purpose. Your daughter, who has not known peace of her own, will need to bring peace to others. She is the key to the prosperity of all the worlds. If she dies, we will all be thrown into darkness. I do this for her, and for us all. Sometimes to walk in the light, you need to first travel through the darkness."

"Why would you hide this from her?" he asked. "The woman I know would probably prefer the villain-ous approach."

"She would, but…it's complicated. My voice carries very little weight with Reagan. It has to do with a torturous situation."

He'd had about as much circuitous talking as he could take. "Fine. Send this vampire to me. I will see what can be done."

"There are two things I need first, however." She held up a crooked finger. "In addition to being able to *See* you."

"A deal with the devil? How droll."

"Yes. One, if Reagan should ask you to turn the vampire Vlad over, you must do it, whatever the cost."

He smiled and put up his hands. "Easily done. I enjoy betraying creatures that think too highly of themselves. Two months ago, I had planned to kill him, so really, in the grand scheme of things, he's making out quite well. I will first need to use his forces, however. I need those numbers."

Her eyes got a faraway look, and her gaze roamed into the sky. "If Vlad is delivered to Reagan, then Darius will need to make a choice. A choice that, if incorrect, could ruin their future."

"What is this choice concerning?"

She blinked at him. "Something about Darius's shared past with Vlad. I can't get a clear picture."

"And the outcome we are hoping for?"

"No clue."

"Dare I ask whose future? Reagan's or Darius's or Vlad's…"

She just shook her head. He stilled in annoyance.

"The second thing I must ask is for you to hold off your visit." She pointed at the ground. "Come back later tonight. Find her, and go to her unannounced."

"Find her, as in…you don't know where she'll be?"

"Correct. I have no idea. But it must be tonight, and then not again until…" She flexed her fingers. "Fogginess. You are blinding me!"

He barely stopped from rubbing his temples.

She squinted and chewed her lip. "I could really use some acid."

"If I don't allow you to get readings on me…"

"Reagan will die."

"You're sure?"

"No."

He felt his eyebrows rise. "Then what assurances do I have in trusting you?"

"A wing and a prayer."

CHAPTER 3

"JIMMY, LISTEN TO me, I know all about it." I stood beside the merman bouncer outside the Purple Bear. Penny had to pee really badly, so I figured I had a few moments to chat through the whole merpeople sex thing before I needed to get her drunk enough to forget about her first real Garret experience. The other time with him hadn't counted because she'd been too new to magic to feel the full weight of his annoyance.

"Yeah?" A big man with a unibrow and a permanent scar, he stood with wide legs and squared shoulders and basically scared underaged people with his mere presence.

He eyed my stringy ponytail. My hair had dried during the hundred-mile or so drive back into town, but without a brush, it gave the decided appearance of having been wet at one stage.

"How's that?" he asked.

I briefly described my watery voyeurism.

He shook his head and grabbed a young man's ID, checking it out before giving it back and jerking his head, allowing the man admittance into the bar. An older woman and man with him paused with raised eyebrows, obviously the kid's parents. They were probably thrilled they could now go to bars on family vacations. Jimmy waved them on.

"That won't make you any friends," he finally said.

"I already don't have any friends. I seem to break them all." I couldn't stop my gaze from drifting down to his crotch. "Question—"

"Don't start asking questions," he warned me, eyeing a couple of young women who'd stopped in front of the bar and looked in. They noticed his gaze, frowned, and started moving along. "That stuff is not talked about outside of our people. Just like the two dozen other times I've told you."

"Right. Got it. But is your junk the same size now as it is in water?"

"Fucking hell," he murmured, taking a middle-aged man's ID and barely flicking his eyes at it. He waved him in, along with the next few people in the party.

My gaze drifted down to his crotch again.

"How would I get my fucking pants on if it was that size all the time, Reagan?" he growled, the words nearly indistinguishable. That answered that. I was a little relieved for him.

"Do you have a mate?" At his scowl, I put up my hands. "That question is between friends. I won't tell."

"We're friends now?"

"Best friends, yes. Always have been. I lied earlier when I said I didn't have any. I have you." I gave him a wide grin.

He huffed out a laugh. "No, I do not have a mate." He glanced around. "Yes, I have tried every season since I was of age. The more powerful mermen can usually lure two or three women a season. I manage two, usually." I opened my mouth for the next question, but he seemed to know in advance what I was going to ask and then some. "No, matches aren't easy to find. Yes, sometimes you can tell when you're on land, but not always. When you find your mate, it's for life. Even if you split, you ain't gonna have kids with no one else. There is no point in even heading out to the water at that point."

"Mhm, mhm, hmm." I tapped my chin. "Lure, huh? Is that the feeling that made me horny?"

He rubbed his shaved head and ran his large hand over his face. "We shouldn't be having this conversation."

"I know, but honestly, I've got so many problems, I won't even think to tell anyone all of yours."

He looked down at me and furrowed his brow before huffing out another laugh and shaking his head. "You do got a lot of problems. I've heard."

"No, no." I put my finger in his face. He swatted it

away. "You first, then I'll tell you anything you want. Anything at all. Secrets? I'll spill them."

"Why do you care so much about my kind?"

"Mysteries were made to be solved, bud."

He sighed. "Yeah, that thing that made you feel horny is a constant…secretion is the wrong word. It's more like a constant vibe we have in the water. We enhance it to attract the ladies. The more powerful we are…"

"The better it works. Got it. So they come slinking around, and you try for the deed, and…biology shuts you down, or…?

"This is the last one."

"Fine, fine."

"The female's biology shuts us down, I guess you could say, yes. A female has to be ready, and her body knows what pairing would result in a blessing—a child. I don't know how, exactly, but I think there are a few factors, like her age, the guy's age, plus whatever vibes she gets from the male… We'll try and try until we find the right pairing, and then that's it."

"If you mate in the water, does that carry over onto the shore?"

"Yeah. It doesn't always last, because life, but you'll return as a couple and try to work it out. Some people end up with complete strangers. Some people find a mate in the water and have to break off their…situation with whoever they were seeing on land. That's a tough one. We don't often get involved long term with someone from a different species because it can't last. Even if we try to deny the urge to find a mate, we are called to the water. We can't help doing the dance. It's primal."

"Huh. That has made for some sticky situations in the community, I'll bet."

"Very. Your turn." He waved a group of questionable-looking guys on the younger side through. "Did you really get tortured by the elves?"

Memories crowded my mind. The sound of breaking bone, followed by screams. My screams, that seemed to go on and on in the darkness.

"Yeah," I said, turning and glancing at the dying sun. "Those bastards are pieces of shit." Rage filled my gut as I gave him a brief description of what I could remember of their dungeons. Of the pain that had threatened to strip me of consciousness. Of the hard stone floor where they'd left me after each session, two and three sessions in the day and night.

"And Lucifer pulled you out?" he asked, pulling me out of the darkness. Sometimes I got trapped in it, in the memories of the pain that part of me hadn't thought I'd ever escape.

I blinked a couple times before I gathered myself enough to answer. "Yes."

"You were really trapped down in the Underworld?"

"Yeah but...it was a good kind of trapped. I didn't feel like I was a hostage. I mean...I *knew* I wouldn't be allowed to leave, but given what I was doing and how long I was there, it didn't short-circuit me."

After I explained a little more—he *had* told me his secrets, after all, and fair was fair—he issued a long, low whistle and rocked back on his heels.

"That's some shit," he finally said.

"Yeah."

"And now you and the vamp are joining with Roger and them fae to go to war?"

"Yes," I said, and then unclenched my fist, thinking about standing in front of the elves and daring them to come at me again and see how it worked out a second time.

But then, I was supposed to be a peacekeeper, wasn't I? I was supposed to stop the Underworld and the Realm from destroying each other.

What a shitty job for a person who'd suffered at the hands of those horrible fuckers.

Then again, my father would've killed Darius, Penny, and Emery, not to mention Ja's posse of elder vampires, had I not interfered. My father had allowed another of his kids to torture my druid pal, Cahal, once upon a time. Was he any worthier of being saved than the elves? Could I make that distinction when push came to shove?

Because the thing was, I liked my dad, but I did not like those elves. Not one bit.

Basically, I was not the person who should be at the crux of this thing. I needed to go back to my job as a bounty hunter and let the big dogs handle everything.

If only.

"I still need to connect with the fae," I said. "We're supposed to be doing that in the next few days. Time to get ready. Playtime is over. Or so they tell me."

He stepped in front of me, his face deadly serious. "We've known each other a long time, Reagan Somerset. Years. I've dealt with your shit more times than I can count. You always start trouble in this bar. *Always.* You owe me." He paused dramatically. "Can I take a ride on your dragon?"

I released a breath, and let it flow into laughter. "If Roger lets you visit the super-secret lair where they're staying, or if we win this war and they're allowed into the Realm, or if I ever patch stuff up with my old man and we can go freely into the Underworld, then yes, you can ride Archion. He would tolerate you for a time, especially if I tell him about all the mermaid stuff."

Jimmy stared at me for another beat, nodded, and stepped back. "That would be fucking amazing."

I laughed again and continued into the bar, finding Penny on a barstool with a shot of whiskey, straight, sitting in front of her. Her shoulders were slumped, and a grumpy expression had taken up residence on her mug.

"It's not that bad." I scanned the bar before I took a seat next to her, not seeing any familiar faces. That was good. They wouldn't know to stop the bar fight I was keen on instigating. Jimmy would let me get away with a whole lot with a dragon ride on the line, I had no doubt.

"It is absolutely that bad, and you know it. What a stink-faced, weaselly little turd." She took a sip of her drink, then grimaced spectacularly.

I drummed my knuckles on the bar. "You're right. It is that bad. He sucks. I'll start a fight in your honor."

"I'm starting to understand why you're prone to them, with associates like that snarl-toothed dong we just had to endure."

It was hard to hide my glee at Penny's ill humor. Usually she didn't let it get to her this badly. She'd probably been happy to pull off a job of her own, for once, and then that dickface Garret had gotten in her way.

"We'll do another one." I nudged her with my shoulder. "We'll take another bounty-hunting gig and handle it without interference. I'll stand back and let you take point, how's that?"

She didn't say anything, but her shoulders lifted a

little.

"Reagan." Trixie sauntered down the bar, a few new tats decorating her chest, merging into the older ink flowing down her arms. The light from the bar sparkled off the stud in her right nostril and her blue hair had been cut at her cheekbones. "Back to cause trouble?"

I made like I was thinking. "Probably. How about a hurricane?"

She lifted her eyebrows. "Going big, huh?"

It wasn't rare for me to drop by for a hurricane, but hurricanes meant trouble if I planned to stay for a minute. I did love me some trouble. I missed demolishing stuff in the Underworld. In the Brink, you couldn't just destroy buildings with abandon and rip down walls. People got angry. The best you could do was kick in doors, and even that turned people off. It was very restricting.

"Yeah." I hooked a thumb at Penny. "She had a bad day. I'm drinking in solidarity."

A look of warning flared in Trixie's eyes. "Penny, I can't have you destroying this bar. I heard about the accident at the Mages' Guild…"

Penny and Emery had been at the Guild for most of the time since we'd returned from their excursion into the Underworld. She'd only come to NOLA because we were about to start the next phase of the Skirmish of the Worlds, and she wanted to regroup with the Bankses and me.

"What accident at the Guild?" I asked, sending an accusatory look her way. "You didn't tell me about any accidents."

"It was nothing. I was just trying out a spell and it backfired." She downed her drink.

"Leveling a building is what you call backfiring?" Trixie gave her a flat look and walked down to the other end of the bar to make my drink. They had premixed hurricanes for tourists, but those were watered down and kinda lame. I needed the real deal, and Trixie packed a helluva punch in her drinks.

I turned on my barstool to catch Penny's expression and noticed the mood of the whole bar had quickly changed. Conversations had halted, eyes snapping up and tension curling through the air. This wasn't because of Penny's misdeeds.

I felt the newcomer's presence in the prickles of danger at my back and shivers of warning crawling up my spine. The gush of raw power. The intriguing mystery of a sex life undisclosed.

"Roger." I gave Penny a brow furrow to tell her we'd return to this conversation, then swiveled in the other direction on my barstool.

The alpha of the North American pack stood framed by the door, broad shoulders nearly spanning from one side to the other. His built torso slimmed down into trim hips before exploding out into powerful thighs. The guy was built like a tank, but he moved forward as deftly as a dancer, lethal grace in every step. He was not a guy you took lightly, unless you'd been in the trenches with him, crawled through hell, and lost any remaining fucks you had to give.

"Bang any pretty ladies lately?" I asked with a grin. Just call me fuck-less.

His dual-colored gaze, one blue eye and one green like a faded dollar bill, swept the area. His attention lingered in two places, and I wondered what he was thinking. Clearly he didn't like the look of someone in our proximity. Since he'd been taught how to shield his thoughts from me, though, the details remained a mystery.

"Reagan." He stopped behind the open barstool to my right. His gaze fell on Penny. "Natural Dual-Mage."

I frowned and pinched my lips. "Since when do you greet her with her magical type?"

"Because of my influence within the Mages' Guild, the Guild insisted I need a title," Penny said. "I've refused, of course, so they—and now the shifters—are using my magic as a signifier. It's ridiculous. This is what gave the mages a big head in the first place. Does no one learn from the past? I don't want this organization to turn out anything like the last one. If we pick titles, we might as well follow up by highlighting people's levels. That'll create a hierarchy, which leads to competition and the desire for advancement, which leads to showboating, which leads to greed... It's a slippery slope, and this is how it starts."

I nodded slowly. "She has a point, Roger. That last Guild was a cesspool, or don't you remember standing by in Seattle, doing nothing because you weren't powerful enough to take them on while they broke all the rules?"

His gaze took on a hard edge. My stomach curdled. I could take him in a fight, and had, but even so, the man could freeze water on a hundred-degree day with that look.

"Also...why don't I get a title?" I nodded at Trixie when she placed my drink on the bar in front of me. She grabbed the bottle of Jameson and poured Penny another shot without asking.

"You have a title. Chief Shitshow," Roger said, nothing on his face to show that he'd just made a joke. Apparently shifters thought cracking a smile would invite someone to challenge them. A bunch of ninnies. His eyes stopped sparkling from his less-than-funny joke. "We are set to convene in two days at our compound in Montana. Darius has all the information. The Realm is restless, and we've had word that the wheels are starting to turn. The battle seems to be drawing near."

"A commune, how fun. Who is 'we'?" I asked, just to make sure we were on the same page. I took a large pull of my hurricane.

"The first and second Arcana have all their people gathered—those who aren't hidden away in the Realm. We'll talk more about that when we meet—"

"Should I give us a privacy spell or something?" Penny asked, glancing around.

Roger didn't scan the bar again, unlike me. Most people were shooting him furtive glances, a few clearly lustful, and a couple were staring into their drinks like the sheriff had just waltzed into the saloon. Not one of them set off my danger bells.

"No need," he replied. "The elves' people aren't good at blending into populated Brink areas. They stick more to the shadows and the outskirts. There's no one in this bar to worry about."

And that was the reason for the scan. Got it. Though I could've told him this place was clear. I was pretty sure Penny could've done the same, though she probably didn't realize it. Danger had a way of shouting at you when it was present, and we'd been in too many dangerous situations not to notice.

Roger pulled out the barstool beside me like it had done him wrong. He moved in front of it and sat, just a regular guy…if you couldn't feel the pulsing power and danger emanating from him. Or didn't notice his poise and readiness, like the world might explode and he'd save everyone here when it did.

"Can I get you something, alpha?" Trixie asked, leaning her hands against the edge of the bar.

"Cosmo. In a tumbler."

Penny leaned forward and looked at him from around me. "Cosmo?"

He met her assessing stare. "Have you tried them? They taste pretty good. Better than your drink."

"I am not drinking whiskey because it tastes good. I am drinking it because it tastes like a punch in the face. After the day I've had, and the few months that preceded it, I just need a punch in the face from time to time." She made a soft, irritated sound in her throat. "The devil's bells and tackle, I need a donkey kick to the throat, actually. Is there a drink that is like a donkey kick to the throat?"

I tapped my glass.

"Yeah," she said with a nod. "Maybe I'll get that next. Anyway, Roger, I'm impressed, that's all. You're a big, rough-and-tumble guy, but you're clearly secure enough in your masculinity to drink a pink drink. I respect that."

"Not totally, though, right?" I said. "He got it in a tumbler…"

"I always spill with martini glasses," Penny responded. "I get it."

He didn't respond for a second. Then: "My pack has levels, and we have structure...but that hasn't resulted in a cesspool or corruption. If the leadership puts the pack—or organization—first, and lives and dies by honor, then the pack will thrive. That kind of leadership fosters respect. A title won't set you on a path to corruption, Penny. Levels won't destabilize all you've achieved. Instead, those things will help people understand where they are and where they are going. You'll get some bad apples, yes. Any organization will. Good leadership means recognizing those bad apples and throwing them away. Good leadership means helping their people step up the ladder in a safe environment that praises hard work and growth. As a friend, let me encourage you to be as open in your leadership as you are in your magic. Feel it out, and judge what's best. Don't let the fear of what *could be* tarnish what is."

Penny blew out a breath and sagged a little. "Yeah." She took a sip of her drink. "Damn it, I'm really starting to like you, which is annoying, because you scare the poop out of me." She pushed off her stool and turned toward the back of the bar. "I'm going to go pee."

"She just peed. She's going to compose herself, is what she really means." I stared after her for a moment. "I have been sorely out of the loop. What's all this now?"

Roger thanked Trixie and then sipped his pink-red

drink. "You've been purposely kept out of the loop. We need your attention on the big show."

It was for the best. I had less experience than Penny when it came to running an organization. Less interest, too. Except that wasn't totally true.

My mind flipped to Lucifer, who'd wanted to teach me to help rule his kingdom. A pang hit my middle, and I couldn't help wishing things had been different. Wishing I might've stayed a bit longer, under different circumstances, so I could decide if I actually wanted that role and would be any good at it.

I'd never been a big-picture sort of person, but I'd also never been given the opportunity. I'd had to hide most of my life, sticking to the shadows and minding my own business. Now, with my magic out in the open, I didn't really have a purpose anymore. I didn't think bounty hunting would feel like enough for me. Not anymore. And now that I'd settled my curiosity about the whole merpeople thing, I didn't even have that mystery to occupy me. If I wasn't going to take a role in the Underworld, what would I do? Penny had her thing, and Darius had his, but I wasn't a mage or a vampire. I didn't fit anywhere up here.

"Anyway," I said, reaching for my drink.

"She needs a long vacation and a lot of bubbles," Roger murmured, his gaze following Penny.

I chuckled. "Probably."

"And you need to get on the battlefield."

I nodded slowly. "Probably."

"You have some rage to work through."

"Did you suddenly turn into a counselor or what?"

"My job is to keep a lot of different personalities working cohesively together. With the fae, that is simple. Working with Romulus and Charity is seamless. We have our initiatives, we have some extensive preliminary plans, and we have our desired outcome. We will need to keep Lucifer at bay and force the current elven regime to step down. Once that is done, we can help the elves and the Realm rebuild and restructure their government so that it is fair and just, with Romulus and Charity as the chief peacekeepers."

"Well, bully for you."

"You and your jumpy natural dual-mage are wild cards. Karen is nervous a lot lately, and it concerns you two. She won't tell me everything, though, and I'm thinking that's because of Penny. She wants to protect her daughter."

"Do not talk to me about Karen and her bullshit prophecies. She can suck it. She and that red-haired lunatic sent me to get tortured."

"And then get rescued and trained by your biological dad. I can feel your power now, Reagan. You don't need a title because there is absolutely no mistaking what you are. Even humans can feel it, or don't you realize they are giving you a wide berth?"

"They've always given me a wide berth."

"That's because you used to have crazy eyes. Now you seem much, *much* calmer. And that only makes you seem more dangerous. Which you are, obviously. I need to know you are in it for the team if you step out onto that battlefield with us. This is already a very precarious situation—I need to know that you'll help us bring it home."

"I'm going to have to. You can't do it without me."

"True. We need you. More than anyone, we need *you*. Darius has assured us that no one else can take on Lucifer and win. The mages could give it a shot, but without you, they would fall short."

"Aw shucks."

"But I'm worried about your festering rage over what the elves did to you. The elves need some restructuring, like the Mages' Guild did. They need new leadership, and we have to gut all the bad apples—"

"That's a bit of a mixed metaphor…"

"But they are necessary to that world. If the fae are restored to their role as guardians of the citizenry *and* the ruling party, it would create a much more peaceful, safer environment for the Realm. If the Realm is left to Lucifer or, worse, the vampires, then there will be incredible turmoil, worse than there is now. I truly believe that. I have no dog in this fight other than wanting peace and justice in the Realm."

"Like in the Brink?"

"Like in the magical portion of the Brink. I can't do anything about the rest of this world."

I pushed out a breath as Penny came back. He was coming from a genuine place—I didn't just hear it in his voice, I *felt* it—and what he'd said made absolute sense. It was the outcome we'd all agreed we wanted before I was captured. Before I went back to the Underworld. My logical mind said he was right.

My logical mind wasn't always in control.

"Heard," I said. That was about as much as I could offer him. What they'd done to me was inexcusable. Unforgivable. And not just because it was unjust, but because it was a common occurrence in that place. They'd tortured countless others before me, showing them no mercy. No common decency. Allowing them no dignity.

"But tell me this: what do you plan to do about the shifters they've taken?" I ground out as Penny sat down. "They've tortured your people. You don't want vengeance for that?"

"I do." A growl laced his words. "Badly. And I will have it in the form of change. I will see those responsible for the carnage torn from their places and exiled. Or killed, if they don't go quietly."

Fire raged in his eyes and his voice, but it was something behind it that captured my attention. Pain, not just for the shifters he'd left behind, but for me. Roger was the ultimate alpha—he looked after his people to the fullest extent, at times sacrificing his own wellbeing for theirs. He internalized their pain so that they could release it. It was all in there—a beast of festering rage that he kept on a tight leash.

If he could stuff his down, surely I could do the same?

I nodded, feeling the fire lick up my middle.

Then we understand each other, Roger thought.

"We do," I replied, wondering what would happen if I lost that vein of logic.

He downed the rest of his drink, pulled a wad of cash from his pocket, and leafed two hundred-dollar bills from the top. He set them on the bar and called Trixie down.

"Open the bar for the regulars until that runs out." He knocked on the wood and stepped back. "Reagan, natural dual-mage." He turned and walked out the door.

"I still want a title," I called after him. "A cool one."

"That guy makes me nervous," Penny mumbled when he'd gone.

"He makes everyone nervous. I think that's part of his job description."

"He just manipulated you. You know that, right?"

I sagged against the bar. "No, he didn't. I heard what he had to say and internalized it. He made good points."

"He just handled you like a child. They're all worried you're going to fly off the handle and go on a killing rampage with the elves. Cahal made a painting of what you looked like after they got through with you. He's not the type to lie."

Cahal would know. He'd gone to the Underworld with me, and I wasn't so sure I would have made it back without him. After a few days of recouping with us at Roger's super-secret ranch, he'd drifted off into the world like the shadow he was. He hadn't said goodbye, or if we'd ever see him again, or even where he was going. One day, he was just gone.

Which would've been more dramatic if his dragon hadn't been completely fine with being left behind. He'd obviously told her what was up. The dragons were still at Roger's super-secret place, enjoying the new world and the limitless sky. We'd see them again soon. Because there was no way we were rolling into any kind of battle situation without them.

"Cahal paints?" I asked.

She looked at me with her large, solemn blue eyes. It was the sort of look a puppy would give after you swatted it for being bad. "I shouldn't have let you sacrifice yourself. I should have been there with you."

"They would've killed you outright. You wouldn't have been there with me for long. But seriously. Cahal paints?"

"I keep having nightmares about looking back and seeing you in the elves' castle, surrounded. I keep seeing the look on your face when you pushed us ahead of you in the Underworld. Darius was so frantic." Tears pooled at the corners of her eyes. "It's killing me, what they did to you. And I just walked away."

"Good God, Penny, this is a little much for a Tuesday evening. Drink up. Have a hurricane. It'll strip the thinking out of your brain. I'll join you."

"I was supposed to rescue you. And instead, you had to rescue me again. I'm nothing but dead weight."

I swore under my breath. And now we got to the real reason Penny was having a hard time. She was hurting. She was probably scared for the future, too. Maybe we all were.

"Trixie." I nodded to where Roger had sat. "He paid."

"I noticed." She nodded before returning to the drink she was making, and I got off my stool and pulled Penny up after me.

"Hey," she said, a spell materializing in a moment and clouding me.

I wiped it away, unraveling the magic like it was nothing.

"Dang it, I hate when you do that," she said. "I'm trying to resist. Help, this is a kidnapping!"

"Would you come on?" I yanked her out of the reach of her drink then relented. "Okay, down that drink, then we'll go."

"I don't want to go home."

"You don't have a home. You move around way too much for that. Unless you mean Emery?" I paused. "Do you not want to see Emery? Why? What did he do? I'll cut a bitch, I don't care."

"Leave him alone. He's fine. I want to keep drinking and chase shifters around with you. I want to get into trouble and do something foolish."

"No you don't. You'd just feel bad about it in the morning. Come on." I dragged her behind me after she finished her second whiskey, a larger-than-normal pour. Penny had this uncanny ability to make people feel sorry for her and want to protect her. Except for me, of course. I preferred just shoving her into danger and seeing what she'd do.

But right now, she needed a gentler touch. Her oldest friend, Veronica, was staying with Callie for the time being. She'd been collateral damage to Penny in the past, and she figured it was best her friend had some firepower around her, just in case. She'd know what to do if anyone did. Besides, Callie and Dizzy, my other dual-mage friends, were a good distraction, if only because they always bickered.

"Come on, we'll go have Callie make us something to eat." I tugged Penny out into the coming night.

"Oh good. She has a large store of alcohol."

I pulled out my phone, sent a text to Darius so he'd know where to meet us, and headed for the car. As I neared it, a strange prickle of awareness danced across my skin. It flared my magic and fanned it higher.

I looked down the street but didn't see anything except the rolling throng of tourists taking in the new night. I felt it, though, an expectation.

Like something was coming.

CHAPTER 4

"**O**H, HELLO!" DIZZY beamed when he answered the door. He was a guy in his late sixties with a stained blue shirt featuring three rips and one obvious burn mark. His old jeans sagged and collected over his red runners. Gray hair stood up from his head, as though electrically charged, and I could smell the magic coating him. He'd been creating spells.

His gaze fell on Penny, and his expression instantly drooped.

"Oh no, what happened?" He stuck out his arm and turned, shepherding Penny inside.

"She's sad that she followed my orders and left the elves' castle with her life," I said, following them.

I paused in the doorway and turned back. The night paused with me, utter stillness coating the street. Clouds gently drifted across the clear sky, promising a turn of weather to come.

That was what my life felt like right now: the pause before turbulent weather.

A wire crossing the street swayed softly, and a

strange feeling came over me. A pulsing almost, deep down in my blood. A likeness, maybe, drawing nearer. Creeping ever closer.

I frowned, confused by that thought, and continued to peer out into the night. The moon shone down on the placid street. The low hum of a car engine reverberated off the houses, someone probably turning onto the street down the way.

"What's the matter?" Callie stepped out with me, placing her hands on her hips. "What are you looking at?"

"Nothing. It's early for no activity on this street, isn't it? It seems too quiet."

Her brows lowered, and she stepped farther onto the porch, looking down the street to the right, then turning and surveying the left. The sound of the car motor increased in volume, coming closer.

Shivers washed over me, but I already knew who was coming. Sure enough, a black Town Car pulled into the driveway, Darius's surly kinda assistant, Moss, in the driver's seat. Darius would be in the back. I could feel his proximity through our fully restored bond.

More shivers coated me, though, and since they weren't delicious Darius-is-close kind of shivers, I looked away from them and shifted my focus to what was going on inside of me, trying to tap into the sensation. I tilted my head, feeling movement of some kind.

Not organs or anything, but…

"What is the matter?" Darius's deep voice washed over me, somewhat soothing the feeling.

"That's what I asked," Callie said. "She said it was too quiet. I agree. Something doesn't feel right."

I shook my head as Darius's hand slid down my back. "I don't know. It's…" I put my hand to my sternum. "Something is weird."

"Danger?"

I opened my eyes and took a deep breath, unsettled. Moss stood beside the driver's-side door, staring at me with a frown.

"You've been missing me, haven't you?" I called to him, waving like a woman with a handkerchief in the fifties. "You've missed my sass. I know, I grow on people."

His frown deepened into a scowl. He lowered into the car. Clearly he wasn't staying.

"I shall miss you," I said as he shut the door. Any hope of him warming up to me had been dashed when Darius trekked into the Underworld after me, putting his eternal life in danger, yet again. Moss did not like to see his master in peril. He blamed me.

I figured stoking the flames would make it easier for the poor guy to stick to his guns. Also, it was really fun. Always had been.

"Ah!" Callie pointed to a passing Cadillac. "There's

a car." She looked at the sky. "Looks like rain. People are probably just staying in tonight."

"How is your night going?" Darius asked as we headed through the hall and into the kitchen.

I breathed in his mouth-watering spicy-sweet cologne, mixed with the smell of clean cotton and man. A formfitting suit hugged his well-built body, showing off all the planes and angles of his defined muscles.

"Did you have a dinner or something?" I asked as we entered the kitchen.

"A meeting."

"Are you planning my future without telling me again?"

"In a way, yes."

I jerked away from him on impulse, searching his handsome face for more information. His hazel eyes, speckled with green and gold, gave nothing away.

I sighed and let it go. He'd formed an elaborate network in the Underworld specifically to rescue me if I was taken and trapped down there. His plans hadn't exactly worked out like he'd hoped, but his presence down there had helped me keep my head. I had a lot to thank him for.

When we first got together, I'd demanded that he keep me aware of his various machinations, but his maneuverings had an obscene number of layers. To parse them, I'd need to learn a lot of mundane details I had no interest in knowing. Given that everything he did was for us, something he'd proven many times over, I'd decided to let it go. He had the best of intentions, and if they didn't work out, he had me to save him. I could live with that.

Why are you smirking? he thought.

"No reason. Just having a private think. Butt out."

He slipped his arm around my waist as we leaned on the counter. Penny sat at the island, a glass of whiskey with a single ice cube in front of her. Veronica, a cute girl with tight brown curls, a curvy build, and kind eyes, was at her side. Two black markers waited on the countertop between them.

"Hi," Veronica said to me, and her face turned red. Although she wasn't magical, she'd lived on the periphery of our world for long enough to get a few glimpses of magical mayhem. She'd made it through those, but I still tended to make her nervous for some reason. I had no idea why, because I always took care to mind my crazy around her—Callie's orders.

Penny heaved a sigh. "Yeah. We should probably go now, or I won't be able to see the signs." She was clearly answering a previously posed question.

"Where are you going?" Callie demanded as she filed into the kitchen.

"Neighborhood watch." Veronica, sporting a supportive expression, rubbed Penny's back and then got off her stool. She took the two markers, waited for Penny to stand, and handed one over.

"This will make you feel better," Veronica told her as they headed out. "It always makes me feel better, at any rate."

Should we let them go? Darius thought to me. *Penny doesn't seem completely...at ease.*

I gave a shallow nod so Penny wouldn't catch it. In this mood, if anyone messed with her or Veronica, they wouldn't get a chance to be sorry—they'd be dead too quickly.

"I do not get how correcting the grammar and punctuation on handmade garage sale signs would help anyone feel better," I said as they turned the corner. "If that is their definition of a neighborhood watch, they didn't have a very rough neighborhood growing up."

"Of course they didn't have a rough neighborhood growing up." Callie opened a cabinet and pulled a glass out. She eyed Darius.

"I would love a cognac, if you have it," he said.

She set the first glass down, reached a little higher, and brought down a snifter.

"That woman was sheltered within an inch of her life by her mother," Callie said, moving the glasses to the island and pulling out two bottles, one for Darius and one for me. "And Veronica fixes those signs because she is an editor and hates seeing grammatical errors. It's ridiculous, but it's their thing." She poured my glass and handed it over, then turned back for Darius's.

"About as ridiculous as a sixty-year-old woman wearing a gold, faux-velvet sweat suit with 'money maker' written on the butt?" I asked with a smirk.

She handed Darius's glass to him and ignored the comment. "If it makes Penny calm down a little, it's okay by me."

"She is incredibly wound up," Dizzy said, standing at the island. His protruding belly flattened against it. "She did the right thing, leaving Reagan to that horrible fate, but—"

"Would you stop calling it a horrible fate?" Callie demanded, picking up a half-filled tumbler of whiskey from the far counter by the stove and finding a stool. "It only makes things worse."

"*Well?*" he demanded, raising his voice. "You were there. It looked like a horrible fate. But we had to go, I was saying. Otherwise they would've killed us."

"Ms. Bristol was exemplary in the Underworld," Darius said. "I think what she needs is to stand on her own and assure herself that she can be a hero if she needs to be."

"She tried today, but that weasel Garret at the MLE office got in her way. What's going on with the Mages' Guild?"

"That's another thing." Callie took a sip of her drink as Emery walked into the room. After spending years on the lam, hiding from the elves and the previous corrupt Mages' Guild, Emery had learned to be the right kind of dangerous. He was also quite easy on the peepers.

He ran his hands through his wet hair, his graphic T-shirt smelling fresh and his sweats without a single spill. Clearly he was right out of the shower. He must've worked out earlier, or maybe done arduous spell working while Penny was being annoyed by Garret.

"She's got far too much on her plate." Callie got up and moved to the fridge. She took out a beer and handed it to Emery. "You do too, young man. Far too much on your plate. You can't hope to head up the Mages' Guild *and* be Reagan's right hand. It'll never work."

"Where's Penny?" Emery asked.

"Neighborhood watch with Veronica," Dizzy answered.

Emery nodded and popped the top on his beer, his blue-eyed gaze coming my way. "How'd it go with the bounty hunter gig?"

I briefly explained, watching as a grin worked up Emery's face. He loved Penny's antics almost as much as I did. I also let them know about Roger.

"Penny thinks he's manipulating me," I finished.

Emery held up a finger. "You glossed over the

merpeople part of that story." He sat down at the island and leaned forward. "What happens when they're in the water? I tried to find out once, and one of their males almost killed me."

I held my breath.

"Really?" He squinted an eye at me. "You're *really* not going to spill?"

"Oh my God, I want to. I really do. But I can't."

"Ask Cahal," Darius said, his smooth, deep voice sending a shiver down my back. I leaned into his hard body. The guy could still get to me. All this time together, and it still felt fresh and new. Exciting. Or maybe I was just horny. Hard to say. "He doesn't seem to have any qualms regarding spilling other creatures' secrets."

"Still mad about the unicorn slip, huh?" Cahal had given up the vampires' secret means of creating new vampires to Roger, of all people, although he'd also revealed another interesting tidbit: new shifters could be made—not birthed—with the use of dragon blood. I grinned up at Darius. "Speaking of, what's going on with them? We're pretty sure Vlad's going to try to bogart them, right?"

"The unicorns are their own creatures. They will choose what course they will take, though they are partial to Vlad. We will need to meet with their matriarch before long and plead our case. I have already spoken with her, but she has requested your attendance as well. If the elves are defeated, there is a question on where they might roam. Everyone has interests in the coming war, including the magical creatures."

My heart leapt, my stomach flipped, and a stupid grin worked up my face. I hadn't seen them since my first visit to their territory, back when I was helping Darius solve a case. They were the vampires' best kept secret (until Cahal had blabbed, clearly not afraid of vampire retribution). I'd wanted to get back there for a long time, but it just hadn't worked out.

"Totally," I said, gushing.

"When we need to move the dragons, we'll fly them to the unicorns' land on the way to our destination. We might as well hit two birds with one rock."

"Got that saying wrong, but what's this now? Move the dragons?"

"I sure would like to see a dragon," Dizzy said with glittering brown eyes. His smile lit up the room. "Imagine! I had no idea they even existed! Wouldn't you like to ride a dragon, Callie?"

"Have you lost your mind? I'd fall off inside of a minute. You would, too. You'd forget what you were doing and slip right off."

"How can you forget that you're riding a dragon?" he replied.

"How can you forget that there is a flowerbed between your shed and the house? I don't know, but you manage to trample through it at least twice a day."

"We'll meet Roger at his packs' compound in central Montana," Darius said as the dual-mages continued arguing. Emery switched seats on the island so he could hear us over the bickering of the older married couple. "A few of my people are setting up accommodations there now, blacking out, that sort of thing. I'll only bring those obviously loyal to me. Vlad is employing the same tactic with his vampire allies. At present, there is no real way to discern numbers. Many are still on the fence, waiting to see how things shake out."

"They'd rather join with Lucifer than Roger," I said.

"Yes, for obvious reasons. Roger and I are working amicably together now. We have an understanding. I doubt we will ever trust each other, though."

"Yeah, but...you don't trust anyone."

"I trust you, *mon amour*." He kissed me on the temple. "Vampires are practical, though. They will choose the side most likely to win. We'll need to have a good showing. Anyway, the pack has close to a hundred thousand acres in Montana. The dragons should be happy there. There's plenty of game to hunt and space to fly."

"But they'll need to go through the Realm to get there," Emery said.

"Yes." Darius slowly took a sip of his cognac. "We

obviously can't have dragons flying over humans, even if the journey wasn't too far for a single trip. No, we'll have to take them through the Realm. We are plotting the fastest ways, hoping to fly over the least amount of enemy troops."

Shivers racked my body. Enemy troops. The battle was coming soon, and the battle lines were being drawn. I'd been in a lot of skirmishes at this point, some larger than others, but this was the war to end all wars. I'd unabashedly use my magic, and unfortunately have to combat someone just as strong but a lot more experienced. Not to mention the elves, whose king and queen were just as strong as me and also a lot more experienced. I was the newbie in all of this, and I was expected to take on the masters, one of whom I really didn't want to fight. Not after getting to know him.

"It'll be fine," I muttered, and drained my glass dry. Callie hurried up to refill it. She must've known what I was thinking.

"When are we leaving?" Emery asked.

Darius rubbed my back supportively, which I thought was a little odd because I wasn't *that* shaken up about kicking this off, until he spoke.

"I want to speak with the *Seers* tomorrow," he said.

"Nah." I pushed away from him and took Callie's proffered drink. "They didn't do such a bang-up job the last go-round. If I was going to end up in the Underworld anyway, I didn't need to make a pit stop in Elf Torture Land. I could've revealed myself to the demons, and they would've taken me with them, handy as you please. Penny wouldn't be having nightmares of leaving me to die, Cahal wouldn't have to paint torture porn or whatever he gets up to, and I wouldn't have to choose between taking my vengeance on the elves and saving the fucking day. The *Seers* can chew on rocks for all I care. I don't want to hear what they have to say."

"Our friendship with Karen has certainly been…strained since we got back," Dizzy said softly.

"I'll say," Callie grumbled, thunderclouds on her face. She and Dizzy tried to brush it off, but they hadn't fared much better than Penny when it came to leaving me behind. I heard thoughts that slipped, felt it in their tight hugs, and saw it in their sorrowful eyes. I was physically tortured, but they'd been tortured emotionally. It had probably left a bigger scar on them than on me.

"Let's talk about what you said earlier," Darius said smoothly, and I braced myself, recognizing that cunning gleam in his eyes.

"Which part?" I asked suspiciously.

Emery drained his beer and pushed it in front of him. Callie moved to the fridge to get another. Clearly this would not be a sober affair.

"Roger manipulating you," Darius responded, suddenly on point.

I waved it away. "He didn't. Penny was just overreacting."

"That's what's so fascinating," Emery said, studying me. "If it was Darius, or me, or even Lucifer, who's supposed to be the master of lies, you'd clue in to what we were doing. You might not even register it as manipulation, but you'd instinctively know someone was trying to tell you what to do, and you being you, you'd push back. I've seen it time and again. But Roger so *obviously* turns you in the direction he desires and pushes, and you bat your eyes like a lost lamb and go with it."

"First, I did *not* bat my eyes. When have I ever? Second, I didn't agree to anything other than showing up on the battlefield with them. Honestly, you guys, he isn't trying to get anything besides help. His reasoning was...reasonable. My logical side gets it completely. I just have to work a little to keep that side of me in control, that's all."

"Ah." Darius's lush lips wrapped around the edge of his glass, and I tore my gaze away. Now was not the time for randy thoughts.

Emery nodded like Darius had actually said something meaningful, and I wondered if suddenly I wasn't the only one able to read thoughts.

"What *ah*?" I asked, feeling incredibly stupid and

very annoyed because of it. It had been so much easier when I didn't have friends to confuse and annoy me. So much easier. And less painful. And less conducive to feelings of impending doom.

"Lead by example," Emery said, accepting the full bottle from Callie. "He explained his reasoning, which is backed by his morals, and sold it to you with his personal guarantee that he will follow the same set of rules. You know he's a trustworthy guy who will put his life on the line for you, if need be. He drew on your trust to elicit an assurance that you'll abide by his moral code. That you'll fall in line and act like a team player." Emery turned to Darius. "It works because of the whole *a pack is mightier than one wolf* mentality. She's never had a pack, so she has never confronted that sort of mentality."

"You guys seem to be missing the point where I didn't actually agree to anything," I said.

"She is used to people manipulating her for their personal gain, and not for the gain of a group as a whole," Darius murmured, and I could see the wheels turning.

"No, no." I waggled a finger at him. "Don't you get any ideas." I turned to Callie for help. Maybe Roger was trying to get me on board with the team, but he *had* been reasonable. I still didn't see the problem.

She was looking at me with a thoughtful expression.

"You're so used to being surrounded by the likes of *his* kind"—she pointed at Darius—"that you always assume people's motives are to use you. Roger isn't trying to use you—"

"That's subjective," Emery cut in.

"He's trying to unite you with the rest of his team, and I'm sure that feels good to a person with your…background." She was about to say "issues," I knew full well. "You don't pick up on that kind of subtle maneuvering, because he really is trying to look out for you, in the best way he knows how. Your primal urge with a guy like him is to let him protect you." She dropped her voice to a mumble. "I'd want to let him, that's for sure…" She dabbed her forehead.

"I can see that," Dizzy said, frowning at her. "I probably would've said yes to that shifter too. Then again, he's the sort of guy you don't really want to say no to."

"The problem, of course, is that he doesn't understand his enemy," Darius said, watching me acutely. Damn it, I shouldn't have said anything.

"Exactly," Emery said, war in his eyes. "The elves in charge are morally bankrupt. They do not care about anyone, save themselves. They aren't stupid, either. Roger is naive when it comes to the really dirty, gritty places of the Realm. Places the elves have cultivated with their longstanding mistreatment. He can't possibly know the extent of the vileness he's about to face. He's not prepared for it, and if he tries to chain you to his cause like this, he'll get a rude awakening right before his forces are completely wiped out. He might be trying to do the right thing, but he's not fighting fire with fire in this case."

"I agree, *mon coeur*," Darius said to me. He moved his words to his thoughts.

I did not realize your desire to be part of a greater unit. I should have, with your reliance on Penny and your growing esteem for Roger. With the loyalty you've cultivated with Cahal. I was shortsighted. Soon we will establish some roots and build us a life like the one you crave. I promise you.

"But for now," he continued out loud, leaving me confused and touched and longing for a life that didn't involve hiding, the fear of discovery, or constant feelings of impending doom. "For now," he said, capturing my attention again, "we need to get past this last hurdle. And to do that, you need to work the way you always have—and that means being headstrong and impulsive. You know every player in this war. Now you have but to act, and let us help you bring about change."

"Curse breaker," Callie said softly.

"Yes, but..." Dizzy rubbed his temple. "Charity had that vision that said we were supposed to stop the two leaders from killing each other."

"Charity had a vision of the shifters and fae standing between the leaders, true enough," Darius said. "They all stood together, as you recall. But Reagan and the natural mages, and my vampires, were separated out. The shifters and fae have their interpretation of what that vision meant, but that doesn't mean it is ours. We weren't *Seen* to be standing with the rest of them for a reason. Reagan has different motives, and she needs to hone down what those are."

He was right, though my motives were still a bit hazy at the moment. Things had gotten so big, so confusing, that I wasn't handling this whole situation the way I usually would.

Although, in my defense, this was a situation unlike any I'd ever imagined. A situation born of pain and confusion. We were all flying by the seats of our pants, not just me.

We'd better figure it out soon, though. Time was running out.

The doorbell chimed.

Knock, knock… I heard, and my blood ran cold.

CHAPTER 5

"NOBODY MOVE," I said softly, a whip crack of command in my voice.

You are supposed to say, "Who's there..."

I knew who was there. Lucifer.

My breath came in short bursts. Emery pushed up from the island, his body tense in places and loose in others, ready for action. Darius stayed perfectly still, watching me closely. Callie and Dizzy put down their glasses. Clearly no one intended to heed my command.

Oh, it seems you have some friends coming to call, I heard.

"Penny!" I burst into action before my thoughts could catch up with my legs. I didn't know whom I was rushing out to protect, Penny or Lucifer, but I did know that if I didn't get there in a hurry, someone was going to die.

"What's going on?" Callie yelled as I sprinted down the hall toward the front door. Darius kept pace behind me, with Emery hurrying after.

I reached the door and ripped it open, finding Lucifer on the front stoop, wearing the white button-up dress shirt and jeans he always did, turned to face the person who'd stalled on the walkway leading to the house.

Penny stood within a gathering cloud of magic, spells twisting and turning around her, vicious, pumped full of power, and ready to do some serious damage. Rage shone plainly on her face, burned brightly in her eyes.

At the edge of the property, Veronica peeked out from behind a bush and a wall of spell, sectioned off from the battle that was about to unfold.

"Wait—"

Penny loosed the spell, which she sent surging and twisting through the air, straight for Lucifer.

I flung out my hand, but Lucifer had already whipped his hands out to react. His magic ballooned out, a complex weave of fire and ice, so finely wrought and artfully crafted that I wanted to sulk at my paltry attempts.

Her spell slammed into his wall, sizzling through parts and sliding off the rest. He braced, the muscles in his arms bulging, his body shaking slightly with the onslaught. He heaved forward, pushing his magic toward Penny, fighting her spell back toward her.

"Stop!" I shouted, my magic slicing into the mix. I halted my father's efforts and then latched on to

Penny's spell. I followed it home with my magic, unraveling both it and the churning cloud of magic above her. "Emery, go calm her down."

Are you here to wage war? I asked Lucifer.

"No. I come in peace." He paused, and a little smile twisted his lips as he magically wrestled with me, pushing back at my efforts to cut through his magic. "Take me to your...leader," he said, grunting as he thwarted my attempt to punch through his barrier.

His magic speared at me, and I flung it away at the last moment, continuing to work at his push, now aimed at me. Wanting to crush me. To wipe me from the earth.

He was teaching me, even now.

Sweat beaded my brow and determination steeled me as I fought back, figuring out how to work around him. Loving the feeling of fighting with my magic. Of sparring with death threats instead of the equivalent of a wooden sword.

"She's still fighting him," I heard, the words barely registering through my focused attention. "Damn it, Emery!"

A concussion of air pushed me. A body hit a car in the driveway—probably Emery—and then another stream of Penny's magic sliced through the air. This time, it wasn't just rage behind the spell, but fear and hurt and vengeance...laced with love and devotion to our friendship. To me.

She was also borrowing heavily from Lucifer's and my demonic magic.

The spell boiled and fumed, twisted and grew. The stream turned into a gush, and hellfire erupted in the air and washed over Lucifer, cutting through his efforts and blasting him back into the doorjamb. It crackled across his skin and turned to fire along his scalp, burning away his hair.

"Penny, whoa!" I stepped in front of him and held up my hand, meeting her hellfire with my own to stop the onslaught.

She cut off, panting, rage still burning brightly as she beheld Lucifer. "Why are you stopping me?"

"Hellfire won't kill him, remember?" I paused to make sure she wasn't going to throw another spell. "Also, I was just sparring with him. It wasn't for reals. Sorry, I should've said something."

She dropped her hands, and her body sagged a little. "Are you shi—" She scowled. "Suck a toe, Reagan. You could've let me know."

I almost pointed out that she had been about to swear, but I pulled back. "I know, I'm sorry. Hang tight, though—we still don't know why he's here. We might have to kill him yet."

"Yes, that possibility is never out of the question." Lucifer laughed and straightened up, smoke curling from his head and his eyebrows wiped clean off his face. "Mighty magic. You have earned your place at my daughter's side." He offered her a bow. "I must ask…can all mages do hellfire?"

"No." I didn't leave my place, mostly between him and her. "She has a rare gift. If she's close enough, she can…borrow someone else's magic, essentially. She can tap into the kind of magic they do and weave it into her spells."

His brow twitched upward. "Fascinating. And the angelic magic…where did you acquire that? After killing that accursed druid, I hope."

I answered for her again. "No, she robbed it off a disgusting little Redcap goblin we killed a while back."

"Oh, fantastic." He beamed at her. "Horrible little creatures, those. Almost as bad as the wretched angels."

Callie and Dizzy stood just inside the door, capsules in hand, ready to throw some spells. Darius was off to the side, the wariness I felt through the bond not showing on his perfectly composed face.

I squared off with Lucifer again and met his eyes. "Why are you here?"

He put up his hands. "I was telling the truth a moment ago—I come in peace. Alone. I wanted to speak with you again. See where you live and what you're doing. That is all. I understand if you don't want to see me."

He was the enemy, at least one of them—everyone agreed on that. He was one of the powers I'd have to fight on the battlefield. That I would have to best in order to keep the worlds somewhat balanced. I should send him away, or maybe even try to kill him.

But instead I let out a breath, looked at Callie and Dizzy, and lifted my eyebrows. "Can you fix his hair, and also can he stay for a minute, or should we move this to my house?"

"You *cannot* be serious," Penny said on a release of breath.

"Babe," Emery said softly, trying to subdue her.

She stuck out her arm toward Lucifer. "He trapped her down in the Underworld, planned to kill us, *chased* us with the intent of kidnapping her again, and we're supposed to invite him in for tea and crumpets?"

"Let Reagan handle it," Emery murmured.

"Your loyalty to her is commendable," Lucifer said to Penny. "And you're right, of course. I am a deplorable specimen. I'm best watched at all times. I simply cannot be trusted...except when it comes to my blood. Reagan is my daughter, my heir, and I hope to make amends. As much as can be expected, of course, since war is coming. It seems we won't be on the same side. As for my hair..." He ran a hand over his head and then down his face. Thick, dark hair sprouted and grew, covering his head and forming perfect eyebrows. "Easily remedied."

Penny's brow lowered. She cocked her head at him. I doubted she was used to the villain coming right out and saying where he stood. Vampires certainly never did. Apparently shifters didn't either, that tricky bastard Roger.

Or maybe she was just jealous of Lucifer's ability to grow his own hair back. What I wouldn't give for that trick…

"You know what…" I nodded, looking at Darius. "Let's move this to my house. If things go south, and Penny has to blow it up, it'll give Darius a reason to make it even bigger."

"I'd like that," Lucifer said, and stepped back. "I'd also like to try some of your Brink whiskey. Let's see what the Underworld failed to live up to."

"A lot." Penny crinkled her nose at Lucifer. "A whole lot, that's what. It's a mind bender down there, and I don't mind saying it."

Unable to help a laugh, I walked toward Darius. "The Underworld broke Penny's brain."

"The elves did, actually," she said. "The painting Cahal drew certainly helped."

I quickly explained what Cahal had apparently painted.

"Ah. Yes, the state she was in…" Rage and anguish flickered in Lucifer's eyes. Fire curled into the air around him. "The elves will see retribution for that. But that is for another day. I will meet you at your house, Reagan. I was there earlier in the day, but you'd gone out. The *Seer* told me to come back later."

I slowed as I reached Darius, turning back to face my father, but decided I didn't want to ask questions. The Red Prophet had been hanging around my place, which was fine because she never mentioned her prophecies. I didn't mind her weirdness—it was growing on me, actually, especially considering how much it irked everyone else—but I could not tolerate her magic. Not anymore. I was a person who held grudges, it turned out. Torture could do that to a person.

Into our cars we went—Darius, Penny, Emery, and me in my car, followed by Dizzy and Callie, who'd refused to stay behind. Poor Veronica had been left at their house alone, guarded by an impenetrable ward, which was definitely for the best in case things went pear-shaped. I took a couple deep breaths and prepared to invite my father into my world.

Darius slipped his hand onto my thigh. "It is encouraging that he decided to visit. He does not seem to harbor ill will."

"He's always like that," I responded, clicking on my turning signal. Somewhere above us, Lucifer flew in his demon form, a very handy way to get around town. "He's chill until he isn't."

"He probably wants to talk you into helping him take down the elves," Penny said, looking out the window. She held Emery's hand.

"Probably," I replied, getting onto the highway.

"So he can find you anywhere?" Penny asked. "There is no hiding from him?"

"Not unless she uses that spell we did," Emery murmured.

He was talking about a spell that could magically make me disappear. I could assume a new appearance, wipe out the feel of my demonic magic that allowed my father to track me, and drift into the shadows. If my mother had had access to that spell, I knew she would've used it on me to give me a normal life. After she'd passed, I likely would've used it on myself. But now?

No. I liked who and what I was. Even if Lucifer and I didn't end up getting along, I wasn't going to hide from him. I wasn't going to slink away and turn into someone else. I'd worked hard to become me over the years, and I wouldn't change because of some daddy issues.

"Seems so," I said.

Penny clearly read the *not gonna happen* behind my statement, because she murmured, "There has to be a way to mask her magical signature without changing her. Like camouflage. A temporary thing…"

I took the exit, close to home now. Adrenaline and nervousness fired through me.

The car was quiet as I rolled down my street. I loved this little corner of the world, just like I loved my magic and myself. I wanted to share it with Lucifer. It might not be much, but it was mine.

He landed as I turned off the car and pushed open the door. Mikey stood near his stairs, a hard scowl affixed on my father. He looked like he was about ready to run—seeing a demon turn into a man before his eyes probably wasn't sitting well. Smokey waited in the shadows of the cemetery across the street, watching the goings-on. Mince, a guy that lived a block over, strolled down the street toward us, his eyes downcast, looking at his phone. He'd missed Lucifer landing.

"Long time, no see," I said as he came closer.

He glanced up, his face creased with annoyance from whatever he'd been looking at on his phone. His nose was wide and a bit crooked from being broken so many times during his boxing years, and a bit more padding lined his stomach than the last time we'd seen each other. His gaze shifted to my front yard.

"Smokey said that whack job is gone," he said.

He meant the Red Prophet. He wasn't a fan.

"Is she?" I looked at Smokey, crossing the street to us. "She took off?"

"She said she had to intercept the musings of a

madwoman or some shit," Mikey said, his stare still on Lucifer. "That guy was here earlier. Claimed he was your old man."

"Yeah." I came around the car with a straight back and raised my chin in case Lucifer looked down on my home. "He is."

Callie and Dizzy parked behind my car and got out, bickering about something. They cut off when they saw Lucifer standing at the base of my stairs.

"We havin' a party?" Mince nodded at Lucifer, then smiled at Darius, showing off a chipped front tooth. That was new. "Hey, bro. Where's your fancy car?"

"This ain't stuff you want to get messed up in," Mikey said to Mince in a low tone. "The new guy makes the Red Prophet look like a saint."

"What?" Mince stopped, squinting at Lucifer. "Why?" He took a step back.

"He's fine." I gestured at Mikey. "Lucifer, this is No Good Mikey, obviously Mikey for short." I pulled out my keys.

"What the fuck did she just say?" Mince stepped back again, now turned sideways, ready to run. "What kind of dude calls himself Lucifer? Because Lucifer is fictional." He bent at the waist a little, his features comically wide. "Lucifer *is* fictional, right?"

"And that is Mince." I motioned to him. "They aren't magical, and aren't real fond of things that are."

"Wonderful to formally meet you, Mikey, Mince." Lucifer smiled at the now-frozen Mince. "Yes, my name is Lucifer. I do not run hell, although some don't see much of a difference. I am not fictional, as you can see, though I doubt I resemble the stories you've heard as a child, either. I never wear red hats over my horns, for example. My horns are black." His image rolled into his demon shape, black wings snapping out to the sides. He had glowing red eyes stuck in a bony face with two horn nubs at the top of his forehead. I was nearly positive he could make this form look nicer, since he could effect any form he wanted with his magic, but he clearly liked dramatics. Or maybe he used his human look for the Dr. Jekyll version of himself and the demon form for Mr. Hyde.

"What the fuck?" Mince took two quick steps backward. "Reagan...*what the fuck*?" He squeezed his eyes shut, then opened them up as wide as they went, rubbing them and trying again. Lucifer's image rolled back into that of a human, with his white button-up and jeans. "Nope." Mince shook his head, clearly not quite able to turn away just yet. "Nope!" Finally, he turned and ran.

"I'll see ya later," Mikey said, walking the other direction. "This shit is not my forte."

"And that's Smokey." I nodded at Smokey, who was gleefully watching Lucifer, probably hoping he'd do some other magical trick. A light burn marred his bald head, and his face looked sunburnt. Suddenly I wondered what had happened earlier. Whatever it was, it clearly hadn't dampened Smokey's mood. "He's not magical either, but he doesn't mind it like the others."

"Fantastic to meet you, sir," Smokey said. "It's an honor."

"Out of curiosity, why didn't you choose a magical neighborhood?" Lucifer asked, offering Smokey a small bow.

"I've had to hide my magic, and it's easier with people who don't know magic exists." I led the way up the stairs. "I'll introduce the others inside."

"You've had to hide your magic," Lucifer repeated softly, following me. "Why is that?"

I turned the key and opened the door before stopping. "We have a very strong ward. I'll need a blood offering to let you through."

Lucifer's gaze trailed to the frame of the door. "If you insist, though I can get through this if you'd prefer."

I stepped into the house. "You can see the magic?"

"I can feel it because of its power. It's expertly wrought, I can tell. By a mage, yes?" He turned and looked at the grim faces of Penny and Emery. "Those mages, I would assume? The angelic magic thrums within it."

"Would you wreck the spell to get through?" I

asked.

Lucifer thought for a moment. "Most probably. I don't think I could pass without disrupting it. I could try…"

I furrowed my brow. "So you wouldn't need to tear the spell down first?"

"My power trumps theirs. I've pushed through a lot of wards in my time. I'm good at getting around or through them."

"I guess I won't have much protection if the elves decide to come calling," I murmured as I pulled a knife from the holster on the side of my leg and nicked his finger. He didn't flinch.

"Only the most powerful of them, and they wouldn't bother doing the dirty work themselves. Are they here? In town? I can send up a host and clear them up easily if you'd like. It would be my great pleasure."

I let his blood drip onto the tripwire for the spell and had him pass through. "Not the elves specifically. They've sent spies, I've heard. They aren't actively engaging yet, though Roger—the alpha shifter I'm working with—doesn't think that'll last."

"Probably not, no." He entered my house and his gaze traveled over the living room and then down the hall. He followed me into the kitchen, noticing the table, the countertops, and then the pantry.

"Have a seat." I motioned to the table, figuring I'd

treat him like anyone else. When it was time for whiskey, we usually sat at the table to drink it and shoot the shit. I pulled down glasses as the others filed in, the latest remodel making that possible. Penny took a seat opposite Lucifer, her eyes hard. Dizzy took a chair next to Lucifer, and Callie settled in next to Penny.

"No drink for me, Reagan," Emery said, drifting to the counter and hoisting himself up on it. He clearly planned to treat Lucifer as he would a new vampire.

Darius lowered into the chair on the other side of Lucifer, leaving the seat at the end for me. Wariness swirled within him, and I knew he was intentionally putting himself as a buffer between my dad and me. On the surface, though, he couldn't look more confident.

"The mage scowling at you is Penny," I said as I put the glasses down before retreating to get the bottles of alcohol.

"I seem to have two mages staring at me." Lucifer glanced between Penny and Callie. "I am getting the impression that I am not very popular among your friends."

"Not really, no." I poured two fingers of whiskey for Lucifer and then the same for myself. Callie tapped her glass, and I poured for her and then Penny.

"Wine for me, Reagan, thanks," Dizzy said, his customary smile absent.

After pouring Darius's cognac, I grabbed a bottle of

red from the pantry.

"The younger one staring at you is Penny," I said, finally sitting down. Usually Darius would help prepare the refreshments, but he clearly wasn't comfortable enough to move freely around the space. It seemed I was the only one who felt zero wariness in Lucifer's company.

"Hello." He tilted his head at Penny. "You were the mage that laid waste to the entrance of my kingdom, correct?"

"Yes," she said without bashfulness. "I didn't mean to the first time. I did mean to the second."

"Of course. As I said earlier—you have mighty magic."

"Emery is over there on the countertop," I said. "He's her dual-mage partner. You might've heard of him as the Rogue Natural."

"Ah." Lucifer nodded at Emery. "A rare treat. Yes, I have heard of you. You caused some disturbance with the elves, correct? Reagan thought you would enjoy my castle. Didn't you say that, Reagan?"

"Yeah. They wouldn't mind if you did an illusion to mess with them," I told Emery.

"Mind? We'd welcome it." Lucifer laughed. "I do so enjoy getting visitors lost in the castle. It's been too long."

Emery nodded but didn't say hello.

"This is Callie"—I motioned to her—"and Dizzy."

"We've met," Callie said with a hard expression.

Surprise flitted across Lucifer's face. He studied her. "Remind me, if you would. I don't recall."

"When you were involved with Amorette," she replied. "We were her friends."

"Yes, I remember now! Forgive me." He smiled at her. It wasn't returned. "A grave loss for everyone, but no one so much as Reagan." His eyes turned apologetic as his gaze flicked back to me. "I apologize for my actions in your mother's garden. I overstepped and used your pain abominably. I hope you can forgive me."

"It's possible," I said, warmth budding in me because he'd realized his error without being told. "This is Darius. I believe you planned to kill him and my mage friends."

"I did, indeed, yes. That would have been a mistake, hmm? You would not have forgiven me for that." He turned and inclined his head at Darius. "Your reputation precedes you. You have made short work of learning my kingdom. You know it quite well in a short period of time."

"Not well enough, or I wouldn't have found myself in a cell, waiting for death," Darius replied smoothly.

Lucifer laughed. "This is true. You are the child of Vlad, is that correct?"

"Yes," Darius answered.

Lucifer took a sip of his whiskey, and his face pinched. "This is quite a bit different than what we can offer in the Underworld. I can see what you mean, Reagan." He blew out a breath.

"It's like a punch in the face," Penny said, clearly fond of that comparison, and leaned forward and looked at Lucifer closely. "You are incredibly nonchalant about almost killing us. You don't seem sorry at all."

Lucifer spread his hands. "You tore down my magical walls, snuck into my kingdom, and intended to deceive me. Death was justified. It's for the best it didn't happen, but that doesn't change the offense. You have not apologized because you had good reasons for your actions, and I will not apologize because I did too." He shrugged. "And here we are. My hope is that Reagan can forgive me, and we can put it behind us." He met my gaze. "I wondered if I might have a few moments of your time?"

"Not on your life," Callie said immediately as Penny started shaking her head.

"It's fine." I pushed back my chair and stood, Darius with me. Emery hopped down from the counter. "You guys, it's fine. He didn't come all this way to kill me, and he won't be able to kidnap me out from under your noses."

"Very true. I mean Reagan no harm." Lucifer

pushed his chair back and stood with me. "Not now, and not ever. It was a bad judgment call to try to force someone like her to stay in my kingdom. Tatsu has made that abundantly clear to me." Tatsu was his dragon, and I was surprised to hear that she didn't agree with Lucifer. "We have things to discuss, though. Things that have nothing to do with the coming war."

I grabbed my glass and used my free hand to gesture to the living room. "We can sit in there."

Emotion rolled through Darius, but he made no move to stop me when I left the room. He also made no move to sit back down. Neither did Emery.

"Your friends are very protective," Lucifer said as he sat on the couch. I took the armchair on his right. "That speaks highly of your connection with them. Your neighbors are the same way. I can see why you were eager to get back here." He moved his hand through the air. "Your home is beautiful. It suits you perfectly. The location is interesting as well. This is a very vibrant city that speaks to me. I'm glad to be here."

I bent my head in acknowledgment, pushing down a smile and trying to ignore the weird glow of pride in my chest. I'd wanted his approval for reasons I couldn't explain.

He paused for a moment to sip his drink. His face pinched again. "I'm not sure I like whiskey. It is, indeed, like a punch in the face." He smiled and put it on the coffee table. "I owe you an apology, Reagan. I read the situation with you very badly. Those antics would've worked on a great many people, but I am a proud parent to know that they will not work on you. I do think of you as my daughter, I hope you know that. You are my blood. You proved that in so many ways in the Underworld. I hope I don't make you uncomfortable when I say that you belong there. You were meant to rule, and I hope you'll choose to come back someday." He leaned back and crossed an ankle over his knee. "I have made it clear to my subjects that you are royalty, whether you live there or not. You are my daughter, and you will be treated as such. It is your birthright."

The warmth glowing in my middle swelled and flowed through me. I had wanted this olive branch. Ever since leaving the Underworld, I'd yearned to go back.

I swallowed down the lump in my throat but didn't respond. I wasn't quite sure what to say.

"I invite you to return and stay for a while," he continued. "I've left the borders opened. You can come and go as you please, wander wherever you may. You have no limits—no restrictions. I will offer you no warnings or advice, as you surely don't need them. I would just ask that you treat the kingdom with respect."

"Of course," I managed.

"I left your vampires alone when you were last in the Underworld. They were allowed to follow you out in peace. All but the one that had been captured. He, I returned to his maker and a horrible demise. In the future, if vampires come in with you, they will be welcomed. If they are not, they will need to report to me and state their business. I hope you don't mind, but they are cunning. Until this business with the elves is settled, I'll want to keep my eye on them."

So he'd let Ja go. I glanced toward the quiet kitchen, everyone clearly listening in. That was a good little tidbit for Darius. Maybe he could wrangle another favor from her or something.

"First, they aren't *my* vampires. None of them. And if they aren't Darius's, then they are definitely up to no good. You're right to keep your eye on them at all times." I pointed toward the kitchen.

All of them, I thought so the others wouldn't hear. *Darius loves me, but he's still a vampire. I'd be grateful for a heads-up if he's wandering around down there. He doesn't share his business as often as I'd like.*

A ghost of a smile curved Lucifer's lips. *Wise. You'll now have a network to rival his. We can easily keep tabs on him.*

Cripes. I needed to remember whom I was talking to.

"I hope, someday, that you will take a position of leadership within our kingdom," Lucifer went on. "We can work you in slowly, or throw you in the deep end and see what happens."

"I'll think about it," I said, and maybe I was crazy, but I actually meant it. "There's a war coming, though, so I really should deal with that first."

"Yes. About that." He adjusted himself in his seat. "The elves will be trying to kill you, you need to realize that."

"I do, obviously."

"And I will be trying to kill them."

"Right. Makes sense."

"If you get in my way, I will go around you, or kidnap you for real this time and stow you somewhere safe, but I will not go through you. You have nothing to fear from me or my people. I wanted to make that clear."

"Are you going to ask me to join your side now? I got manipulated by a shifter earlier today, so everyone is taking their shot."

"No. I'm done trying to manipulate you. You will go your own way. As will I. I will say this, however: I don't need that accursed druid's painting to know what you looked like in that dungeon. To remember the broken body lying on that cold, hard ground. To know how long it took you to recover. That is etched firmly in my memory. Either you will claim vengeance for that, or I will do it for you. I will not tolerate mistreatment like that, not to my blood. They will suffer for what they have done, and if I am not mistaken, we are not the only ones who wish to claim our vengeance."

His eyes flicked to the kitchen. His words became thoughts.

About your hellfire-spewing friend. Make sure that she doesn't tip too far into rage, or at least does not stay there too long. She might want to get vengeance as well, but if you value her, don't let her. She is not like us. She can't venture too far into the darkness and still make it back to the light. I can see how her death or insanity would affect you badly, so I offer that advice.

I shook my head and looked away. I liked this sonuva bitch more and more as I got to know him. I loved how his evil blended so well with the good, and how he was completely unabashed about either side.

"I probably would join your cause, if you weren't working with Vlad," I joked, huffing out a laugh.

"Hopefully you will join me after we wipe the elves from the Realm."

He was joking, his tone light, but rage suddenly blasted through me, and I wanted nothing more than to stand in front of his army and command them to march. I wanted to lead them straight to the castle to finish what I'd started—*burn it to the ground.*

"Turns out I'm not adjusting so well to being tortured," I said, wiping my hair away from my face.

"I would like to make a joke about that, but I'm not adjusting so well to you being tortured, either."

"Not as well as you adjusted to Cahal being tortured?"

"You will never let that go, it seems," he replied. "I will say, however, that he was in a day spa compared to what you endured. I've never seen that druid so pale as when I saw him looking down on you in that dungeon."

"That's really no excuse for letting your son torture someone."

"Even the druid? I have a very hard time feeling bad about him, you must realize. The angels took pity on him—surely we're even?"

I frowned at him, and he laughed.

"Where is he, by the way?" he asked.

I shrugged. "He took off."

"Of course he did," Lucifer said darkly. "And just so we're clear, I fully expect that druid to attempt to kill me, like he tried to kill my last heir."

I lifted my eyebrows.

His smile was cold. "Didn't tell you that part of the story, did he? Hmm. I'll save it for him. You're a good enough judge of character to tell if he's lying." He cocked his head. "You mentioned hiding your magic earlier. You have the magic of the Underworld—why would you hide it?"

"Oh, I don't know. Maybe because I knew you'd show up, drag me down into the Underworld, and try to trap me there..."

"Yes, that's a pretty obvious answer. I would've had a much better time at keeping you down there when you were younger, though. I call that a missed opportunity. Now I have to go about it with decency. So much more hassle."

I had to smile at that. "Way more hassle, yes. Maybe a better outcome, though."

"Let's hope." He glanced at the kitchen again. "Now, should we go back in to your friends, or let them eavesdrop a little longer?"

I rose, and we re-entered the kitchen together. Darius pulled the chair out for me.

Lucifer sat and threaded his hands together on the table. "Darius, tell me more about your relationship with Vlad. I have been instructed to turn him over to you if Reagan asks. It seems there are some skeletons in his closet regarding you."

Normal people would've gone unnaturally still at that word bomb, but Darius didn't seem at all affected as he lowered into his seat. "Who has mentioned this to you?"

"That nutty fae with the red hair. We have secret dealings—I can't tell you what they are."

I shook my head. "Don't listen to her. You might end up in a pickle."

"Like you did?"

"Exactly like I did, yes."

"I do not like their brand of magic. I can agree with you on that." Lucifer looked around the table. "I might try the wine. I remember liking that brand of alcohol."

Emery turned from leaning against the counter to grab a glass.

"Given you are the mate of my daughter," Lucifer said to Darius, "I would advise you to find a way into Vlad's closet. It doesn't seem as though you will like whatever you find. I assume it's no secret that I am using him for his forces—I'd like this matter resolved before long or it will interfere with my killing all the elves. Please note that I will use his forces regardless. Taking him won't change that, not now. If he isn't leading them, one of the others will. That's the joy of creatures that are not at all sentimental."

"So then…it's all about you?" Penny said.

Lucifer grinned at her. "Of course. Did you expect the master of the Underworld to be altruistic?"

Penny frowned. I laughed at her confusion. Lucifer's irreverence had a way of disorienting a person.

"Noted," Darius said, and rolled the brown liquid around his snifter, his tell for when he was thinking.

"So, tell me." Lucifer glanced around. "What did you really think of the Underworld? Pros and cons. I'm looking to make some improvements."

It was amazing, watching Lucifer thaw the room and make everyone comfortable with his presence. Even

Penny warmed up, shedding some of that rage she'd carried around like her magical cloud ever since leaving the Underworld. When he left a couple hours later, everyone was speaking like old friends. Emery hadn't ventured any closer, but he was chuckling regularly and had even smiled a time or two. Callie huffed a good bit, of course, but I could tell her heart was no longer in it.

When it came time to leave, Lucifer gave me a hug, which somehow wasn't awkward, and told me he'd see me on the battlefield, if not before. He also said he hoped to see me in the Underworld when I was ready.

"It is incredibly hard to hate that man," Penny groused after he'd gone. "He was going to kill me. He was headed to the *jail cell* I was being held in to kill my fiancé and me, and now I kinda like him. What kind of magic *is* that? You're not that cool, Reagan. I have to say it—you're simply not that cool. I don't trust him."

"You shouldn't trust him, and he was always incredibly charming," Callie said. "And incredibly dangerous. You have to be careful to remember what he is capable of."

"I guess that is kind of like a vampire, though," Penny murmured.

"We're going to see on the battlefield what he is capable of," Emery said. "But at least we don't have to worry about him killing us. That's a relief. Of course, there is still Vlad, and I don't think for one minute that

Vlad will feel beholden to Lucifer's wishes."

"No, nor do I," Darius said.

"Do you have any idea what Lucifer was talking about with the whole skeletons-in-Vlad's-closet thing?" I asked him. "I assume he didn't mean that literally. Or not just literally."

"No. I'll need to speak to the Red Prophet. Vlad is capable of great treachery, but I thought I'd uncovered everything in our long history. Possibly I was mistaken…"

"Great, we're headed into battle with even more questions," Callie said.

"The greatest question of all is for you, Reagan," Emery said, and the room quieted down. "What will you do about the elves? Will you go Roger's way and play nice, or Lucifer's way and kill them all? Because if you go Roger's way, you'll still need to stand between your father and them."

I got the feeling that he and Penny hadn't come to New Orleans to "regroup" at all, as Penny had said. I got the impression Emery wasn't sure which way the wind blew as it concerned me, and he'd wanted to come before everything started to figure it all out.

Joke was on him. I still didn't know myself.

I shook my head and finished my glass of whiskey. "Sometimes the best plan is no plan at all."

CHAPTER 6

LUCIFER LANDED A few yards away from the circle of women called together to send him home. He didn't want to chance going through the Realm, not even with a demon host. From the last reports he'd received, the elves were on the move, preparing to track and kill anyone in the Realm who might pose a threat to them. In all likelihood, they were also preparing to go after the fae, the shifters, and probably Reagan herself, in the Brink. Lucifer had warned her and the vampire of that probability. Meanwhile, he'd need to carefully watch his own borders.

Time was speeding by rapidly now. He wasn't yet ready to battle, but soon he would have no choice but to rise to the occasion. He would not allow the elves to dominate him a second time. They would be beaten down, and they would pay for the pain they had caused Reagan.

"Are we ready, ladies?" he asked the collection of dark-magic practicing, devil-worshipping humans. They were grateful to serve and so good at putting together basic summoning circles.

"Will you spare us your time, my lord?" one of the women asked, wearing a see-through chemise that showed her budded nipples.

"We would love to pleasure you, my lord," another said, wearing a shapeless dress pulled up to her hips, where she sat with her legs crisscrossed. He could tell there was nothing on underneath.

His desire stirred—his subjects were *very* grateful to serve. They'd said as much.

"Next time," he said, waiting off to the side for them to be ready. "I cannot spare a moment on this trip."

"Yes, your grace," the first woman said, brushing her fingertips across her chest. "We are here whenever you have need. Give us another few minutes, and the circle will be ready."

He waited, thinking over all he had to do. His forces were being organized and outfitted for battle in the Underworld, but they'd received a lot of interest from various groups in the Brink, though they would be quite rusty. Some of them had never fought at all. They'd need a quick tutorial. Soon he'd need to bring in Vlad's host of vampires as well, hopefully before the turmoil between Vlad and Darius boiled over.

His thoughts drifted back to Darius. Stoic and genteel, the vampire had a very polished surface, like Vlad. Also like Vlad, he had a deep, dark, savage underbelly.

Lucifer could read their kind incredibly easily. Their darker elements spoke to his violent side, and their unique set of strengths spoke to his passionate side. Darius was whip-smart, too, and incredibly cunning. Lucifer hated to admit it, especially given how close he'd come to an irrevocable error, but Darius was a good mate for Reagan. He'd protect her, strive to make her happy, and, most importantly, keep her alive through her hopefully many long years.

Her friends were well suited for her, too. The younger dual-mages were particularly powerful, thanks to the woman's unique gift, that touch of angelic magic, and a survival instinct earned the hard way. He'd heard many things about that Rogue Natural, including how much the elves hated him. And now the man was connected with his daughter. How very sweet. Yes, those mages would make powerful allies for her.

"We are ready, my lord," one of the women said.

Lucifer checked the circle, noting the correct use of the symbols. He stepped inside and waited while the women started to chant. The writhing was a bit dramatic, but whatever kept them answering summons…

The magic swelled and he had a brief feeling of falling. Blackness rushed in around him. Air pressed against his body. In a moment, his feet touched down on marble, driving his weight down to one knee.

He blinked and stood, glancing around his monitoring chamber. Images flickered of the various areas of his kingdom. His assistants waited to the side.

"Welcome back, Great Master," Victoria said, its legs a little shorter than usual, likely because of all Reagan's taunting. "How did it go?"

"Better than expected." He started forward. He had a lot to do. "She will come back here, I have no doubt. Not until after the war, though."

Victoria followed him closely. "Did she share her plans?"

"No, but my resolve is unchanged. If she is in any danger at all, she'll be removed and taken to safety. I will not lose her. I can crush the elves without her, and any others foolish enough to stand in my way. Tell Vlad time is up. Get his vampires down here and whatever other creatures he is able to secure. We will get ready to move."

"Yes, sire. I will put the plans into effect."

PENNY STARTLED OUT of a deep sleep as a warning thrummed through her body. She sat up in a rush, Emery doing so a hair later. The ward!

She leapt out of bed in one of Reagan's spare bedrooms—she had three after the latest upgrade—and hurried to the window, ripping back the blackout curtains. The morning sun glowed in her face, making her squint. Nothing moved along the side of Reagan's property, the budding day still and quiet. On *this* side of the house, anyway.

Another warning blared through her, locking up her joints for a moment and slithering down her back. Someone was using magic to poke at the ward now, trying to figure out a sneaky way through.

"Are they mages?" she asked, suddenly out of breath as she pulled on sweats.

"It's impossible to say. The elves have a lot of powerful creatures at their disposal, and they're experienced in dealing with wards and spells. I ran from more than you can count." Emery shrugged into a shirt and grabbed his shoes.

The warning came again, manifesting in slight physical pain. They were working at tearing down the ward.

"It's a solid ward," Emery said as Penny threw on a sweatshirt. "It'll take a long time for them to get through. We should be okay."

"It won't take nearly as long for Reagan to burst out of here and attack whoever is on her property."

Penny threw open the door and rushed down the hall to the master suite. Once there, she didn't bother with theatrics—she cranked the handle and pushed the door open just as Emery swung around the top of the stairs and took them two at a time. Inky black greeted her, zero light making it into this room.

"Reagan," she said, closing the door behind her and fumbling for the light switch.

"Yes."

Sheets moved in the darkness. A hand slid under Penny's, reaching the switch first, and she flinched away. The light flicked on, and there was naked Darius, much too close.

"Good God—" Penny pushed to the other side of the closed door.

Reagan pulled on her leather pants. "What do you have?"

Darius zoomed across the room, glancing at the clock before pulling on his clothes. He wouldn't be able to do anything, though, not at this time of day.

"We don't know. Someone's trying to get through the ward, kind of sneaky-like."

"Sneaky-like, huh?" Reagan said with a little grin. That meant terrible things. "I wonder if it could be a coincidence that this is coming so soon after Lucifer visited…"

She pulled down a sports bra and shrugged into a tank top. She didn't bother with weapons, just snapped her fanny pack into place and headed for the door.

"Should I call someone in?" Darius asked, dressed and in the middle of the room, probably feeling helpless.

Grateful not to be in that position for once, Penny pulled the door open a crack and stepped into the still-dark hallway.

"Nah," Reagan said, following her out. "If they're trying to be sneaky, that means they're not ready for a serious altercation. Surprise! I'm always ready for a serious altercation."

Penny hurried down the stairs, Reagan behind her. The feeling of the ward being tampered with dug between her shoulder blades—someone was pouring substantial power into breaking the spell.

Emery stood in the hallway by the back door, looking their way. He pointed, his gaze on Reagan. She nodded, and Penny had a feeling he was silently communicating something.

Reagan flattened her back against the door, looking to her right at the curtain covering the thin back window. Emery stepped up to Penny and leaned in close, his lips to the shell of her ear.

"On the back porch. Four of them. They look humanoid from what little I could glimpse, but it's an illusion. I can see the magic shrouding them."

"What's the end game?" Penny asked as Reagan leaned closer, trying to look through the gap between the wall and the material.

"They might think Reagan is alone and the four of

them can take her," he whispered.

Reagan shook her head and straightened back up, her voice low. "They must know I'd be with Darius, and if they asked around *at all* they'd know you guys were also around. You always stay here when you're in town. Plus, they're trying to come in, not draw me out, away from Darius." She shook her head again. "They've been sent to gauge my preparedness. If they make it back, great. If not…" She shrugged, anger burning hot in her eyes. Penny had a flash of how good it had felt to release that hellfire. "The elves don't care about their underlings. They won't lose any sleep if they don't come back."

"The elves in charge, at any rate," Penny said, knowing her mother kept *Seeing* that Reagan should spare the majority of the elves at all costs. That she must prevent Lucifer from mass killing.

She hadn't brought that up to Reagan yet, though. She knew it wouldn't be received well, what with how the last batch of *Seeing* had turned out, not that Penny could blame her. She probably shouldn't have said anything about Roger manipulating her. Given what she knew, that had been shortsighted. Though Reagan likely would've clued in eventually.

"Sure," Reagan murmured, stepping away from the door and then turning. "Should we come up with a plan?"

"Run out there and kill them?" Emery suggested, magic curling around him.

"I like the way you think." Reagan pushed her palm against the wood, leaning in close, reaching down to the lock. She paused, and then everything happened all at once.

CHAPTER 7

I FLIPPED THE lock and yanked open the door, pulling it wide. Large hands curled around my upper arms and pulled me back a moment before I was about to burst out of the door. A jet of magic zipped by my face and slammed against the doorframe, blistering the wood.

These fools were trying to fight Lucifer's daughter with fire. Clearly they hadn't been prepared for this mission. They were probably mercenaries or hired goons.

I'd just thought the word "goon." What was happening to me?

"Thanks," I murmured to Emery, just so he wouldn't think I was ungrateful. He couldn't have known that spell would've done nothing but strip my eyebrows.

I bent and dove, rolling out onto the porch and popping up. I slammed air into the strange-looking old-man forms, all exactly the same, with balding heads, white whiskers, and disproportionate bodies. If I couldn't feel the difference, I'd have thought they were demons.

The short bodies, half my height, flew backward, their magic dying on their fingers. I ran forward immediately, but Penny's and Emery's magic got there first. A vicious spell ripped at the creatures' skin and tore at the magical illusion. Orange trousers and plaid shirts disintegrated. Underneath, brown and black spots speckled pasty white skin, like some sort of very ugly animal. Long, pinched faces with large mouths full of sharp teeth hissed at us as the creatures fell to their hands and feet and scrabbled to face us in pairs.

Another spell bore down on them, magic shredding their skin and stabbing down through their backs. The creatures howled, and the one nearest me lunged forward, hands out to grab. I erected a wall of air and then sliced through its neck with an air blade before lighting it on fire. I had the feeling that Penny and Emery were going to dispatch the other ones, so I'd better get all my rage out now or I'd lose my chance.

The howl turned into a scream, cut off quickly. Magic kept stabbing the three others, much more gruesome than my approach, though I couldn't put my finger on why. Green blood welled up and flowed over, dripping onto my porch. The creatures jolted and spasmed, curled down and then rolled over, shaking with the continual onslaught of magic.

"All right, then." I put my hand on Penny's shoulder. "You good?"

Tense, she broke my connection and stepped closer to Emery, laying a hand on his broad back. Apparently, Penny wasn't the one I needed to worry about this time.

"Hey," she said softly, and Emery shuddered as though coming out of a trance.

He scrubbed a hand over his face, and the magic dried up. The creatures stopped shaking.

Make sure they are dead, Emery thought to me. *Thoroughly dead.*

"Yup. I'm on it." I picked the creatures up with air and moved them down to the grass so I wouldn't get any more green blood on my porch—*ew*—and lit the three they'd taken down on fire. The one I had killed was currently a blackened ball of soot—it wasn't coming back to life, and if it did, it wouldn't be very effective without extremities. Or a head.

"Didn't like the look of those, huh?" I asked Emery lightly as he stared down at the burning mess of magical creatures.

"That message was personal," he said in a hollow voice. "They know I'm here."

"Wait, wait." I put out the flame, squished the creatures' remains into pieces to make sure they were thoroughly dead, and then ushered Emery back into the house. "Darius should listen in."

I closed and locked the door behind us. The tampering hadn't gone on long enough to do much damage to the ward, but sometimes a lock helped people feel safer. Especially people who had tramped though the Realm without a door to lock for so long.

"Why would the elves send a personal message to you?" Penny asked as we climbed the stairs and met Darius in the hallway. Frustration and annoyance boiled within him—he didn't like standing on the sidelines. "You're not really one of the focal points of this thing. Also, why was it a personal message?"

"After my brother and I played that practical joke in the elves' castle," Emery said, "they sent those things after us. When I was on the run a couple years later, they were constantly on my heels, it seemed like. They're easy to kill, but they can eat through a ward pretty fast. At least the kind of wards that I used to build back in the day. Ours are better and much stronger now. I'd wake up as they were eating through, sometimes almost too late. I lost a lot of sleep because of those things."

"What were they?" Darius asked.

"Snellax, cave dwellers." Emery ran his fingers through his tousled hair. "The elves treat them like hounds. They didn't use illusions to hide them in the Realm, but then they didn't need to."

"Reagan, secure the house and then put some coffee

on," Darius commanded softly. "Penny, help her."

I frowned and turned toward the stairs. Nothing had been left open but the back door, which was now locked, and we were religious about closing all the blackout shades and curtains before bed. He would know that the downstairs was safe for him. It meant he wanted a moment alone with Emery.

"He does that sometimes," Penny said quietly as she followed me through the house, double-checking everything. I actually wanted to go outside and survey the grounds, as well, see if there was anything lingering in the area. Maybe something had been watching, and it would now skulk away to make its report. "He has flashbacks to those days on the run, or something triggers a memory and he loses himself a little."

I nodded as I entered the kitchen and pulled out the coffee pot. "Makes sense. He had a hard life there for a while."

"Yeah," she intoned. "I don't see why the elves would pick him out of the lineup, though. Like…why specifically mess with him, you know? Why not you? Or me? Or Roger and the fae?"

"We don't know that they haven't gone after Roger and the fae." I pulled down the coffee filters. "Let's hear what Darius has to say. He probably knows something he didn't fill us in on yet."

The coffee had started to percolate by the time Darius entered the kitchen with Emery, both of them with hard expressions.

"Verdict?" I asked.

Emery quietly pulled out a chair and sat next to Penny, who started rubbing his back.

"It could be the elves," Darius said, pulling open the pantry door. "They have a history of mental warfare. They know Mr. Westbrook's weaknesses, and it is a small thing to send a warning. But there are other creatures who would wish to unsettle Emery, and Penny with him. Vlad, for one. Possibly a mage who is dissatisfied with the new order. Without more information, we can have no way of knowing who sent those creatures, or if they were even meant for him. Someone might've just wanted to check the strength of the ward."

I leaned against the counter, studying him as he pulled out ingredients for sandwiches.

"What aren't you telling me?" I asked, crossing my arms over my chest.

He put bread onto the counter and pulled open the refrigerator door. "I have nothing concrete, but it seems it has begun."

"It… Meaning the start of the war?" I asked.

"This is the first attack, and it was mild. There will be more, each more intense than the last. That is a guess, but…"

"It's a good guess," Emery said, and I pulled mugs

from the cabinet.

"The elves have had watchers that Roger and Romulus haven't disbanded," Darius said. "They reported back, obviously. Now the elves are stepping up their game. That, or Vlad is. I have word that he is ready for Lucifer to say the word, and then he'll move his forces to the Underworld. Goblins, trolls, some minotaurs— there are many from the Realm that have already headed down there. Vlad will pull more of them still. A great many want to see the elves torn down."

"And there's the problem. If we tear down the elves totally, then who would take their place?" Penny asked in a small voice.

I poured two cups of coffee and delivered them as Darius answered.

"That is the question. Vlad is hoping to climb atop that throne himself, of course."

I huffed and poured a cup of coffee for myself, though I kind of wanted something stronger now. In my heart of hearts, I was hoping Lucifer's forces would be evenly matched with the elves, and I would be free to tear down that damn castle brick by brick. I'd get my revenge and wouldn't have to get between two forces that obviously needed to duke it out. But if Lucifer had more power, and he decided to take the world for himself—or worse, the vampires...

"I hate that I am thinking of siding with Roger," I

muttered. "Kinda."

"Just think," Penny said before sipping her coffee. She winced at the heat. "Your dad could take over and put you on the throne instead of Vlad."

Shivers racked me as Emery and Darius's gazes slid my way. No one said anything.

And now I knew what people really feared. It was just that no one else had had the balls to say it outright.

"What's next?" I asked Darius, picking up my cup. I didn't intend to dignify that with a response. "If this is starting, we're in the wrong place. We need to get to Roger."

"Yes. I was thinking the same thing. Callie and Dizzy will be en route soon. We need to get the dragons and head to the unicorns' territory immediately, the Island of Eternal Light, before Vlad is called down to the Underworld. He'll try to take them. They are herd animals, and they trust him. If we aren't there first to give our testimony, they'll likely follow him."

"And paradise will await them down below, compliments of my father," I said, feeling urgency take root. "Lucifer won't take kindly to me heading into the Underworld to lure them back."

"He said he wouldn't trap you down there, though," Penny said.

I smirked. "You don't really understand the guy we're dealing with. He's not like Roger—he's not hero material. He won't harm me, but if I tried to mess up his plans, he would have no problem stuffing me away in luxury while he handled what needed to be handled. That should remind you of someone *else* we all know, and a certain desert island we all spent time on…"

"And all this time, we didn't realize you had daddy issues," Emery said, his good humor thankfully breaking through the black mood those things had put him in.

"Yeah, right?" I took another sip of my coffee. "The things we learn about ourselves."

"We'll head out tonight." Darius piled turkey onto a sandwich. "We'll use today to get everything in order." He placed the other slice of bread on top, cut it, and delivered it to Emery.

"What sort of trek are we going to face once we're in the Realm?" Emery asked.

Darius was silent for a moment. "We won't take the longest and safest route to the unicorns, because the journey would sap the dragons, and they'd likely be tired by the time we reached the portal closest to the shifters' territory in the Brink. My reports seem conclusive that the elves are watching that portal closely. They aim to prevent anyone from using it."

"We'll need to fight our way out?" I asked.

"Yes, it seems so," he answered softly. "When we leave, we will likely have to fly over camps containing the enemy. If their fliers are faster than the dragons, we could be arriving to a host of waiting enemy, ready to attack."

"Their fliers aren't faster than dragons," Penny said, "especially because they won't see us coming. You can ride with me, and Emery can ride with Reagan. Our spells will keep us mostly hidden. If they do happen to see us as we fly over—sometimes our invisibility spells don't work for all creatures—then we'll burn them all. Or Reagan, you can kill them horribly. When we get to the portal..." She shrugged and finished her coffee. "Well, at this point, we're no stranger to fighting our way out. That's not the problem."

"And what is the problem, Ms. Bristol?" Darius asked.

Penny looked at me. "How to get Reagan to go along with the *Seers*. I get the feeling she's not going to like what they have to say."

CHAPTER 8

"CHARITY'S VISION CHANGED again," Emery said as we got out of the taxis in front of Roger's secret hideaway in the woods, which had also become the dragons' secret hideaway. He studied a text message as Darius opened the front door with a key Roger definitely didn't know he had. Given he didn't need a key to open locks at all, I had the feeling he was silently boasting. "It seems this time you aren't in the picture at all, and neither are we. The *Seers* are feeling very grim, even the Red Prophet. In the vision, the fae and shifter forces are overwhelmed by demons and vampires."

We'd managed to get our affairs sorted in record time, probably owing to our constant on-the-go status for the last bunch of months, and got in a decent-sized nap before we loaded into Darius's private plane to head out here.

"I'd thought the fae's quest visions or whatever didn't change," Penny said as we walked into the wide hallway and headed out to the backyard. "Hers seems to change at the drop of a hat."

I checked the knives strapped to my leg and adjusted the pouch around my waist, holding a plethora of spells in casings.

"When are you going to give up that fanny pack?" Emery asked with a groan.

I held out my hands, looking down at it, then scowled at him. "How dare you," I said dramatically. "Show respect for the *pouch*. It is a pouch. Not a fanny pack."

"Do you know what the difference is?"

"Delusion," Penny supplied. "That's the difference."

"You don't even need it," Emery continued, obviously having quite the grudge against my useful bodily attire.

I patted it. "In case I need spells, I got spells. Stop being jealous."

He rolled his eyes. "Your horrible fashion sense aside, the *Seers* think the Underworld magic is messing with things." Emery tucked his phone away. "They can't get a reading on Lucifer. Not even when he went to your house, Reagan. Karen thinks he is changing the game, and Charity's visions are changing with it. His magic defies the use of *Sight*, apparently. That's what Karen says, anyway."

"I wish my magic would defy *Sight* as well," I grumbled, spying Cahal seated at the patio table with an open book. Darius had gotten in contact with him a few days ago, because of course he'd known how to do that, telling him to stick to the Brink in case we had to make a move. He'd made a follow-up call shortly after the attack this morning. Clearly Cahal had wasted no time. "Well, look what the cat dragged in—if it isn't the great painter himself."

Cahal picked up a unicorn bookmark from the patio table and fit it into the pages before closing the book and looking at me. "They had a right to know what the elves did to you."

"Why? What possible good can it serve?" I glanced at the tree line, not seeing the dragons. "Where is Archion, do you know?"

"They are hunting, and then they will digest so they have energy for what's to come," Cahal answered. Darius had filled him in on our plan, such as it was, instructing him to tell the dragons if he got here first. "And the good it serves is to let your friends know what the elves are capable of. If they did that to you, they have done it to others."

"Many others," Emery said.

"It'll also help them understand the risk that you might lose your mind and kill them all," Cahal continued.

"Kill everyone and take the throne, huh, Penny?" I raised my eyebrows at her before turning back to Cahal. "Apparently that is one of the worries."

"A worry born of ignorance—they didn't see you in the Underworld for long," he said. "The Realm is not your home. You'd be miserable there, and you'd make the world worse."

"Super. Lovely to have you back," I said. I took a deep breath of clean mountain air to try to still my nerves. It didn't work. "So the dragons are up for joining us in battle?"

"Yes," Cahal answered. "I hear Lucifer visited you?"

"Last night, yeah. He was easy and charming and ready to compromise." I sat down to keep from pacing.

"I think I will make us a little something to eat while we wait," Darius said, and disappeared into the house.

"He backed down, then," Cahal asked, studying me closely.

"Not about killing all the elves, but..." With the help of Penny and Emery, I went over the meeting from the night before, not glossing over any of Lucifer's reactions or words.

When I finished, Cahal nodded as though a question had been answered.

"What?" I asked. "Good, bad...?"

"Good, for both of you, I think. He tried to be over-bearing, you rebelled, and now you both know where you stand. If we weren't about to head into a large battle that might change the shape of two worlds, I'd say great things came of that meeting. As it is...we'll see what happens."

"Yeah," I said softly. "And everyone wants a slightly different outcome."

"That's how it always goes, Reagan," Emery said. "And no one will get exactly what they want."

I looked at Cahal, tempted to ask about the last heir. Then…I decided against it. The guy had been tortured. The angels had come down to help him—the *angels*! They'd clearly been on his side, and Lucifer obviously had a soft spot for his blood relations, including my half-brother. Bottom line: it was drama I didn't need to know about. It was a past that still haunted Cahal. He'd never been anything but good to me and my friends— his ghosts could remain private.

TWO HOURS LATER, the dragons returned, leaving us only a few hours to get to the Realm before sunrise. The urgency to get moving cut into my joy at seeing Archion again. The more I thought about it, the more I suspected that the visitors earlier had been a bad omen. Darius was right—more would come, not to mention we were fighting the clock when it came to those unicorns.

There really are unicorns? Archion thought as we lifted above the trees and headed toward the portal. Emery sat behind me, hands on my shoulders. He was clearly worried about maintaining contact to hold the concealment spell.

Yep. They are a bit bigger than a horse.

What is a horse?

Oh yeah. He was quite sheltered when it came to the Brink.

You'll see. Roger the shifter might have one.

I tensed as we neared the portal, reaching back to touch Emery's knee for no reason. Penny and Darius fell in behind us on Saphira, and I assumed Cahal was taking up the rear on Coppelia. He didn't have a mage friend to cloak him with an invisibility spell, but thanks to his shadow magic, he didn't need it.

The elves' fliers are no match for a dragon, Emery assured me as the portal clawed at me, checking my magic and sucking my energy. The orange world of the Realm waited just beyond. *Fairies and phoenixes and lamassu—none of them can compete with a dragon. They won't even try, especially if Lucifer's heir is riding on the back. They'll know you can slap up solid air and cut them down, no problem. Save your anxiety for when we need to cut through the elves' forces to get through the portal near the shifters.*

Wise words from a guy who would know.

I nodded, though he probably didn't see, and thought to Archion to pull back a bit and wait for Darius to take the lead. He knew the way.

You look majestic on the back of that dragon, Darius

thought as they flew by. *I don't think I ever mentioned it.*

He had, a few times over, often when naked and kissing up or down my body. I tried for a grin, which probably looked more like a grimace, and then we were falling in behind him.

Have you decided what you'll do about the elves? Emery thought as we made our way, the orange filaments in the sky flying past us. Trees and flowers dotted the way below until we cut across a stretch of flat land with very little landscaping. Clearly people didn't often walk this way, and if flying creatures did, the elves didn't care about them. Good news.

I debated giving a half-truth, or making light of it like I usually did. It was a trauma that was in my past—I didn't want to worry the people I cared about by bringing it out in the open. Other people, the ones who hadn't been there and weren't traumatized by it too, didn't seem to get that trauma didn't just evaporate at the light of day; it had a habit of lingering. But if anyone could understand what I was going through, it was probably Emery. The elves had mentally tortured him for years, keeping him on the run, not letting him sleep or rest, helping the shitty mages who used to control the guild by keeping him moving.

I heaved a sigh.

"I want vengeance so badly I can barely think," I said, turning my head so he would hear. "I still wake up in that dungeon, hearing screams that I know are mine. Fighting hopelessness. Waiting for death. After they were done with each session, I looked up at the dank ceiling and begged for Darius to come. I cried because I didn't feel our bond. Because I was utterly and totally alone. And then, for the next session, I had to pull it all back within myself, stuff it down, and pretend like I didn't care. I broke a little, I think. Or maybe I just need more time to get over it." I let the wind dry my glassy eyes. "Or maybe what I need is vengeance."

Emery was quiet for a long time. The land passed far below us in a blur. I had an insane urge to rip the sky away and kill all their stupid illusions.

Penny sides with Roger about what to do with the elves, and I get it, he thought. *I know the Realm needs a ruling force, and someone from the Realm needs to be that ruling force. Why elves, though? Why not the Arcana? Why not Charity? The fae aren't amazing in some respects, but they aren't so corrupt it has diseased the whole of their ruling party and most of their people.*

He had a point.

Someone needed to head up the Mages' Guild after we tore it down, he went on, *but we didn't worry about that when we were doing the tearing. We fought our enemies and dealt with the fallout in the aftermath. So why are we doing this any differently?*

Another good point. I said as much.

I don't know, he finished. *I've had firsthand dealings with them. So has Vlad. So have you. I'm sure Darius has more opinions than he is sharing. He sees the folly in allowing the vampires or Lucifer to sit on the throne, but he hasn't weighed in on what he thinks you should do, right?*

"No," I answered, and it was amazing that he hadn't. Usually, Darius would talk me through a situation much more thoroughly than I'd like, going through the possible ramifications of every decision, but I got the feeling that he was letting me fully captain this ship. While he'd made it clear he would fight by my side, he didn't plan to point me in any particular direction.

I wondered about that. Maybe this situation had gotten too big for even him, and he wanted to see which way the wind would blow before making a call. Or maybe the days of manipulating me were long since done.

I was not sure I believed either of those.

Regardless, it was becoming increasingly apparent that no one knew what was best. Roger and the fae didn't understand what they were up against. The king and queen's enablers weren't about to out themselves as bad guys, so a lot of them would end up back in positions of power. And where was the representation of the other creatures in the Realm if only the elves ruled?

Shifters didn't even have proper representation now, and they'd all worked dutifully for the crown. Had for many, many years.

I rubbed my temples. The whole thing was giving me a headache, but this time I couldn't just shove the mess aside and go hunt something. This time I was all in.

So what did I really want in this game?

I wanted to be able to come and go to the Underworld, a right that Lucifer had granted me, and to learn enough that I could help him rule. For that to happen, the Realm had to be stable. The dragons and other creatures needed to be able to roam freely. Royalty should once again visit one another across world lines, and they should share ideas.

"Why does this all rest on my shoulders?" I was ashamed that my tone came pretty close to a whine.

Because you're a power player now.

"I don't know that I will fight my father."

It doesn't seem like he has any interest in fighting you. He has a grudge match with the elves, same as you. Same as the elves do with him. No one is innocent in this, not even me.

I laughed without humor. "You made an illusion, Emery. Give me a break. Lucifer's castle is full of them. For funsies."

Different strokes, he thought.

Different strokes was right.

We've said it before, but I believe you're overthinking all this. I think you need to handle things the way you usually do.

Show up and kick ass.

"I have to grow up sometime."

Maybe. But when there is no right answer…

"Stop making good points. It's getting annoying."

He chuckled as I clued in to our surroundings. I recognized the rock area near the vampire lair, full of big boulders and wandering rock beings. We flew over the path that wound from it, our trip drastically shorter thanks to the dragons.

My stomach curdled as I saw the figures zooming through the lands, headed in the direction of the nearest Underworld entrance. Vlad's people, it must be, and they were on the move. The sheer number of them was enough to push my heart up into my throat.

"We've run out of time," I yelled, leaning forward to push Archion a little faster. Ahead, Saphira had put on the jets too, meaning Darius had also noticed the exodus.

We soared along the path that led to the unicorns, passing the waters that held flesh-eating serpents. Last time I'd been this way, Darius thought it odd there weren't any sentries. I didn't know if it was odd or not now, but they were equally absent.

Warm light rained down on the unicorn lands up ahead, not actual sunlight but close enough. The small island, surrounded by swampy water, was covered in lush greenery, from leafy trees to wide meadows. They weren't natural, those too-green trees, but created from magic. It was something I hadn't noticed the first time I was here, since the illusion was done so well.

Saphira circled, and we followed, Cahal behind us. Great, regal beasts herded together below, silky-smooth fur catching the soft light from the faux-sun. One neighed, shaking its head and white mane before rising on its rear hooves. The gilded horn sparkled.

"Wow," Emery said with a release of breath.

I'd have to agree. They were lovely in the way the dragons were magnificent. Imagine riding into battle on one of those beauties: your enemy would stop with a dopey smile that wouldn't leave their face until your unicorn friend plunged that beautiful horn into their middle.

Figures stood within the greenery at the southern tip of the island, most wearing black and standing as still as statues. One figure was huddled close to the largest unicorn in view, standing amid the poppies and daisies on a bed of plush green grass. I couldn't see the face, but I recognized the stature of our great buddy Vlad.

"Land." I tapped Archion. "He's trying to make off

with the unicorns! We have to stop him."

Saphira landed first, but Archion ignored me and did another lazy circle around the island.

Why aren't you landing? I asked as I peered down through the trees. More unicorns stood within, but they weren't grazing or moving toward the vamp visitors. They were staring northward.

Frowning, I looked in the direction they did, not seeing anything to raise suspicion...at first.

Wait, I thought, turning to look over Archion's shoulder. *Something is...*

Archion adjusted his course, flying east to west, giving me a sideways view. Boats dotted the murky sea. Five rowers to a boat and at least two dozen boats. They weren't manned by vampires, though—those willowy forms with their permanently windblown hair could only be elves.

"Look." Emery pointed ahead of us. Dots moved along the eastern pathways, too far away for any detail, but they had humanoid forms. They could've been vampires, but they were coming from the opposite direction as the Lair, and with the elves coming from the north...

"Hurry," I yelled, tapping Archion's shoulder in the direction I needed him to turn. "Get back to the others. The elves are going to try to wipe out the unicorns and probably anyone else around."

"Vlad was almost too late," Emery said, gripping my shoulders as Archion put on a burst of speed.

We sailed to the southern tip and dipped down.

Get off now; it'll be faster, Archion urged. *I need to look for a larger landing place. Take the mage.*

I whipped my right leg around, grabbed Emery's arm, and jumped. Rather than follow, he tried to yank me back, almost ripping my arm out of my socket.

"Come on," I yelled, using my magic this time and forcing him off Archion.

"Warn me next time," he hollered, his voice tight. "I don't usually just leap off dragons mid-flight."

"How would you know?" I sped us toward the ground quickly. "You've only ridden one twice."

"This…is…terrible," Emery said as the ground rushed up to meet us.

I slammed on the hover-brakes as Darius and Vlad turned to look at me. Penny stood off to the side, head back, eyes wide, her attention firmly fixed on the unicorn matriarch rather than her fiancé's dive through the air.

"Reagan, so good of you to—"

I cut Vlad's posturing short. "Elves! Quick, elves are coming!" Something occurred to me. "Shit, we should've warned the unicorns on the north side of the island. Will they know to run? Will they be fast enough?"

Vlad's eyes narrowed marginally, as if he suspected a trick, and honestly, maybe it would've been a good one if I'd thought I could pull something like that off on a vampire. Darius, however, knew better.

"Where are they coming from?" he asked, surveying the vampires around us. "How many?"

I closed my eyes and repeated what my perfect recall had printed onto my brain.

"Is this everyone?" I motioned around the clearing at the vampires standing idle.

Vlad's head snapped right, where his second-in-command stood in her leather bustier and spiked high heels. "Send someone for backup. We don't have enough to keep the elves at bay for long."

"No." I put out my hand, sparing a glance for Darius and hardening my resolve. "No." I met Vlad's eyes. "Take a team and get the unicorns out of here. Get them down to the Underworld. Find my father and tell him they need protection. Tell him to make them comfortable."

Darius studied me for a moment, but he didn't question my command. He turned and nodded to Vlad.

"How magnanimous of you," Vlad said, nodding at his assistant. She zoomed off and started barking orders.

"It isn't about me." I turned to the great beast beside us, the matriarch, her radiance stopping my breath for a moment. Her soft mane fell down her velvety neck, glowing in the sun. Her deep eyes took me in. "You saved my life once. It's my turn to save your...herd." Man, I hoped she'd be cool with me calling them that. "Go. Hopefully one day we'll meet again."

She neighed and shook her head, drawing my attention to that foot-long horn.

Clouds rolled and boiled above us, and I looked up in confusion as I turned back to the others.

"An enemy has set foot on the island," Darius said, stripping off his clothes, Vlad doing the same thing beside him.

"It seems the elves aren't here for tea and a friendly chat," Vlad said.

"Reagan, take them by air," Darius said.

"You plan to fight them by foot?" Emery asked as the unicorns started to move, running toward a team of assembling vampires directing them south toward a land bridge.

"We are their protectors, Mr. Westbrook," Vlad said, dropping his folded clothes to the ground, "a troth we take very seriously. They have young ones that can't run as fast. We need to give them a fighting chance."

CHAPTER 9

UNICORNS RACED FROM the trees north of us, neighing, their hooves stamping the ground. Those young ones Vlad spoke of galloped with four left feet beside their mommies, some of their legs wobbling and most not coordinated enough to run at high speeds.

More unicorns of all sizes burst from the sides of the island in a mad panic to get out. One took a great sniff as it thundered by, tilting its nose into the air, its nostrils flaring.

"Penny can stick to the ground with me," Emery started, "since Reagan can use her magic from—"

He cut off as the unicorn skidded to a stop, its hooves cutting into the grass and churning up dirt. Another unicorn bumped into its rump. It slowed as it circled past, then looked back at its pal before continuing on its way. They clearly didn't like the idea of leaving anyone behind, which was probably why the matriarch still stood beside the vampires, her head swinging, watching her herd head south.

The unicorn that had left the stampede regarded me

with shining black eyes as it stomped at the ground. It huffed, blasting me with its hot breath, before bending and sniffing me. I watched that horn come within a foot of my head, not impressed by this turn of events.

That must be Lucy, Darius thought, and I remembered the foal whose mother we had saved. The foal had rubbed against me, which was apparently a no-no—vampires were forbidden to touch without permission, and mothers rarely gave it—and then went to Darius.

I grimaced as it—she—nudged me with her nose. The matriarch stamped her foot and nodded her head, clearly annoyed. Or warning me? Lucy did it again, though, now snuffling my temple with her nose. Her horn stuck out above me, and if she crashed her head down, I would be sorry.

"Apparently she wants you to pet her," Vlad said with a flat expression, his suspicious gaze sliding to Darius.

"Right, okay, but there's danger coming, Lucy," I said out of the side of my mouth, and rubbed her nose. "You need to get going."

"She has a human name, too. Interesting," Vlad quipped.

The flow of unicorns defecting from the trees had slowed. The sky boiled, angry black clouds announcing that bad news was coming. At the rate the elves had been moving down the path, they should've been here by now. Then again, if they'd noticed the dragons, they probably realized they should wait for backup from the boats. Vlad and Darius had clearly known the elves wouldn't immediately rush in.

Lucy neighed, stomped the ground, bumped my head with her nose one last time, and ran after the others. The matriarch's head was still now, and she stared at me. She was not impressed.

"Look, I'll explain later. Just get out of here, would you?" I motioned her on, not wanting to run for Archion and show her my back. I didn't want that horn through it. Then again, at the rate these beasts were fleeing, I wasn't sure about their prowess in battle.

Cahal jogged up, offered a bow to the lead unicorn, and pulled his sword from its place on his back. It glittered like the unicorn's horn. "I will fight on the ground. Coppelia will follow Archion's lead in the air."

"Ah. The druid is back." Vlad smiled, and it was like we weren't under attack and running out of time. This freaking vampire was too cool for his own good. "It seems you've chosen your side again."

Cahal's eyes were so hard that I was surprised they didn't stake the vampire where he stood. "Yes. I like to win. I intend to have a perfect track record."

Vlad's smile sent a chill through my body. He glanced at the matriarch unicorn. She bobbed her head and then pushed through us, taking up the rear of her herd.

"Excuse me," I mumbled, knocked to the side. Clearly I was on her shit list.

"What's the plan?" Penny asked, pointing at Darius. She probably knew I didn't have one.

"I'll lead the team on foot," Vlad said, looking between Penny and Emery, at the vampires that hadn't gone with the unicorns. He looked at me. "Heir." It was the first time he'd officially recognized me by title. Huh. "This is an illusion. I assume you can take away their hiding places?"

"But then we'll also take away yours," I said.

"We don't need them." His form shifted into a pasty monster, Darius following his lead. The vampires to the back did the same, readying for battle.

I patted Cahal. "Give 'em hell."

"With pleasure," he murmured.

"Penny, you good—"

I cut off when she hurried north with Emery, not needing me to shove her into battle anymore. "Cat's in the Cradle" was playing somewhere, I just knew it.

I delved into the magic on the island, feeling its connection to the sky and careful not to sever it lest I expose everyone to what had to be dawn by now. Once that aspect of the illusion was protected, I hovered into the air toward Archion, already picking at the rest of the illusion. The overall design was some great work, large in scope, but they hadn't equipped it with any fail-safes—once you started pulling on a thread, the whole sweater would unravel.

Why are the other riders on foot? Archion asked as I took out a bushy tree and let him lift into the sky. This was a place designed for unicorns—there wasn't enough open space for the dragons' great wings.

We need more numbers. They'll take the ground, and the dragons can provide cover from the sky.

You might leave my back?

Possibly. One can never tell what will happen. Fly close to the tree line.

I continued working on the illusion, pulling faster now, wiping away the trees first. The ground began to shift into a flat, sandy surface. I watched over Archion's shoulder for any stray unicorns that might have been revealed, but they'd all made it out. Most of the boats had docked, but a couple of them lingered in the murky water, their rowers pulling for all they were worth. They wouldn't make it.

Can you handle the boats? I thought, seeing Darius lead the charge through the quickly disappearing trees. I skipped ahead in my thread pulling, working at the edge of the swamp where boats had docked. The illusion started to falter as Archion pumped his wings and gained speed. He swooped low, opening his maw and spewing fire across the boats still headed toward shore.

Magic blasted us from behind as flames enveloped the rowers, all of them stopping and throwing their hands up to ward off Archion's wrath. Then they stopped moving, not able to combat fire. Good news for us.

Magic slapped us, then crushed. Archion faltered, tilting dangerously toward the right.

I turned toward the onslaught and found two elves standing side by side with their hands up. Saphira was right behind us, though, just cresting through the unraveling trees, and she didn't hesitate to act. Her flame washed over them, catching them unaware. They spasmed and tried to turn, but it was too late. In moments, they were incinerated.

More and more trees cleared, leaving squatting elves caught with their pants down, so to speak, looking around wildly for cover that no longer existed. Coppelia slammed them with fire next, dipping low to get good and close. She wasn't as powerful as Saphira or Archion, but it made her no less eager to join the battle. She charred the sandy ground and set fire to any trees that hadn't yet cleared away.

I don't like elf magic, Archion thought, gaining altitude now that the other dragons had handled the immediate threat. *It makes me very angry.*

He didn't sound angry in his thoughts, and I had a suspicion this type of anger was cold and calculated. He was about to go on a killing spree. I was game.

Fire at will, I thought, watching Darius in his monster form zoom into the vicinity of the elves. He caught them as they turned to look up at the dragons, probably intending to combine their might against them. They were likely better at magical cooperation than old-school mages, but not the mages Penny and Emery were training up at the Guild, who would *hopefully* be meeting us at Roger's shifter compound. Hopefully because Vlad had a way of infiltrating people you thought were loyal and turning them to his cause. It would be very interesting to see which sides people chose in all of this.

Myself included.

Can you protect your friends? Archion thought, swooping low again.

Yes. Burn the shit out of those bastards.

He roared, using his special brand of magic to freeze up everyone but Penny, who was behind Cahal one moment and in front of him the next. She'd become amazing at the *mind over matter* side of things.

As we neared, I covered Darius with ice magic. Archion blew fire, scorching elves and the ground alike. The elves on the periphery managed to jump to safety, but Darius was on them a moment later, slashing his claws through their middles or stopping to wrench off their heads.

Pick me up in a minute. I pushed up to standing and then jumped, allowing myself to free-fall for a moment, until I got below the oncoming dragons. Fire slashed into the exposed ground to my right, charring elves and sand, while I covered a spell-slinging Penny, and then Coppelia breathed fire to my left, and I shifted my protection to Cahal and Emery.

A shock of magic slammed into my back, knocking the breath out of me. Pain trickled through my middle and twisted, like it would snap my spine.

I'd felt this magic before. It would not, in fact, break my spine. They'd had to bring in a higher-powered elf to even make me scream, and when that wasn't enough, they'd resorted to breaking my fingers and other bones by hand or using weapons. This pain was nothing compared to what had come later in those dungeons. I could ignore it easily.

The elf crouched in the few bushes that my magic had not yet eaten away.

Another burst of magic came at me, but I pushed back, free-falling for another moment to get into range before shifting to a hover and blasting the creature with hellfire. It seared through the illusion and the elf both, cutting a line through its chest and unraveling the bush. Whoever did up this illusion had done a bang-up job, but wasn't trying to protect it from magic like mine.

Archion flew at me, and I turned around.

Now, he said, because Penny and Lucifer had both made us look like amateurs when they'd done this, and Penny *was* an amateur. We clearly had to practice with vocal cues for the time being.

I dropped onto his shoulder and nearly bounced off. He tilted to keep me on, and I grappled for a better hold.

You need to line up better, I told him.

You need to hold your hover a little stiller, he barked back.

It was clear neither of us planned to accept responsibility for that nearly failed attempt.

A spell swept a line of running elves. It sliced through them at an angle, killing a few of them immediately, and severing limbs on a couple of others. An arm blew off. One flew backward, *sans* right leg, and into the murky water. A wormlike creature with fins and little legs exploded out of the surface, chomping the body with its sharp-toothed maw before rolling onto its side and falling back into the water with a splash.

Archion pumped his wings to gain a bit of altitude and keep away from the water's surface. I just stared for a moment with wide eyes. That would not be a fun way to go.

Of course, neither would facing Penny and Emery when you'd wronged them in the past.

One of the elves was trying to crawl away to God

knew where, but Emery stalked toward it, his face closed down into a terrifying mask of rage.

Cahal waited behind him, his sword out and dripping. Three elves popped up from behind an unraveling group of bushes near him and ran for it, but Cahal caught up with them easily, whipping his sword around and cleaving them with a few skillful slashes. Darius went after a few others, jumping and landing on their backs, ripping and tearing.

I think they got this, I said, looking over the island. There were still a few spots of vegetation to the south, the west, and the east, where Vlad should be fighting. Beyond, no boats filled the swamp and nothing walked the paths.

Let's go check on the other group.

We flew that way, and I realized just how much three dragons could tip the scales in a battle.

Vlad had a dozen or so upper-middle-tier vampires. They were strong and fast and experienced, and yet their battle hadn't ended. They still fought a dozen or so elves, Vlad moving incredibly fast—swiping at one, turning and sticking a second in the chest, and launching at a third, teeth ripping at the jugular.

A band of elves had broken off, racing for the path.

They are probably the track-and-report squad, I said as Archion sped after them. *Or else they thought they might intend to do some damage to the unicorns and the vampires already on the way.*

I guess we'll never know.

He bore down on them, offering them no way to dodge or scoot around the outside. His flames rolled over them, blistering in intensity.

It's almost too easy, I thought as he made a loop around.

Half of the demons in the Underworld won't be bothered by fire, and I can't kill with Glaciem *magic. Not to mention that they have dragons as well. Very experienced dragons. If we are battling them, it won't be easy at all.*

I blew out a breath. There was that. And also the fact that the more powerful elves might be able to knock him out of the sky with their magic. We'd have to cross that bridge when we came to it.

Vlad and the vampires were too close to the enemy, all of them spread out, so I wouldn't be able to shield them if Archion did a fly-by flaming.

I'm headed down, I thought. *Kill whoever you can, however you can.*

The vampires, too?

I laughed. *Tempting, but no.*

I leapt off and free-fell a good ways before putting on the air brakes. My feet touched down, and then I was running, throwing air knives at the nearest elves. The first knife sliced an elf in the neck, dropping it to a knee. The second missed, and I disintegrated it in midair.

When I reached the kneeling elf, I kicked it in the face and lit it on fire before running toward Vlad, smashing the second elf between two bursts of air.

"Push them away," I yelled, grabbing one with magic and tossing it into the air. Archion swooped down just in time, like a dog after a ball, and cracked bones between his teeth. We might not be great at midair landings, but that move had to earn us some style points. "Or crowd together, and I can cover you with ice."

Vlad stuck an elf in the middle with his claws and ripped upward. He flung the creature off and grabbed another to fling, apparently for me. I lit it on fire. Easy-peasy.

He darted toward the others, barking a few words I didn't understand, and they broke away from their fights. Once they were close enough, I covered us all with ice and stuck up a thumb for Archion to go scorched earth. Or…scorched Realm, I guess.

"Dragons are quite the asset," Vlad said, in his human form again. He stood naked and slightly disheveled beside me, blood leaking down his arm. "You have…three, correct?"

"We don't *have* any of them. We work with three of them. How many do you work with?"

His gaze was cool as fire coated the group, flaying the elves on the outside of my spell.

"You made quite the impression on Lucifer when you were down there," he said as Archion passed. The vampires rushed forward, killing the elves while they were down.

"Yes, I did," I replied, stepping farther away. "Take a hint."

The island's illusion continued to unravel, but no enemies remained standing. The elves lay in twisted, blackened messes along the charred sand.

Silence settled around us, the vampires catching their breath. One zoomed away as a few changed back into their human forms, and I assumed he was going for clothes. Vlad wouldn't be so stupid as to pick a fight with us right now.

He put out his hand, indicating the barren ground. "Thank you," he said, his voice smooth and silky, his stupid face unbearably handsome. It was very disconcerting, like appreciating the look of a lion. Dazzled one minute, dead the next.

Archion landed not far away with a rumble in his throat and smoke coming out of his nostrils. It was a warning for Vlad.

"For helping us protect the unicorns," Vlad continued. "I know that you hoped to win them, or some of them, to your side. And you might've, but now they are beyond your reach."

There it was—there was the dig.

"The elves are clearly starting to play dirty," I responded, ignoring it. "And I don't have a side. Apparently I'll be standing in the middle."

Darius ran into the area, slowing when he saw us. The dragons sailed lazily overhead, Penny and Emery on Saphira and Cahal on Coppelia.

"The elves are starting to play dirty, yes," Vlad said, glancing at Darius. "From reports I've received, their…foul play won't be relegated to the Realm. If you truly plan to stand in the middle, you might watch yourself."

Darius tilted his head down a bit, coming to a stop next to me.

"One last thing." Vlad shifted his weight a bit, his gaze on Darius now. "Who led the other vampire group into the Underworld?"

Darius's arm came around my waist. "Someone who isn't to be trifled with. Someone who doesn't have a side in this conflict but is pretending to choose ours at present."

Vlad's eyes sparkled, and I bet that he knew it had been Ja. I mean, who else could it be? Ever since Penny had awakened the extreme elder from her old-age fugue, she'd been sticking her fingers in everyone's affairs.

"We should go," Darius murmured to me.

Before I turned, I looked Vlad straight in the eye

and said, "I didn't tear down the whole illusion. But the elves might do so on the battlefield." I looked up at the sky, then back down at him. "Choose my father if you want to, but I guarantee he won't protect you if the sun makes an appearance. Not if he doesn't have to. I, on the other hand, will give my life to protect Darius. If you stand next to me, you will stand in shade. Either way, you will never sit on the throne."

CHAPTER 10

CHARITY STOOD AT the front of the gathering and looked at the assembled troops. Shifters in animal form waited in a horizontal line of ten, facing the portal within the shifter compound. Two lines of warrior fae stood beyond them. After that stood a row of grim-faced mages, the Bankses included. They wouldn't be kept away, no matter their age...or sweat suit clothing choices.

This crew wasn't their full arsenal by a long shot, but these individuals had been handpicked for their experience, power, and determination under fire. They didn't need many right now—they needed a quick, hard punch to create an opening, and then intense cover while Reagan and the others made the journey into the Brink.

Roger stood halfway between their people and the portal, nude and waiting for word. He faced the two constantly arguing *Seers*, who stood to Charity's right. Romulus stood beside Roger with a composed though expectant expression on his face.

"We need time to get them through the portal," Karen shouted at the Red Prophet.

A battle scene flickered through Charity's mind, but she squinted to clear it, not letting it materialize. Her visions were coming often, always changing, like a TV on the fritz. It was not normal for their kind, and given she was only half fae, she'd heard whispers questioning whether she could be trusted at all.

Short answer: no. Not when it came to predicting the future. Though the Red Prophet had said the frequency of the visions indicated the battle would likely be coming soon.

Well, no shit.

"Hey," she said to Roger and Romulus as she approached.

"It is a fine line between *enough time*...and *too much* time." The Red Prophet looked at the sky. "We have made a huge boon today, though only one will have realized it, and he ain't talking."

Karen slammed her hand down on the TV tray propped up in the dirt. Her crystal ball jumped. A few tarot cards fluttered in the breeze. The left side of her folding chair dug into a soft patch. "I don't care about what happened earlier; I care about what will happen in ten to twenty minutes. My child is approaching this portal from the other side with her merry band of idiots, and I need to get her help so that she can make it through. *Focus.*"

"Yes. I can see how this might be a troubling time for you," Red Prophet said slowly, as if she was trying to calm Karen down. The two were like cats and dogs, the rabid variety.

"Hello," Romulus said, his eyes crinkling at the corners. He was always happy to see her, which was miraculous, since nobody else was happy at all. The other warrior fae weren't just questioning her visions but the whole enterprise. Apparently they'd forgotten the elves' mistreatment and their trespasses against both Charity and Romulus.

Of course, since most of them had been hiding in the Flush, they'd only heard about those things secondhand. They probably thought Romulus had made it up to support her.

Whatever the case, her people were shaken up, but there wasn't much she could do about it at this point but stay the course. This had to be done for the good of all.

"How are you?" her father asked, which meant she'd at least mastered the fae art of appearing not to give a shit. She was getting very, *very* good at hiding her extreme anxiety and turmoil over what was to come.

"Great." And she'd gotten very good at lying, too. "Everyone is primed and ready. It doesn't sound like they have an exact time—"

"Five minutes," the Red Prophet yelled, and put out her hands before bending to the side and windmilling her arms. She went all in with the dramatics when she did this stuff. It was tough to take after a while.

Karen's lips pressed into a hard line, and it came as little surprise when she started shuffling her deck. Wind whirled up from the flat ground, bringing the smell of cultivated lands and the distant cows. This was a working ranch in some respects, but thankfully there was so much acreage that the shifter predators could move about freely—or congregate around the portal—without disturbing the livestock.

With a sudden movement, Karen slapped a few cards down, her gaze straight ahead. Her eyes flicked downward and then shifted back and forth, reading her cards. She nodded with a sigh. "Five minutes. From…"

"Now!" the Red Prophet called.

"N—" Karen scowled at her. She clearly couldn't be rid of the fae *Seer* soon enough. They'd probably both retire after this.

Romulus looked at the waiting force before stepping away and gracefully pulling his sword. Roger's skin bubbled and boiled as he reduced down into a large wolf, much bigger than his natural counterpart. Charity felt the song of battle pick up on the breeze. She looked through her people to find Devon just behind, a big black wolf working his way up the ranks. He wasn't ranked highly enough to be standing up here with them yet, but she knew it wouldn't be long.

His yellow-eyed gaze bored into hers, and excitement and anticipation washed through their magical link, fueling her adrenaline and strengthening her resolve. Her answering confidence swayed back to him. She didn't know about the visions, and she couldn't help what her people thought of her, but fighting and battle had always made sense in a way that required no description. It was in her blood. Before long, her people would realize that. The shifters already had.

She turned to face the portal, on the other side of Roger from her father, and drew her sword. The song of battle increased. A vision flickered through her mind, but she cut it off and chased it away. *Not now.*

"Three minutes…" Karen called, staring at her watch. Her muscles were tight and her eyes hard.

"*The elves are turning one by one, hurrah, hurrah,*" the Red Prophet sang softly, still bent over but her outstretched arms still now. Lines formed around her eyes, squeezed shut. "*The elves are spooking one by one, hurrah, hurrah. The elves are prancing one by one, the heir will come and cut their fun, and we'll all go marching down, to the field, to chop out their hearts.*"

"That went downhill fast," Charity murmured.

The Red Prophet started in on a spirited rendition of the next part of the song, but Charity focused on the battle drums in her mind, beating in time to her heart. The world went still and all sounds ceased for her but for that drum. But for the inner song of battle flowing on the breeze.

"One minute, counting down," Karen said over the Red Prophet's singing.

The Red Prophet cut herself off abruptly, then said, "It will be she that saves the day. Not with the sword. But with the soul."

"I didn't *See* that," Karen replied. "I don't even know who you are talking about."

"You don't *See* all, and soon that will be very apparent to all who matter," the Red Prophet replied.

"Keep it up and you won't *See* anything. You'll be too busy falling from someplace high. You might heal fast, but when all your insides are on the outside, I doubt you'll heal fast enough."

"Threats. What fun."

"Thirty seconds," Karen shouted, her frustration and anger at the Red Prophet drowning out her worry for her daughter. She might not know it, but the Red Prophet's antics were actually helping her push through the fear for her child.

"Go!"

Charity took off running, shoving through the portal at the same time as Roger and Romulus. Magic sucked at her energy and ran its claws across her middle, but she ignored it out of practice. A swell of enemy appeared before her amid the puffy green trees and colorfully speckled flowers on the sides of a limestone path. At least four dozen elves waited there, their power thrumming around them, and a troop of centaurs waited to the side, swords in hands and hooves stamping. Looked like Vlad hadn't grabbed them all. Some were still loyal to the crown.

Two large forms flew through the air, great wings beating at the sky. Sun shone off their glittering scales, and smoke curled from their great maws, curling upward. Dragons. Holy shit, they were fantastic. Charity was suddenly incredibly envious of the people sitting on their backs, leaning over to look at what was unfolding down below.

Charity rushed forward as their people gushed through the portal behind them, traveling in twos and threes. She pulled her sword to the side, ready to swing at the back of the first elf, when the blue dragon roared. The sound vibrated off her body before digging inside, freezing up her muscles and clamping her jaw shut. The white dragon swooped down, belching fire at the gathering enemy. It seared across the lines, blistering skin and forcing out high-pitched wails of agony.

The roar stopped, and Charity unstuck her feet from the ground, shaking and suddenly winded. Crap, that was intense. She'd had no idea they could do that.

"Marshal your will to overcome the dragon's magic," Romulus yelled through the din. "Except the fire—will alone won't keep you from burning to death."

The elves at the front threw up their hands, and the dragons' great wings stilled for a moment before tilting away from the onslaught of magic, each turning in a different direction.

"They've assembled a lot of power here," Halvor yelled from behind as more of their people pushed through the portal. "They must've known the heir and the dragons were coming. We have to take out these elves."

Fire erupted from the pale orange sky, and only then did Charity see the third dragon, smaller than the others and pink, with a musclebound man on its back. The fire cut through the line of elves, sending them running. This dragon's fire wasn't as powerful, however, and only a few perished in the blast. The rest scattered, spreading out, giving the dragons less of a tightly focused target. It did the trick against the elves' attack, though, cutting it off so the larger dragons could regain their composure and lift higher into the sky.

A lion's roar reverberated through Charity, signaling that Steve was on the scene and ready to go. She grinned maniacally, cutting into the back of one elf before kicking the chest of another so she could land a kill strike on a third.

Another dragon roar loosened Charity's bowels, and she clenched and balled up a little, worried she'd crap herself right here on the battlefield. What her dad had said echoed through her mind—*marshal your will.* She fought the effect of the roar as a dagger enlarged in her field of vision.

She dodged the strike and swiped with her sword before rolling across the ground and popping back up. The dagger now lay on the ground with the elf's arm. Roger snarled before lunging, tearing out its throat.

Another group of elves to her right were poised to throw more spells at the dragons. These ones conveyed a confidence that suggested they actually had some experience. Maybe they were old enough to have fought in the last battle with Lucifer. They'd be trouble for him in the coming conflict.

She ran that way as the figures on the dragons above jumped, falling through the air.

Charity knew one moment of blind terror, worrying that the elves had thrown the riders to their deaths, and then the figures dramatically slowed within ten feet of the ground. Reagan had them.

A sword sliced through the air, and Charity barely spun in time. The blade cut through her skin, pain welling up and sending tingles down to her fingers. Fucking ouch.

Devon flew through the air, his paws hitting the elf

in the chest and his teeth clamping over its face. He ripped his strong neck from side to side as he took the elf down, wrenching the head loose. That ended that problem.

Charity threw up her hand and called down lightning as more elves turned toward them, finally registering that the attack wasn't just from the front and now splitting their forces.

Good. That had been the plan.

Reagan and team pushed forward from the front, clearly targeting the strongest elves in order to protect the dragons. Bodies started flying upward, thrown by an unseen hand. The blue dragon dipped down and snatched one out of the sky with its big teeth, chomping and ending the screams. Another dropped down beyond the crowd. The blue dragon let out another roar, slowing the roiling mass of bodies, then rained down fire.

Charity hacked through two elves, paused for Devon to take down a third, and caught sight of the druid coming toward them, aiming for the same force of elves they were battling. Sword moving so fast it was a blur, he walked forward as though marching through the jungle, determined though graceful, hacking through elves as if they were nothing more than vines. Her small hairs stood on end at the display, his cool efficiency with killing something she'd never seen before, not even with Halvor.

Another stream of fire rained down from the sky, rolling over Penny and Emery as they shot magic at their foe. It enveloped them but didn't hinder their progress. They were obviously protected by Reagan. The elves around them, however, were burned to a crisp.

Reagan ran through the middle of a cluster to Charity's right, throwing invisible knives and stabbing with an invisible sword. Hellfire bloomed from her hand, punching through an elf in front of her. An elf to the side of her froze and then squirmed before its body flattened in a spurt of entrails. Gross.

A centaur barreled through three fae, their swords slicing down its side but not stopping it. It thundered toward Reagan, his horse shoulder at head height and his long sword held at the ready. Charity sent a ball of lightning zipping across the melee. It smashed into his bare chest, and lightning erupted all over his body before the magic turned to fire. He screamed and stopped, beating at himself and dropping his sword.

With a sweep of Reagan's hand, his head was lopped off and fell to the ground. She glanced Charity's way and bent her head, a small bow in thanks.

Another roar that threatened to loosen Charity's bowels distracted her attention before she renewed her determination, running at a group of elves pushing toward Emery and Penny.

Charity sliced through one's back, pulled her sword back, and stabbed through another's chest. She pulled down the lightning, stabbing them in the heads with electricity as the natural dual-mages shot spells at the centaurs.

A huge roar echoed through the landscape, larger than any dragon, vibrating in her ears and turning her blood to ice.

She snapped her head right to see a huge T. rex stomp down, its big foot passing through the middle of a centaur. A magical distraction, then. Callie and Dizzy had stepped up their game with its size and sound.

Steve the lion pushed up to her side and lunged, smashing into an elf that had been intent on sending Charity into the afterlife. It screamed, showing its teeth, before the lion smashed into it. Devon was there a moment later, taking out another elf that had been running for help.

Charity needed to pull herself together. She'd thought she was ready for battle. She'd thought she was experienced enough to be an incredible asset. She had to stop getting frozen up by dragons and distracted by large-scale magic!

Another plume of fire rained down on the right, followed by a burst on the ground, Reagan working seamlessly with her dragon. Cahal strutted toward two centaurs, swinging his sword over his head and slamming it into the holster strapped to his back. He shrugged out a bow from who knew where, followed by an arrow from the sheath next to his sword, and then nocked and shot in one incredibly fast, smooth motion.

One centaur reared up in shock and got an arrow in his underside. Another arrow, nocked and shot inhumanly fast, blossomed in the neck of the second.

Charity sprinted and ducked, running under a third centaur while stabbing upward. Hot liquid spilled down on top of her, and she dove and rolled as the creature screamed and stomped her hooves. She'd rather not be trampled by a horse-woman, thanks.

Back up in a flash, she sliced off a foot and dodged a kick, seeing Devon in trouble with another centaur. The bastards were big, and given that Cahal still hadn't taken his two down despite peppering them with arrows, they were obviously tough to kill. She dodged another flailing kick, pushed in, and stabbed again, tearing the underside out. That had to do it.

Devon yelped as a hoof took him in the hindquarters, and molten fear cut through her. Dodging an elf, ducking around Cahal, she dropped her sword and slammed her hands together. Hellfire shot out, blistering in its intensity, and struck Devon's attacker on the right shoulder. She ripped it down and across, cutting the thing in half.

Cole the yeti roared, lumbering over to protect his alpha, but it was done. The top half of the bare-chested woman slid off the bottom, ruining a pair of very nice breasts. *Sorry, lady. You chose the wrong side.*

Charity picked up her sword, and Steve joined the yeti, targeting the final centaur on this side of the battle. They didn't need her help, so she looked for the next elf to strike.

Bodies littered the ground. Her dad stood among them across the way, Halvor at his back, bloody and disheveled. Roger was up near the natural dual-mages, his sides heaving as he caught his breath, and Emery and Penny seemed to be doing what she was: looking for another fight. Reagan and the monster version of Darius stood in the middle of a group of downed centaurs, both smeared with blood. The two of them were a helluva force to be reckoned with.

Silence descended on the battlefield as the dragons flew overhead.

They'd won their victory, but it was only the first in what would surely be a long, grueling fight.

CHAPTER 11

"I SWEAR, I cannot take one more second with that woman," Karen said, sitting across from Penny at the long table in the mess hall at the shifter compound.

I sat on the other side of Emery from Penny, leaving enough of a gap that it looked like I was giving him space, when really I was politely getting as far away from Karen as I could. She was in a mood, and if she talked to me, *I* would be in a mood. That grudge I felt was still going strong.

Cahal sat across from me, leaving a sizeable gap between himself and Ms. Bristol. He didn't care about being polite.

"I don't get it," I said, looking at his plate filled with vegetables. "I don't get it. You don't eat meat anymore? A guy your size?"

"She is intentionally trying to jam up the works," Karen continued. "I just know it."

"Centaurs are vegetarian," Cahal replied.

I held out my fork and lifted my eyebrows. "Yeah, and they suck. And the ones who attacked us are dead.

Terrible point."

"They're big, was my point," he replied as Karen continued to unload on Penny. "Death weighs on me after a number of years. I cycle through various eating styles. Currently, I don't wish to kill another living being if I don't have to."

I leaned on an elbow as I surveyed him. "You're kidding, right?"

His eyes were flat as he popped a buttered carrot into his mouth.

"You just cut down a whole bunch of living things." I finished chewing and sawed off another portion of steak. "Eating horse is taboo, and eating man is taboo, but if they weren't, you could've had your fill out there from your killings." I paused. "Is eating elf taboo?"

"Over the line," Emery said, chuckling. "That's just wrong. And probably not helping your argument."

"I don't need help making my argument," I replied. I poked at my steak, a little too rare for my taste, but I didn't plan on mentioning it. If you complained about the food in the shifter commune, you had to get into the kitchen and help cook. Given Darius was busy checking out the vampire quarters and probably wouldn't bail me out even if he wasn't, I didn't intend to raise a fuss. "This delicious steak is making my argument."

"It would be more prudent to eat centaur," Cahal said, cutting his potato, skin and all. He didn't scoop out the middle like normal people. "They are hard to kill. They are not raised to be food, like the useless animal you are eating."

"Well, that's just offensive to cows." I shook my head and sighed, tired but still going strong. The flight to the portal had thankfully been uneventful, and the help of the friendlies at the end a surprise bit of awesome. That might've been a tough battle, but it had ended up being manageable.

A few things stuck out, though. "They *were* hard to kill, but they went down eventually. The elves nearly bringing down the dragons, though…"

The guys fell silent in time for me to hear Karen rattling on. "I'm not sure I trust her, honestly. Sometimes the magic reveals a few paths to choose from, and she'll just throw in another one willy-nilly. It's almost like she just wants to throw everyone into danger so that the bad guys win. It's madness. I'm starting to wonder if she is losing her faculties."

I shook my head and looked away, my guts churning. Then I put down my fork. I would give my house to not know what came next. I had this sinking feeling that it wouldn't be great.

Because in today's battle, only the first few strikes had felt good, like I was seeking vengeance against the elves. When the dust, or in this case soot, settled, I hadn't felt vindicated. I hadn't felt better about what had happened to me. If anything, I hadn't felt anything for myself at all. My only emotion was relief that my friends had made it through safely. The worst they'd been dealt was Dizzy's pulled hamstring (the older dual-mages had stayed on the outskirts of the action, thankfully).

Sadly, though, in this last skirmish, people *had* gotten hurt. No one I knew, but three fae and two shifters had gone down. It could have been much worse if we hadn't outmatched and outnumbered the competition. In the final showdown, I doubted we'd outmatch either of the other forces. And if today was any indication, I wouldn't be worried about vengeance; I'd be worried about protecting those I cared about.

Emery's words from the beginning of our journey came back to me. Why should we go into this with an agenda about preserving the elves' rule? Why not just tear down everything and let them build it up?

Sitting here, now, the answer was frustratingly simple: because you couldn't leave an entire world unstable. The Mages' Guild was basically a corporation of magical people. If it weren't around, there would be instability, sure, but the mages would still exist within a greater framework of law and order. They would have the shifters to keep them in place, and the Magical Law Enforcement, and the non-magical government. Those overarching systems would help avoid a complete clusterfuck. Plus, the corrupt leaders hadn't been replaced with individuals from a different species, just a more solid organization of the same type of magical person.

This was a different situation. The people battling the elves mostly didn't live within the greater part of the Realm. They didn't know the unique challenges and trials involved in leading such a place. They would have to learn it all from scratch.

In the meantime, the world would plunge into lawlessness. Without direction, the fae wouldn't know how to police. The Realm was also impossibly vast, and they couldn't watch every nook and corner. In the shadows, the demons and vampires and whoever else crept into the open borders would take advantage of the lesser species that couldn't defend themselves. The strong would take advantage of the weak.

And sure, that was already happening, but at least right now the people of the Realm only had to worry about the elves. Take away their heavy-handed leadership, and you had a vacuum. So what was the answer?

Balance.

It was like the word had been whispered into my ear, and it kept pinging around my head.

Balance.

The worlds needed balance.

I had to protect my friends and family, make sure

the Underworld didn't wipe out the elves, or vice versa, and force balance into the worlds.

How the literal fuck was I supposed to do all of that, though? We were going to get crushed in the middle of those two forces.

I held up my hand. "Karen, all due respect, but Penny isn't going to help you pull your weight with the Red Prophet," I said, cutting into her chatter and realizing Cahal's eyes had been boring into me this whole time. He could look really creepy and stalkerish sometimes.

Karen swung her head around with slightly widened eyes. My stomach flipped. She was a woman you really didn't want to mess with. Magical or not, you always needed to watch your six where Karen was concerned. I'd just excited her crazy.

"Is that right?" Karen said quietly. Too quietly, like she might plan on finding some scorpions and putting them in my bed. "And what do you know about it?"

"Well, she probably knows that you recently sent her to the elf castle to be taken and tortured," Penny said, shocking me mute. She didn't usually stand up to her mother. "Then taken again and trapped. That's what she probably knows about it. Mother, honestly, you'll just have to do the best you can. We'll all have to do the best we can. You can help Roger, Romulus, and even Darius, but when it comes to Reagan, I doubt you'll get very far."

"Penelope Bristol, don't you sass your mother."

"Mother, I've had enough." She threw her napkin down and pushed to standing, stepping over the long bench.

I looked at Emery to see if we were all standing, or if he'd maybe try to calm her down instead. Given he sat frozen, clearly he didn't know what to do.

Cahal stood, though, like a cobra rising from its coil. He picked up his plate.

Apparently we were leaving.

"You have no idea what it's like in the thick of things," Penny continued, showing those ragged edges she'd gained after visiting the elves and touring the Underworld. "You don't know what it's like to watch your friend sacrifice everything for you and be unable to stop it. To spend months trying not to blame your own flesh and blood for the pain you were put through—that *she* was put through. I don't blame you, Mother, just so we're clear. I trust in your gift. But a lot of what the Red Prophet has said has been right, too. And now Charity's stuff is on the fritz, and my Temperamental Third Eye has gone nuts... It seems like something is interfering with your *Sight*, with everyone's sight, and this time I don't think the fates are going to lift their skirts and reveal their wares."

My mouth dropped open. A little smile played across Cahal's face.

"There is clearly not one right path, and that's good, because the last time there was one path it didn't work out that well for a few of us. You're just going to have to figure out your thing with the Red Prophet on your own." She picked up her plate, took a deep breath, and then finished, "As soon as the war is over, if we're both still alive, I am going to marry Emery, and there is nothing you can do to stop it." She nodded. "So there."

She turned around and stormed away.

I grabbed a fistful of Emery's shirt as Ms. Bristol's crazy eyes slowly slid to him.

"Go, go, go," I muttered, grabbing my plate with the other hand. "Let's go, let's go!"

"Excuse me," Emery said, picking up his plate and stepping over the bench.

I hustled him away, but we were close enough to hear Cahal behind us. "Ma'am, Penny is right about a couple of things. First, there will be many paths. In war, there always is. Sometimes there will be no right answer. Sometimes...you will need the Red Prophet to put in motion things you might not be comfortable with advocating. As for the second..." He paused for a while. "In my opinion, the fates are indeed interfering with your *Seeing*. And if not the fates, then Lucifer himself, and any of his people he's managed to smuggle into this compound. Be prepared for blindness."

I frowned at him when he joined us toward the

plate-drop area. A few shifters nodded to us as they exited the cafeteria-style area, most with plates. We'd beaten the dinner rush, which was good news judging by the amount of food these people had on their plates.

"What did you mean about Lucifer interfering with their *Sight*?" I asked, dropping my plate into the brown rubber basin at the dirty-dish station on the east wall, away from the line of shifters waiting for their turn at the rapidly emptying buffet.

"He has that ability, as do you. As do a couple other creatures."

"He certainly didn't tell me that," I muttered.

"What other creatures?" Penny asked.

A brick of a guy stepped in front of us, over six feet tall with a muscle-stacked body and a face that would make angels weep, wondering what had gone wrong with his genetics. Half his head was shaved and the other half long. There was probably some significance other than *I'm bad at fashion*, but I didn't much care to find out.

"Ma'ams, sirs," he said in a gruff voice. "This is a shifter-only eatery. You'd probably be more comfortable in the cafeteria set up for the mages and fae."

"Why?" I looked around at everyone minding their business, getting food and sitting down to eat it. "What's so special about this place? Are you just about to group together for a circle jerk, or something?"

His eyebrows flattened over brown, close-set eyes. "We have a housing unit for the shifters, and one for guests. That's the way it has always been done."

"I guess you're not so different from the fae at the root?" I asked, but of course he didn't know what I was talking about. Roger would, and I would definitely rub his face in it, just for funsies. When Devon's pack first brought Charity to visit the warrior fae, they'd been relegated to crappy guest housing far away from the other residences. Samesies on our second visit. "Anyway, we *are* shifters." I pointed at myself. "I shift into an asshole." I pointed at Cahal. "He occasionally shifts into a nice guy." To Penny and Emery. "They can make you stop shifting, forever, so you should probably just let them do what they want."

"Joe." Steve walked over with his customary grin and swagger. He clapped a hand on Joe's shoulder. "Don't antagonize the pretty blonde. She'll tie your dick in a knot, burn off that stupid haircut, and laugh at your pain."

"But sir…"

A hard edge crept into Steve's tone. "It's good. Leave it."

The man issued a curt nod and walked away with a stiff back.

"The mages and fae actually asked for a different sort of menu," Steve said, gesturing toward the door and then walking with us. "They wanted more options for vegetables and didn't like the meat so bloody. It was easier creating two eateries. Poor Joe thinks shifters are king and came to his own conclusions."

I pointed at him as we walked out the door. "You're tempting me to dash his dreams of being top of the food chain…"

Steve laughed. "Sure, just don't get caught by Roger. He's a bit wound up."

"We're all a bit wound up," Penny muttered.

"Not me. I'm going to go find a pretty little fae and help her forget about her woes." Steve winked and broke away right, sauntering across the grass to another sprawling, rustic building.

Deep night stretched overhead for about two miles, the stars plentiful and bright. Beyond that, the glow of the afternoon shone down. We'd stepped through the portal to a lightening sky, and with Roger's approval, I'd created a cover for the vampires. Penny and Emery had strung up a protective ward that would give the vampires time to get to cover if someone should try to tear down my artificial night.

"Reagan," Cahal said, his voice subdued in the fake night. "You interrupted the *Seer*. Why?"

I snapped my fingers, having completely forgotten about that. "Penny," I said, walking us back to the rooms Roger had designated for us within a sprawling three-story apartment complex that resembled a bunch of log cabins stacked on top of one another. It was really weird and had obviously been here for a while. Roger had apparently inherited managing this place when he became alpha of the North American pack. "Remember that spell in the Mages' Guild battle that judged if people were good or bad?"

Her face screwed up as she thought back. She nodded slowly. "I probably shouldn't have cast it, though. It's not for me, or magic, to judge who is good or bad. And really, are people either good...or bad? After being down in the Underworld and spending some time with your dad, I think everyone has the ability to be both."

I twisted my mouth to the side. "Yeah, I guess," I said in frustration. "It's just...how are we going to get rid of the bad elves so the good elves, or someone else who knows how to rule, and the Realm can step forward?"

"You're not planning on wiping them all out?" Cahal asked.

"You didn't seem to have a problem wiping them all out today," Penny said. "Or...yesterday? My sense of time is all over the place."

"I mean, sure, if they are trying to kill me, I will absolutely destroy them."

I reached the door to the confused apartment building and pulled it open, stepping to the side so the others could go through. Cahal grabbed the edge over my head and motioned me in. He never let a woman enter a doorway behind him, and I'd never asked if it was a gentlemanly thing, or he just didn't trust women. Probably a bit of both, since he was hot but unattached. More than one gal had probably wanted to stick something in his back for breaking her heart, or just cling to those muscles.

"But if they put down their weapons and ask for mercy...if they agree to tear down the restrictions limiting the Underworld, then..." I shrugged. "It's like what you just said, Penny—it's not for me to play god. The Realm needs stability, and killing everyone isn't a good way to achieve that."

"You sound like a grownup," Emery said.

"I know." I grimaced. "Can we still be friends?"

"Oh, we're friends now?" I could hear the laughter in his voice. "I thought I was just allowed to hang around because of Penny."

"Don't ruin it, or you'll be on the outside again," Penny murmured. She'd probably just elbowed him.

"It was spoken like a true leader," Cahal said in a deep voice dripping with respect.

"Gross," I replied, uncomfortable and not sure why.

I stopped at my door, number six, and noticed someone had stuck stickers to the sides of the metal number. Two additional sixes, three in all. Cute.

"I'll see you all tomorrow." I turned the handle and pushed, feeling Darius waiting for me within. He'd probably need blood, and I was eager to give it to him. While naked.

"Yup." The others continued on, heading to their rooms down the hall.

Once inside, I closed the door and locked it. I doubted any vampires would be stupid enough to interrupt our slumber, but someone else might, and I wanted to buy myself a second to wake up before I confronted them. Everyone had spies; I couldn't imagine the elves were any different.

The door to the bathroom was open, and I passed it on my way down the little hallway to the rest of the room. The rectangular interior was basically fashioned like a hotel room, with one large bed in the middle, a desk to the side, and a small seating area.

I stopped abruptly when I saw the individual sitting in one of the two uncomfortable armchairs facing an equally uncomfortable loveseat, upholstered in a green flowery pattern. There went my fake-evening.

CHAPTER 12

"AH CRAP, NOW what?" I asked, starting forward again as Ja looked up, her petite frame and pretty face proving the cliché "you can't judge a book by its cover" accurate. "Come to ask for another favor? Would you like us to get you out of the shifter commune this time?"

She smiled, and I broke out in shivers. It wasn't a pleasant sentiment coming from her.

Darius glanced up as I came around the loveseat.

"Good evening, *mon coeur*," Darius said, standing up out of respect, and then sitting down again as I did. "How was your dinner?"

"Very rare." I watched Ja closely. You just never knew when she'd rush you, I'd come to realize. "What's this about? Trading pleasantries with friends?"

"Your wit never gets old," Ja said, and though it wasn't said sarcastically, she meant it that way.

"We were waiting for you, though I'm not sure why." Darius entwined his fingers with mine and then thought, *She is up to something. Be on your guard.*

"She's always up to something," I said out loud, because that really wasn't a secret, and Ja didn't have any feelings to hurt.

Ja crossed one knee over the other, her pink satin gown very strange for a shifter compound, where the fashion of choice seemed to be a mountain-man style involving lots of plaid. Even Darius had dressed down to a less flashy look of jeans and a gray button-up. A little clutch sat on the ground next to her, and I wondered if she'd just come from a ball or dinner party or something. I didn't mention that, though. I didn't need another comment about my wit.

"Being that relations are somewhat…strained between you and Vlad, Darius," Ja began, "I thought you might want the truth of the past."

What my father had said about Vlad's skeletons rattled through my brain.

"Of course," Darius said after a brief pause, probably thinking along the same lines.

"The nature in which you were made was a lie," she said with a voice as silky as her dress.

I thought back to the story Darius had told me in Seattle, before I gave him blood for the first time. The memory was fuzzy, since it had happened before the vampire bond upgrade, but I recalled that he'd been besotted with a very beautiful woman. He'd wanted to marry her even though it was a bad match for whatever reason. But she was a religious fanatic, and somehow she got it into her head that he was a vampire. Quite ironic, since she ended up playing a pivotal role in him becoming one.

She'd lured him with the promise of a secret rendezvous, only to have him killed when he showed up. The attackers didn't do the job properly, however, and he lay there for hours, near death. It was then Vlad had found him, apparently, and changed him into a vampire.

We hadn't talked about it since that night. I'd honestly forgotten about it. Probably a dick thing to do, but in all fairness, I'd had a lot on my mind.

"Go on," Darius said.

"The woman you suspected did hire those men to kill you," Ja said. "She did think you were a vampire."

"I am well aware, yes," Darius replied.

"She didn't come to that conclusion by herself, however." Ja smiled sweetly. "Did you never wonder why a woman of minimal education became convinced you were a vampire after finding a few artifacts in your home?"

"Thinking people were vampires was very in vogue at the time," Darius replied.

"It was and it wasn't. I remember that time well. I was accused a few times myself, but always by people who had pretty obvious clues to go by, such as always being out at night but never in the day, the deaths of my lovers, that sort of thing. You didn't have those obvious signs, correct?"

Darius watched her, not saying anything.

"A dish with an image, a trinket, and the shape of your bushes?" She clucked her tongue. "Quite a leap."

I wondered how she'd known all of that, because Darius's lack of a reaction confirmed it was true. Her evidence was clearly giving weight to the big reveal that would happen sometime soon. My stomach twisted in anticipation. This wouldn't be good news. I could see the painting on the wall.

"She was a religious fanatic, yes, but the signs she thought she'd found were not obvious. They were occult in nature. Only someone educated would've guessed at their meaning."

"Debatable," he said in a strong voice, but I could feel the turmoil roiling through him.

Her eyes sparkled. She was enjoying this.

"She was very beautiful," Ja said.

"Yes, she was," Darius replied, joining Ja's little dance. The wait was killing me.

"You met her in the village, correct? She pulled the damsel-in-distress routine? What was it that happened, again?"

Darius tilted his head a little, anger starting to work through him. I couldn't tell if it was because of Ja, or being bamboozled by someone he'd almost let himself love.

"Her bonnet flew off, and she rushed into the lane to get it. She was nearly trampled by a horse," Darius responded. "I pulled her out of the way."

"Yes, that's right. That horse—it was pulling a carriage, correct?"

Darius inclined his head. Yes, it was.

"Do you remember the crest?"

So many feelings exploded through the bond that I couldn't comprehend or even name them. "I do not."

She reached down, picked up the clutch, opened it, and extracted a piece of paper. It was the only thing in there. She leaned forward and passed it to him.

He unfolded the paper and surveyed the design without comment.

The suspense was too much. "Do you recognize it?" I asked.

"It is Vlad's family crest, when he needs one," Darius answered as he folded the paper back up. "Ja is insinuating that Vlad orchestrated my misfortune and put me in a position where I would need saving. He kept me alive long enough to turn me into a vampire, his goal since before I'd even met Ernesta, apparently."

Ja nodded.

I closed one eye and screwed up my face. "Except...that seems like a lot of work for a guy that now just invites people to parties under false pretenses, feeds them a drink, and voila, new vampire. Why would he go through so much trouble?"

"Things were different then," Ja said. "We weren't nearly as organized as we are now. We didn't have the same resources. It was important to be a lot more secretive at that time."

Cold anger bubbled within Darius. I should feel bad for him. All this time he'd believed one thing, and the truth was a different thing entirely. I knew I should feel bad, but...wasn't that kind of what he did to people, too? He didn't do it anymore because of me, but he'd turned a great many people into vampires over his long life, and I doubted he'd asked most of them for permission. He definitely had not said sorry. Obviously many had forgiven him, or he wouldn't have been able to gather hundreds of vampires for this coming battle, but still. Being mad was like the pot calling the kettle black.

Ja sat quietly for a moment, watching Darius, who watched her back. It looked like they were silently communicating, but they couldn't—not like I could. Still, they were probably communicating with looks and body language.

"That information changes nothing between us," Darius finally said. "It does not help me in any way."

"Doesn't it?" she asked.

Did I detect a little annoyance in her tone?

"I assume you are referring to the agreement between Lucifer and Reagan, whereby Lucifer will hand Vlad over if she requests it?"

Ja didn't comment, but her eyes had taken on a keen edge.

"What good would it do to kill Vlad?" Darius asked with an indifferent tone, though his anger hadn't subsided. "It won't disband his followers or quell their delusions of greater representation within the Realm."

"Which they should have anyway, and we need to see that everyone is represented in the ruling tier," I cut in, because I'd forgotten that bit, and it should be included in this great plan of balance that I did not, in any way, want to institute. What a stupid position I'd found myself in. This was so not my jam, why had no one realized that?

"Vlad and Lucifer have the unicorns now, with Reagan's blessing," Darius said, ignoring me. "They are building their forces as more and more creatures leave the Realm, searching for someone who will tear the elves from power. With Vlad or without him, Lucifer is setting himself up to sweep through that battlefield and take the prize."

I lifted my eyebrows and studied him. I didn't know what to say. No one had told me the scales had tilted that far in my father's favor. Would we even be able to stop him?

Ja was silent for a long moment, the two back to staring at each other, a game of silent chess. Her eyes slid to me.

"You know, of course, that it will be easy to kill all the vampires fighting with Vlad?" she asked.

"Because the elves might fight during the day and pull down the illusion of the fake sun that protects them, right?"

A glimmer of rage flashed in her eyes.

She thinks you are intentionally being belligerent, Darius thought. *She thinks you are mocking her.*

Little did she know I wasn't smart enough to read her subtlety. I was honestly asking if there was something I was missing.

"Well, then." She uncrossed her legs, still holding her clutch. "I will leave you with a surprise gift, Darius. You will collect it in the next couple days."

"If you wish," he answered, noncommittally.

She stood, and Darius did the same, so I followed suit. I wasn't polite often, but when I was, I was annoyed by it.

Her stare bored into me. "Lucifer has issued orders to remove you from the battlefield—or possibly before. He doesn't want you harmed. Be on your guard if you hope to join the battle." Her eyebrow arched. "You *do* still hope to join the battle?"

"Yes," I replied. "And he won't be taking me anywhere. Someone has to stand up to him."

Her smile was slight. "Good. It wouldn't be wise to grant the Realm's throne to Lucifer. That kind of instability would lead to another war that might bring the worlds to their knees. The last thing we want is to be sequestered to the human lands forever. Their short life spans make them much too volatile as companions."

I scowled at her as Darius showed her out, and then kept right on scowling at her through the door.

"What's the matter?" Darius asked, returning. He lowered into the loveseat and took my hand again, gently pulling me down with him.

"I don't like that she's thinking along the same lines as I am in regard to the Realm. It makes me think I'm missing something."

"Then you won't be getting your revenge on the elves?"

He laid his arm along the back of the loveseat behind me and leaned closer, skimming his lips against my neck. Delicious shivers coated me, and I fluttered my eyes closed.

"I will, somehow. Either on the battlefield or some other time. I'll definitely get revenge. But…I just think it would be selfish to potentially trash a whole world because of my issues. It isn't fair to them. I've had a lifetime of thinking of nothing but myself, and it hasn't gotten me very far. I need to think of others."

He kissed my heated skin, sucking a little. His teeth scratched pleasantly, and his hand trailed up the inside of my thigh. "You are exactly right, and your determination to do right by them can only help your standing within the worlds when you step into your role as ruler."

I widened my legs, breathing heavily. "What do you mean?" I asked, drunk on his proximity, burning from the inside out.

"Lucifer has issued you a compromise." His tricky fingers reached my apex and rubbed. Waves of pleasure washed through me as his lips trailed a line of fire down to my throat. "He is opening the Underworld for you and allowing you the decision to rule or not, live there or not. It's what you wanted, correct?"

"Yes," I said, and it was both an answer and a reaction to his ministrations. The sensation built, tightening me up.

His lips closed over my nipple and he bit through the fabric lightly, enough to apply pressure but not hurt. I groaned, gyrating my hips against his clever fingers.

"I saw you force that powerful *conspector* into submission before we fled the Underworld. You were born to rule, Reagan Somerset, and I don't think it'll take long for you to realize that. You have sacrificed yourself for your friends, put the wellbeing of other creatures before yourself and your plans, and listened to those around you. You are planning to act in a way that benefits entire worlds."

I cried out as I orgasmed, arching backward.

Darius lifted up and kissed my neck again, over my pulse, before shifting his attention to my mouth and running his tongue over my bottom lip. "In such an incredibly short time, you are growing to fill the seat Lucifer has offered you. You will be an amazing ruler, and I will be proud to call you mine."

"Don't be so confident," I said as he yanked the fabric and unbuttoned my jeans. He pulled the zipper down slowly, now kissing along my jaw. "As soon as I get new digs, I'll dump you and level up."

I felt his lips curl into a smile. "There is no leveling up from me, and in just a moment you will scream out your agreement."

Infallible confidence to the last. He was right, though, the bastard.

"I can ask for Vlad, if you want," I said as he pulled my shirt off and tossed it behind him. He stripped my bra next, and his shirt with it. He kissed me, deep and sensual, and I ran my hands up his smooth, cut torso.

He paused for a moment, backing up to look into my eyes. "It would do no good, and I honestly don't know if I could best him. He might kill me instead."

"I'd never let that happen," I whispered.

"I wouldn't let you interfere. But what I said to Ja

wasn't to be taken at face value. She wants me to kill him. Or him to kill me. Both of us are powerful players in the vampire hierarchy, more so than any of the other elders. We have a delicate balance, even now, after choosing different sides. We have helped keep each other at this level for more than half of our lives. I was telling Ja that I would not take the bait and end him, thereby allowing her to move more freely in her pursuits. We will band together to stop her, if need be, and after this, that might be necessary."

"You said all of that while using completely different words?"

His lush lips curled up into a smile. He grabbed the back of my neck and pulled me closer, claiming my lips and my desire. His tongue swept through my mouth, and I pulled open the fly of his jeans. Reaching within, I claimed his hard length and ran my palm along it before gripping firmly and stroking.

He groaned into my mouth, backing off a little, his eyes hooded. "Yes, *mon ange.* I said all of that. She is incredibly dangerous. More so than anyone I have ever met. I knew she'd been a powerful player back in the day, but I had no idea what it might mean. I should not have put her in a position to want to re-emerge into our world in a significant way. Now I will need to put my grievances with Vlad aside and monitor her closely."

He grabbed the edges of my jeans and yanked them

off before ripping away my lacy red panties. He pushed his pants down and then my knees apart, leaving me spread and bare while he lowered his knees to the carpeted floor.

"You're really mad at Vlad, then?"

He ran his tongue up my slick center before enveloping my clit with his hot mouth and sucking, rolling his tongue around. My breath hitched, and pleasure consumed me before he quickly backed off and blew softly, the effect like a light tickle, driving my anticipation to incredible heights.

"I'm not mad about how he turned me. I've done worse, myself. To Moss, as a matter of fact. To many. I do not understand..." He sucked in the sensitive skin on the inside of my upper thigh before moving back to my core. Vampires were incredibly good at having conversations, deep or shallow, while in the throes of passion. It was madness, but did make his history lectures very enjoyable.

I arched, groaning, drinking in the pleasure, my desire pumping higher. My body wound up, right on the edge now.

He pulled back, leaving me teetering there. I whimpered, of all things, throbbing, desperate to spill over into orgasm.

"I do not understand why he kept it from me. He is my maker, regardless of how." He pushed to standing, and I looked at him like he'd grown two heads. Where the hell did he think he was going?

He scooped me up, walked me to the bed, tore back the covers, and set me down gently.

"It is something I will ask him one day." He bent between my legs again and flicked my clit with his tongue. Again. I climbed right back to the edge, pushing my hips up to his mouth, wanting deeper contact, more friction.

He blew again, then flicked.

"Damn it, Darius, fuck me, *please*," I said.

"Your wish is my command," he whispered, once again leaving me right on the agonizing edge and kissing up my stomach. He sucked in a nipple, right on the point of pain. I yelped then moaned, gripping his back, pushing up against his body.

He ran his lips up my chest, all the way to my neck, before pausing just over my mouth. His erection rubbed against me, and I angled myself, trying to capture it with my body. No such luck.

I whimpered again. This was what he did to me, time and again. I loved it as much as I hated it. He was so good in the sack it should be a crime.

"I never did love Ernesta, the woman who betrayed me," he murmured.

"I know," I replied softly, pulling my thighs up high on his hips. My core throbbed almost painfully. "Please,

Darius."

"But I held on to her memory all through this life," he went on, pulling back a little to look me in the eyes. It felt like I was looking straight into his soul. "I held on to the image of her beauty, the memory of her voice, and of my desire to wed her and finally tip into love with her. And then I met you. Everything she was pales in comparison to you. I am nothing without you. Ja thought I would be enraged to find out Ernesta was playing me at Vlad's behest. She thought I would hate Vlad for his role in that betrayal, but I haven't thought about her once since the night I told you of her. Since the night we were first together. I let go of her, then, and held on to you. Loving you came so easily. So quickly. And I've fallen deeper and deeper in love every day since. I will protect you with my life until the day I fall into eternal rest. My love for you will never yield, and my desire to serve you will never waver. I am yours, for all eternity."

I blinked my glassy eyes, my heart swelling with love. He kissed me then, with such feeling and passion that it swept my breath away. He lined up and thrust, filling me completely, body and soul. Almost immediately I exploded and then fractured into a billion little pieces, the sensation spreading through my body. He moved to my neck and bit. I groaned, and then I was building again, wild, ravenous for him. I moved with him, unable to speak but knowing my feelings were pouring through the bond to him.

The next explosion caught me by surprise, and I cried out. He kept going, though, reaching between us to manipulate my clit as he thrust, helping me climax again and again until it felt like we were bonding all over again. I shuddered but kept going, eyes squeezed shut, and held on for dear life.

CHAPTER 13

S HOUTING PULLED ME out of sleep, reverberating through the walls and crowding the space. I sat up in bed as Darius sprang up, dressing in a moment.

"What is it?" I asked, throwing back the covers and rushing to the window to answer my own question. My magic still held, the dark sky stretching above us to protect the vampires. Except for all I knew it could be night. I'd lost all sense of time.

A harried knock sounded at the door, and Darius opened it to a stern-faced Moss. Behind him waited the beautiful Marie and a team of Darius's better-equipped vampires.

"What has happened?" Darius asked as I hurried to get dressed.

"Demons," Moss said, his gaze cutting to me. "A host of them showed up, coming this way. The shifters and fae have stopped their progress, but it's clear they are here for Reagan. They attempted to sneak in, donning human appearances, clearly not realizing shifters can scent the difference."

"It's not like my father to forget something like that," I said, pushing through them and glancing down the hall of the weird apartment building. Penny and Emery came running, their eyes puffy with sleep.

"One of them tried to barter with Roger," Marie said, wearing a pair of Gucci track suit bottoms and a snug top showing off her curves. It was an outfit I never would've thought to put together, but it worked super well. The woman was too fashionable for her own good, especially in the midst of a bunch of shifters who did not care. "They want to take the princess to safety, per Lucifer's instructions."

I rolled my eyes and followed Darius as he and Moss started down the hall.

"Did he honestly think he could come in here and kidnap me?" I asked as Penny made it to my side. "I'm not a broken mess this time."

"It seems they want to…appeal to your sensibilities," Moss said in a deadpan tone.

"It sounds like you don't think I have any," I replied with a grin.

"Is it that obvious?" he murmured.

We both knew he wasn't totally joking, but I still laughed as we pushed out into the crisp night. No light glowed in the distance, suggesting it was after sundown. Wolves and other creatures ran to the north, headed toward the fight.

My magic thrummed, and I could feel demon magic close by, but it wasn't limited to the direction the group was heading.

I slowed, brow furrowed, and picked apart the feeling.

Charity ran toward us with Wolf Devon at her side, her rumpled clothes and hair suggesting she'd been woken up too. She did a double take at me before halting, turning my way.

"What is it?" she asked, Devon slowing.

I shook my head distractedly, focusing on the feeling. There was a second location, and it practically vibrated with strength. The demons were much higher on the power scale, indicating the other group was nothing but a distraction.

"This way," I said, and everyone followed me, including Charity and her growing group of fae. Devon's pack found him a moment later, filing in as more and more vampires joined us. Clearly I wouldn't be confronting the second group without a posse.

"Reagan." Dizzy and Callie hurried my way from the right. Dizzy held up a piece of chalk as he neared. "I have this."

"What will you do with that?" I asked, curving around the next building and then going straight. The second presence didn't move, just stayed in the same location, waiting for me.

"I can lock you in a circle they can't penetrate," he said. "Theoretically."

I grimaced. Good thing I had developed more control over my magic in the Underworld and mastered the highest power level—I didn't really want to leave my safety up to *theoretically.*

"The demons that showed up first were clearly sent to die," Charity said, following close with her sword in hand.

"Or they correctly assumed that Roger is a softy," I replied, the thrum of magic stronger now, pulsing within me.

"Roger might've been hesitant to kill anyone when we first came back from the Realm, but that was only because of where we were in the Brink," she replied. "If anyone breaches his territory here, they go down. He's done playing. Dad is, too."

I could've guessed considering the way they were handling people trying to sneak in through the portal. I'd heard that if someone came through, they didn't return home.

I saw the shapes standing just behind a cluster of trees, five of them in all. They'd chosen humanoid forms that weren't very well proportioned, something I'd seen a lot of in the Underworld. They clearly hadn't been up here in a long while, although none of the demons I'd met seemed too concerned with getting it right. Maybe they just liked being different.

"Why are you here?" I asked as I approached, putting up a hand to motion for those behind me to stay back.

The demon with orange hair sticking straight up turned a bit to face me. Its boobs fell down to its waist, moving within its "I heart San Francisco" sweatshirt. Tan shorts stopped at creamy thighs that didn't match its deeply tanned face, and its knees were red as though from the cold.

"Cute," I said, running my finger through the air over it. "A summer tourist to San Francisco, right? They think it'll be warm and instead it's freezing so they have to buy a sweatshirt?" Darius had taken me a while back, and I'd seen that scenario played out a few times over. "But what are you doing here?"

"Hello, your royal heinous. The Great Master has a few things he'd like me to relay to you. He would've come in person, but he is aware the shifters would not enjoy the joke."

"They wouldn't get it, no," I replied, wondering what he'd actually considered doing to warrant calling it a joke. Simply showing up where he wasn't wanted? Hard to say with him.

"He wishes for me to inform you that the unicorn lands have been created. Tatsu is able to communicate directly with them and had the Great Master fix it up to their specifications. He regretfully informs you, however, that they will likely join his side. He thanks you for sending them his way."

"Super. Way to rub it in," I muttered.

"He'd like me to relay the news that he will be marching on the elves within two days. His goal has not changed—he'll seek to annihilate them. Given how vast his host has grown, he foresees their complete destruction. He respectfully requests that you do not stand in the way."

"Denied," I responded.

"In the event you deny, he would like to remind you that you and your silly friends are not enough to stand in his way. It would put you and them in danger. He urges you to reconsider."

"No."

"The Great Master would like to mention that he will extend the offer a second time during the battle before forcing the issue. If you go quietly at that time, it'll give him the opportunity to save your dearest friends. If not, you will likely deplete his resources, and he will only be able to skirt you and Archion to safety. Your friends will likely perish, stuck between the two opposing forces."

"He sure thinks highly of his situation," Charity murmured, her sword still held up, ready to kill at a moment's notice. "He lost last time, though, right?"

I nodded grimly, but this time would be different. He had more resources than the last time he'd fought the elves, and the elves had less. The power scales had tipped, and he knew it.

I wondered if the elves did.

The demon gave me a somber look. "Forgive my impertinence, your heinous, but you have a duty to your kingdom and your friends," the demon said. "You cannot change the outcome of this war, not with how it is shaping up. You will see the truth of that assessment when on the battlefield. At that time, I urge you to really *think* about this offer. Save yourself, and save your friends. You will then have a chance to help Lucifer lead our people to greatness. It is an opportunity a great many would die to have."

Part of that greatness this demon spoke of would be obtaining the Realm; any idiot could see that. Lucifer wouldn't just wipe them out and walk away, not with the grudge he clearly held. He'd claim it for himself and expand his kingdom. That was what conquerors did.

"Thank him for thinking of me," I told the demon, its words punching me in the gut. My old man was good—he knew dangling my friends in front of me would have an effect. It did. If it turned out that he had the forces he claimed, would he truly be able to stomp on us?

The demons stared at me with unblinking eyes.

"The Great Master requests that you send me back, using the circle provided, or create another one. You have a mage within your employ who can manage such things, correct?"

I slid a glance at Dizzy. How did my father know about that? Someone had clearly been talking, and it wasn't a big stretch to guess who.

"He needs to know what you said," the demon went on. "You can send the others back or kill them—your choice."

"Jesus," Charity said softly. She clearly didn't know how cutthroat demons could be.

Dizzy moved around the five demons, giving them a wide berth. He bent, studying the ground. Callie watched them as she trailed him.

A moment later, Dizzy pointed down with the chalk. "Yup. There's a circle right here." He bent a little more, examining. "Decent work in a shaky hand. Inexperienced, probably. The runes are a little shoddy in some places and the lines aren't totally straight. That aside, it is a very effective circle, I would think. I haven't seen this in any of the books I've been researching."

"Ja was here not that long ago," I said. "She's proficient in circles, right?"

Dizzy rubbed his chin. "Yes, but hers tend to be ancient and neat, I recall. Well drawn. She has a certain few that work well, and she uses them often. I've never seen this one before."

Someone in our camp would've had to draw that circle, Darius thought. *If not Ja, then who?*

That was the million-dollar question.

"How many people would it have taken to bring those demons up?" I asked.

Dizzy turned to me and blew out a breath, thinking. "These demons are high on the power scale. They'd need very little power to beam them up. Callie and I could do it ourselves, I'd imagine. Maybe just me, though that's more doubtful."

And someone summoned the other group, as well, Darius thought.

"Unless the others were brought up first, then the person zipped over here and called up these guys," I said. "An elder vampire's blood would make it easy. The circles could've been made in advance."

"Oh yes, sure, using a vampire's blood would greatly help." Dizzy bent further. "The light is too low for me to tell, though."

I took a deep breath. "We have two days. Let's get everything in motion."

I shoved the demons back with air and fed magic into the circle. I sliced my finger, walked forward, and crouched down, letting a droplet of blood feed the circle.

"It was an honor, your heinous," the demon said.

"He *is* calling you your *heinous,* right?" Charity asked. "I'm not hearing things?"

"Yeah. It's my title of choice. Soon they'll realize how well it fits me." I sent them back to the Underworld with a thrust of power. Nothing to it. That circle was ideal for easy travel, as perfect as if Lucifer himself had designed it.

And he just might have.

"We got problems." I turned and held out my hands, using my magic to force a path through the gathered crowd, careful not to smack anyone or send them flying. "Where's Roger? We need to talk."

CHAPTER 14

PENNY STOOD TO one side of the large, rustic table in what looked like a spacious conference room stolen out of the seventies. The orange Formica countertop at the back, housing a coffee pot and a few sandwiches, matched the strange shag carpet that ran wall to wall. A dusty plant took up residence in the corner, and no one used the spindly chairs positioned throughout the room in little clusters.

Instead, they gathered around the conference table, all eyes on Penny's mom, who alone sat at the table. She had her cards spaced out in front of her, her crystal ball to one side. The Red Prophet sat cross-legged on the surface of the opposite end of the table.

Roger stood across from Penny's mother, his hands loose at his sides and hard lines etching his face. The muscles on his large torso bulged beneath his white T-shirt, his whole body channeling his anger at the revelation that at least one person in his camp was working for the enemy. Given they'd had a problem like this when Penny escorted Charity to the Flush for the first time and they'd never found the perpetrator, it was clear he needed to clean house. Hard to do that with the sudden time constraints, however.

Romulus and Charity stood beside Roger, and the rest of their strategists were positioned around the room, ready to take notes or just absorb the new information.

Reagan exhaled slowly, and Penny could tell she was trying to keep her composure. She hadn't wanted to come and see the *Seers* at work. Darius had pushed, though, wanting her to get the information firsthand and ask questions if need be. He stood behind her, with Emery, the dual-mages, and Cahal close at hand.

Magic swirled through the room, prickling Penny's skin.

"Two days seems right to me," Karen said, her eyes fluttering. The mists in her crystal ball whirled and spun. She slapped her cards down, seemingly at random, then opened her eyes and looked them over. She nodded. "Two days. The elves…" She paused, her gaze flicking from one card to another. She laid down three more cards, two in front of her and one to the side. The third card to hit the table was Death. Her lips tightened. That wasn't a good sign. "The elves are not ready."

"You must take the deal." The Red Prophet stared straight at Reagan, who definitely hadn't wanted to be there but needed to. It was time for big-girl panties. If

Penny had had to go to a demon sex club, Reagan could deal with *Seers*.

The Red Prophet's eyes twinkled. "Take the deal and holster your magic. Make the call."

"She's doing it again." Penny's mom rubbed her temples, breathing in through her mouth and out through her nose. "Before you ask, no, I don't know what that means. I am not getting any of that. Also, no, I still don't know what *the villain's crown is crooked* from yesterday means. She's talking gibberish half the time. I think the stress is addling her brain, I really do. She simply cannot keep up."

"She can be eccentric, but she does have power," Romulus said. "She has never let us down."

"Just so I have this straight." Reagan held up her hand. "You want me to take the deal to save my-self...and put everyone else in danger?"

"Put everyone else in danger, yes. That is the ticket." The Red Prophet gave her a grimace-smile.

Reagan narrowed her eyes but didn't respond.

Penny spoke up. "That wasn't the choice the demon gave, though."

"Leave it," Reagan said softly. "She's putting on the-atrics. She can't hang out at a person's house for a while, terrorize the neighborhood, and expect the shifts in her personality not to be cataloged." Reagan paused for a moment. "She's fucking with me. She knows a secret about what will happen, and she's not telling."

"What kind of secret?" Roger asked roughly.

"I have no fucking idea, but given her level of nuts right now, it's a doozy." Reagan stared at the Red Prophet for a long, tense moment and then tilted her head. The Red Prophet was clearly communicating with her by thinking. "I would not have guessed that, no. So you're playing both sides too?"

"I am on all sides," the Red Prophet said with a knowing smile. "And so are you."

Reagan retied her ponytail, something she did when she was readying for battle. "Keep your secrets. I don't need them." She turned and walked toward the door. "Don't worry so much about turncoats, Roger." She paused when she neared the door. "The Red Prophet made those circles, and it's a safe assumption Ja called the demons. If you see Ja, kill her."

"Now I get why my mother is beside herself annoyed," Penny said, catching up to Reagan as she pushed out of the conference room and went down the hall, heading outside. Penny's watch said dawn was just around the corner, but deep night covered the area. Reagan had really come along with her magic.

"This is bigger than just a war between the worlds, somehow," Reagan said, turning toward the open fields and clear sky.

Darius hadn't followed them, and neither had the

others. They were clearly going to stay behind and hear what Penny's mom had to say, in the hopes her *Seeing* was more coherent. And reliable.

"That won't change my role, I don't think," Reagan murmured, walking out to the edge of her magical night to peer up at the budding dawn. "I miss my quiet life. This has all gotten to be too much."

"I don't miss mine," Penny said. "This is a lot, I grant you, but it is a means to an end. It will be worth it. I can feel it." She patted her pockets, where a couple of her power stones were nestled. Her Temperamental Third Eye had a moment of clarity, the clouds parting to show the way forward. This was right, this path. This was the way of the fates.

That didn't necessarily mean it would lead to a happy ending, though. So the feeling wasn't incredibly helpful.

Thanks, Temperamental Third Eye, as always.

TWO HOURS LATER, they were walking within the patch of magically darkened sky to meet up with Darius and the others.

"Don't want to know," Reagan said as they approached.

"You don't need to," Darius replied, taking her hand and threading his fingers with hers. "Ms. Bristol had a lot of helpful predictions for how the battle would line up, but she kept running into holes. The Red Prophet refused to fill them, if she even could have, despite Roger asking nicely and Romulus demanding. There is something in the works, and Ms. Bristol isn't seeing it."

"The Red Prophet might not be seeing it either," Callie said, wiping her forehead free of perspiration. Her lime-green velvet sweat suit seemed to glow in the low light. Campfires burned sporadically throughout the area, surrounded by benches and chairs, the heat pushing back on the chilled air. Very few people were making use of the areas of respite, though. Many of the mages, who might've enjoyed the comfort, had wandered to the sunny areas outside of the spell, and the other creatures who'd gathered were not as prone to the cold. "She has gone completely loopy. She probably just wants to be noticed."

"I'd hazard a guess that she wants to be forgotten," Reagan murmured, stopping near one of the fires and looking around. She seemed troubled and anxious, but she wouldn't share what had her so wound up. Probably because she'd have to admit to her fears, and that was never any fun. "She liked hanging around Mikey and Smokey, who didn't want to hear any predictions. She was the most normal around them, and when terrorizing the neighborhood. She needs to get out of here."

"We all do," Emery said.

"Where are you all headed now?" Dizzy asked, and it was clear fatigue was dragging at him and Callie. It was dragging at everyone, Penny wagered.

"Roger wanted to get some practice in fighting the magic of the dragons' roars," Darius said. "It's a good idea. It can be done sitting down."

"Oh, I don't know," Dizzy replied. "Penny's dragon always makes me think I'm going to soil myself. I'm so tired right now that I might actually do it."

"You guys go back—"

Reagan froze, her gaze snagging on a vampire who was chatting with two others across the way. He had the usual flawless face and good looks. His shirt and trousers were pristine but didn't quite look high fashion. Penny hated that she now knew the difference. Marie had cursed her.

"What is it?" Darius asked, clearly feeling something through their bond.

"Nothing," Reagan said, taking a step to veer away from the small group of vampires.

That wasn't normal. When did Reagan veer away from anyone?

As though feeling an entire group of people staring at him, the vampire glanced over. His gaze skimmed everyone before snapping to Reagan. His eyes widened slightly, and hunger sparked in them immediately, his body tensing before going loose and fluid.

Shivers coated Penny's skin—a reaction to the new predator suddenly in their midst. That vampire wanted more than just to bite, too, evidenced by the sensual way he licked his lips and let his gaze drift down Reagan's front.

"What is this?" Darius asked in a low, rough tone.

The sensation of danger flared within Penny, yelling at her to run. Or fight. Or throw a spell.

Emery curled his hand over her shoulder and gently pushed her behind him.

"It's nothing," Reagan said quickly. "It was a long time ago. Let it go."

"Wait...what was a long time ago?" Penny asked Callie and Dizzy, who'd stepped up with her.

"It seems we have found my surprise," Darius said, and the sheen and polish of his handsome exterior fell away, leaving a beast in its place. Menace curled through the air. His claws extended from his fingertips.

The breath left Reagan in a whoosh. "She brings up your past to me, and now she is flaunting my past in front of you."

"What's happening?" Penny asked, knowing there was some drama and not getting it.

"Ah." Dizzy patted Penny's arm. "Yes. The vampire from Reagan's past. She mentioned him once. After her mother died, she went slumming, as it were. She walked away and forced him to let her."

"Oh." Penny's breath came in short bursts as Darius turned slightly, facing the other vampire, who wasn't nearly as built, handsome, or put together. There was really no contest between the two. Darius needn't have any doubts that he was the obvious catch.

Except...the way he was gearing up, his shoulders rolling and his jaw firming, told Penny that simple logic wasn't good enough.

The other vampire pulled his gaze away from Reagan with great effort. His stare hit Darius, and given he was clearly less powerful and definitely lower in the vampire hierarchy, he should've walked away very quickly. Any shifter or mage would have. Probably any demon or other semi-intelligent creature. You didn't pick a fight you were surely going to lose.

But this vampire squared up, his body starting to change shape despite his clothes. He clearly didn't have the sort of control Darius did, which suggested he was quite a bit younger. Darius would wipe the floor with him.

"Are they basically going to fight over Reagan?" Penny asked in a harried whisper, a bit scared, a bit weirded out, and a bit excited for some reason.

"No, they are not." Reagan waved a hand, her magic rushing between the two vampires. The magic whispered, *Stay apart. Barrier.* She'd put up a wall.

"Oh, interesting," Dizzy murmured. "That other

vampire must have an addiction to Reagan's blood. Usually it's the human that develops the addiction."

"It was probably on the younger side when it met her," Callie whispered. "She made an impression and obviously didn't kill it when she should have."

"How'd she manage to get away, though?" Dizzy asked. "It didn't seem to know she was here. Any vampire worth his salt wouldn't have lost sight of her."

"Youth." Callie said it like Dizzy was dense. "Younger vampires don't know their ass from their heads, you know that. That's why their makers govern them well past their middle years. She still should've killed him, though. On the sly, obviously, so she wouldn't have the maker breathing down her neck. Now it'll just cause problems. It obviously can't control itself—look at him. No self-preservation. Darius will rip him apart."

"Probably for the best, though," Dizzy replied.

Penny stared with rapt attention, never having seen this side of vampires before. The way Darius had shrugged off his humanity, bent over now with hands fully changed, suggested he was ready to rip that other vampire's head from its shoulders. It was like two bucks fighting for the right to mate a female.

"Darius will *not* rip that vampire apart," Reagan said through clenched teeth. "Starch, walk away," she called. "He's my bond mate. You have no claim here."

"I tasted you first…" the other vampire said, sensuality and desire dripping from each word.

Clearly that had been the wrong thing to say.

"Oh shit," Emery said.

As though he'd been held back by a rope that was suddenly cut, Darius rushed forward. He slammed into Reagan's air wall and started slashing, sending sparks shooting out in all directions. Reagan tensed, and Cahal stalked forward to join her.

"Yes, I fucking know that, Cahal," Reagan said, replying to his thought comment, and another wave of her magic bolstered the first. The other vampire surged forward as well, hitting the other side of that wall and trying to get to Darius. They were mindless in their territorialism, and the magic curling away from them reminded Penny of shifters. It seemed a strange kind of mating dance, heady and volatile, fused with passion and need. A claiming.

"Darius, you have to shrug this off," Reagan said, but he slashed at her magic again, nearly breaking through before she could amp up her wall. "Emery, Penny, help. He can't get to that other vampire, or he'll owe Ja for finding him and bringing him here. We cannot let her have the upper hand."

Magic curled from Emery immediately, forming a sort of diversion spell. Penny jumped in at once, though she wondered if it might be better to just knock Darius out and drag him away. It would be easier.

"Well, how about *I* just go kill that other vampire?" Dizzy asked, dead serious. "Then it wouldn't be on you two. Because honestly, Reagan, it has to be done. This will clearly always be a problem. You should've known that."

"He was shipped off to Europe," she replied. "His maker moved, and he went with. I never thought I'd see him again. Fucking Ja just had to stick her big nose in. You can't touch him, though, because she'll still consider it a win. He needs to be sent away."

"Agreed," Callie said, opening the satchel slung across her chest as she marched in a half-circle to get around the wall. "We can't kill him now. We'll have to send him away, and then *someone* will have to track him down on their own later and kill him."

"Good point, hon." Dizzy joined his wife.

"This is so insane," Penny said, working with Emery's spell, uncomfortable with her reaction to this development. In the past she would've been scandalized. But now, she couldn't deny feeling a thread of excitement at the intense magic wafting off Darius. It pounded with his claim on Reagan, his aching need to protect her against this rival threat. The desire to lay down his life to prove he was worthy of her. It was sexy in a crazy way, and that horrible demon sex club really had changed her for the worst.

"Here we go," Dizzy said as he and Callie worked some plants and then blew some power into them, speaking a spell to life. They weren't natural mages and so needed props and often words to cast their magic.

Emery sent his and Penny's spell forward, layering it over Reagan's. It molted into a sparkling brown-black layer, cutting off Darius's sight and hopefully redirecting his focus.

"Come on, baby," Reagan said softly, still through gritted teeth, walking closer but keeping some distance. "Fire up that big brain and think this through. This isn't the time. You can't let Ja have this over your head."

"Got him!" Dizzy yelled triumphantly, as though reeling in a fish.

Penny tiptoed to the other side, not wanting to miss any part of this. She would chastise herself later.

Invisible bands wrapped around the vampire, keeping his arms tight to his sides and his legs cinched together. He arched and wiggled, flopping onto his stomach and then onto his back, trying to stand.

On the other side, Emery was working another spell, increasing the distraction for Darius.

It was working.

Darius was slowing. His chest rose and fell as he panted. His claws retracted into fingers. And suddenly he was a rush of movement, sweeping Reagan up into his arms. He zoomed off, probably to prove his claim on her…physically.

Penny fanned her face, noticing belatedly that Cahal was staring at her with a small grin.

"What?" she asked, stopping immediately.

Rather than comment, he glanced at Emery before heading around the air wall to Dizzy and Callie.

CHAPTER 15

DARIUS'S LIPS CRASHED against mine, our teeth clashing and tongues wrestling. A surge of unbridled desire ripped through me, pumped up by the feelings of his passion and urgency through the bond and a heady sort of territorialism, the likes of which I'd never experienced before. It dripped fire through my blood and surged adrenaline through my body.

He kicked his way into our room and spun me around, closing the door by slamming me up against it. His body was glued to mine, his kiss deep and urgent, like a starving man going after a meal. He grabbed my tank top and tore it off before shoving up the cups of my bra and sliding his hands over my breasts.

I groaned as his thumbs worked over my hard nipples. He bent down and sucked one into his hot mouth, working my leather pants with his other hand. Buttons undone, he shoved my pants down, my panties caught up with them, and dropped to his knees in front of me. He flung my knee over his shoulder and took to me, licking up my wet heat before flicking my clit with his tongue.

Pleasure surged through me, throbbing in my core and spiraling outward. I tangled my fingers in his hair, gyrating my hips against his delicious mouth. His fingers plunged into me in time with the swirling of his tongue, and my head thunked back against the door as I exploded, fracturing and breaking apart.

Darius pushed up to standing and ripped off his shirt. He was out of his pants in a flash, and then he pulled me closer, wrapping my legs around his waist. Across the room and he dropped me to the bed and moved between my thighs. Heat blistered between our skin. His heavy length rested against my sopping core. His beautiful hazel eyes took me in, and I could see the primal desire pooling in their depths.

"You are mine, Reagan," he said, his tone deep and rough. Fire erupted in his eyes as he lined himself up with me and thrust, filling me.

I cried out, squeezing his middle with my thighs, and he plunged into me with wild abandon. He pushed me into the mattress, capturing my wrists above my head, dominating me with his size and strength. I jerked my hips against his thrusts, drawing more friction, building again.

He ran his open mouth along my jaw and bent a little, scraping his teeth against my throat. I shivered in anticipation, and he bit me. The pain turned to pleasure, his vampire serum mixing with my blood and driving incredible sensations through my body.

I sounded like a banshee with all the moaning and groaning, but I couldn't help it. His primal wildness, his inability to channel any of his usual grace and poise, caught me in the best of ways. I wanted to be *taken*, no inhibitions, no safety net. I wanted this claim just like I had wanted the bond. A vicious part of me understood his need to defend my honor against a rival male. A female part liked his earnestness in doing it.

"Harder," I said, struggling to get closer, to get him deeper.

His breath mingled with mine. His body rose a little so he could give me what I wanted. His hips slammed against me, over and over. He worked one of his hands between us, massaging my clit to give me more pleasure. He drew from my vein again, dosing me with another boost of vampire serum.

He was everywhere at once. Pleasure pulled at every inch of my body, dragging me under. Drowning me in the best of ways.

I blasted apart, yelling his name, arching against him. He shuddered over me, groaning with his release.

The sound of our panting filled the suddenly quiet room. He didn't remove his weight from me, nor did he let go of my wrists, trapped in one of his large palms. He held me there, cupping a breast with his free hand.

"I cannot suffer any other vampire to know your taste, Reagan," he said in a thick voice, the authority of an elder riding his words. "I certainly cannot suffer another vampire teetering on the edge of blood lust because of you. Any time that creature is near you, he will pose a danger to you and a challenge to me. This is not for a human to understand. This is how it is done with my kind."

"Callie and Dizzy said he was too young when…" I let that comment trail off, stayed by the surge of menace in his eyes. He wasn't prone to jealousy, normally, but clearly there were limits.

"He is lesser middle level, not too young to deny his desire for blood such as yours. He has a weak mind, and your blood, magic, and power are a temptation he is unable to resist, it seems. Ja must've realized this. She is devious."

"So she basically sent him here to die?" I asked.

He skimmed his lips against my chin, and I shivered. "She is certainly trying for that outcome. It means nothing to her, of course. She is poking me. Meddling in my life. I could have found that creature before now, and I thought about doing so a few times, but I was respecting your privacy. You didn't want me to track him down, and so I didn't. Well…"

"You did."

He nipped the sensitive skin on my throat. "Yes. He was far enough away that it wasn't an issue. I left it at that."

"And now?"

His kiss was slow and deep. "And now I cannot leave it at that. His challenge was direct, and it was public. You are my bond mate—he is in the wrong on a few levels, particularly in his disrespect of you, and so I will kill him."

The flatness with which he said it, in between gentle kisses and little nips, sent cold shivers up my spine before pooling heat in my core. Good God it was hot when he went all dominant male like this, fighting for my honor and taking me back to his bed like some caveman. I could play the Jane to his Tarzan for the morning. It was just what I needed to take my mind off the Red Prophet's (likely terrible) secrets. Being a wilting flower now would give me a break before I had to strap on my leathers again and be the big boss bitch.

He was still inside me, quickly growing hard again, and I swirled my hips against him. He growled, stretching against me and rubbing his chest along my hard nipples. Their sensitivity sent shock waves of pleasure to wind me up higher.

"You reacted quite a bit differently to Ja's surprise this time than you did after she told us about Ernesta," I said, tilting my chin away so he would kiss down my neck.

"I don't care about my past lovers, just as you don't care about yours. But I will hazard a guess that you would care somewhat more if you walked in and one of my past lovers had my cock in her mouth."

Rage and fire blasted through me, and I tensed up before laughing at my reaction. "It wouldn't be her fault. I'd probably kill you, not her."

"And what if she knew I was bonded to you and didn't want her anymore, and she used a moment of weakness—"

"No, no. No need to elaborate. I was trying to use the PC answer that says it isn't the mistress's fault if the man is cheating. Which it isn't. But no, it certainly wouldn't take much for me to kill a threat."

"A threat to your man…"

"I am currently fantasizing about you being a Tarzan, not me. I'd like to continue to pretend that I am a sensible creature that never flies off the handle."

"Ah. I see. Okay then." He tightened his grip on my wrists and slammed into me, stealing my breath. "Then I will own my mantle and make sure you walk bowlegged the next time we leave this room, how is that?"

"Yes, please," I said, attempting meek. Polite was about as close as I could get. It would do.

I arched my back and said goodbye to the present. For a while, I just wanted to get lost in Darius. On the other side of that pleasure, I knew there would be nothing but pain and blood.

CHAPTER 16

"READY?" I ASKED Penny, channeling nothing but cold determination and a can-do attitude. Battle day. Our futures and fates would be decided.

"Nope." She frowned and tapped her extravagant fanny pack with the various compartments. "Not at all." She took out a red stone and held it in her palm. "I do not want to do this, I'm afraid we're all going to die, and I want to go back to my sheltered life and forget I ever even met you."

"Quite the tune change." I lifted my chin and hovered up onto Archion's back. We'd spent the last two days practicing against the other dragons and their riders. This was because I'd had a moment of weakness and told all the dragons they wouldn't be allowed to come with us.

In my defense, they were three against a sea of dragons. How could they possibly help against Lucifer? I didn't want them to get hurt.

I'd been forcibly ignored.

"Didn't you tell me just the other day that this was

the right path and you wanted to be on it?" I asked as she climbed onto Saphira.

Emery crawled up behind her, and behind us, Cahal was mounting Coppelia.

"I was delusional, and now I have come to my senses. I regret to inform you that I must resign as your bra—a very stupid nickname for a girlfriend, if I might add—"

"Shut up, you love it."

"—stop being your fall guy in the bounty hunter gigs—"

"Garret's fall guy, you mean…"

"—and stop the insanity. *I just need to stop the insanity*," she yelled at me.

"It's going to be—"

"Stop telling me it is going to be okay, Emery," she hollered at him. "We're going to get crushed. You better take that deal, Reagan." She leveled a finger at me. "Donkey turds and old-man farts, you take that deal, and you take me with you, do you hear me?"

Is she always like this before battle? Cahal asked me.

"Yes. Literally always, though she isn't swearing as much this time. I think she might be getting more acclimated."

"I don't think she was quite this bad before the Mages' Guild battle," Emery said, wrapping his arms around her middle.

"Yeah, but there wasn't much warning before that one," I replied.

"Sure. Why not?" Penny muttered. "Talk about me like I can't hear you. It's fine."

I looked out across the large host of gathered troops, everyone in neat lines to go through the portal. Darius stood off to the side with his faction of vampires, all of them in normal human attire with backpacks. Within those backpacks were large sun-repellent blankets that they'd hunker down underneath should something happen to my magic masking the sky. Which wasn't a problem right now, since it had just slipped into evening.

I'd wanted him to ride to battle with me on Archion, but he declined, saying he needed to lead the vampire faction. It seems Charity's vision—or visions, I guess—had been thoroughly theoretical. For all the variations she'd seen, she'd never once mentioned our dragons or the surly druid.

"What's the story with your people, Cahal?" I asked as Archion beat at the sky. "Are they going to be on the elves' side?"

"Druids in general are a peaceful sort of people. There are only a few of us that end up in my line of work."

"Killing people, you mean?" I yelled over the thump of Archion's wings.

He didn't comment on that directly. "They are spread out throughout the worlds and don't often involve themselves in politics. They certainly don't engage in battles of this nature. It's not where our true strengths lie."

"So why are you involved?" I asked as he drifted beside me, waiting for Saphira.

Mostly because I count you and the others as friends. Because I care what happens to you. And because there is honestly nothing more amazing than riding a pink dragon into battle. It also makes my choice completely beyond reproach by my people.

I laughed. Sounded legit.

With Penny finally ready, we flew toward the portal. We'd be going through first. If it were just us against the elves or the Underworld, I suspected they'd be waiting there, ready to pick us off as we came through. But I had it on good authority that the Underworld planned to storm the elves' castle, and I doubted they'd split their forces to stop a much less intimidating group.

That was the logical conclusion, at least, and I really hoped logic held up this time.

Darius looked up at me as I flew overhead. The other vampire had been gone by the time we left the room the other day. I hadn't asked where he'd been taken or by whom, and no one volunteered the information. We could sort that out if we lived.

I felt his love through the bond and took a deep breath to steel myself against the feeling of grave uncertainty of what was to come. If I were to ever get a semblance of a happy ending, it would be on the other side of this battle. The problem was that I didn't see how this battle could go well. I really didn't. Not for us, anyway. It filled me with dread for my future. Dread I pushed down and refused to dwell on.

Roger, still in human form, looked up from his position beside Romulus and Charity. He didn't raise a hand, but that moment of acknowledgment was his way of wishing me good luck. He wouldn't have bothered to take notice of an underling.

He'd approached me a couple hours ago, taking a break from preparing everyone to march.

"It's an honor to fight beside you," he'd said, putting out his arms for what would become a very awkward hug. I patted his back a little, at a loss, until he squeezed me tightly and rocked me from side to side. It had felt a little weird, until he said, "Am I making the vampire jealous? I hear he has a weakness for stuff like that."

"I do not get jealous over mere dogs," Darius replied in a snooty voice.

Roger backed off with a smile, but it faded as he looked at me. "What you said in the conference room the other day has stuck with me. You might've taken a get-out-of-jail-free card in the past, but not now. We never saw eye to eye in the past, but now we do. You are made of solid stuff, Reagan Somerset. I respect you. I respect your position. As I said, it is an honor to fight by your side."

I twisted my lips to the side, a little nervous this might get emotional. How embarrassing. I'd never live it down.

So I just nodded and said, "Ditto."

"Stop chasing my shifters around the bars."

I cracked a smile. "Now you're asking too much."

He laughed and turned to stick out a hand to Darius. "Durant, we won't ever see eye to eye. But I am glad as hell to have you in this battle. You had other options, and I'm glad you chose this one."

Darius took his hand in a firm grip, meeting his eyes. "I had no other options. You are a good leader to your people."

"High praise coming from a vampire," Roger said, stepping back.

"Yes," Darius replied.

"See you out there." And then Roger had left, probably off to find Penny and Emery, making more spells for easy access, or maybe even Cahal, hiding in the shadows or whatever.

"Why have you never weighed in on what I should do during the battle?" I'd asked Darius while strapping on my leathers.

"In short…I don't know what you should do in battle. The *Seers* are not confident, the fae are not confident, and Roger is expending all of his energy on the best practices of defense. There is a very real possibility that this could go wrong. A *very* real possibility. Almost a certainty, in fact."

"I get it, I get it."

"When everything goes wrong, you and Penny—and Emery when he's inevitably dragged into it—are at your absolute bests. When all is lost, you three create miracles. You will not allow yourself to fail, not when it means the failure of those closest to you. Quite simply, I have put my trust in you. I have led you many times—it is time for you to lead me."

And that had finally set the waterworks off. Roger had loosened me up, and Darius shoved me over the edge.

But now? Hard-core badass. Action engaged in leather. Ready to kick some ass and forget their names.

I did a lap, the other dragons flying behind me as we soared over the forces gathered below. Callie and Dizzy waited about halfway down the long line, Steve beside them. They'd wanted to be on the front line, but Roger insisted on keeping all of the mages toward the middle. If elves sprang up out of nowhere, he wanted swords and teeth to quickly meet them, and for the mages to step in as backup.

I doubted elves would pop up out of nowhere, though.

Besides, why would they bother with us? We were about a thousand strong, which was great. It was an awesome force. But the elves had enlisted the help of almost everyone in the Realm, drafting those who didn't come willingly. Anyone who'd escaped the draft but still wanted to fight had apparently headed down to the Underworld. They certainly hadn't come to us. Plus my father had the other half of the vampires (or maybe a bit less, because Darius had gathered a right few), his rage and violence sects, random draft selections from the edges, a host of experienced dragons, a herd of uni-corns—did I need to go on? Why the hell would the elves worry about us when the Underworld was march-ing toward their castle?

A wave of nervousness washed over me, but I shoved it away with a showing of my teeth.

Let's go, I said to Archion, leaning forward to gain speed.

He must've felt my building adrenaline, or perhaps he was feeling his own, because he let out a trumpeting sound before he dove for the portal.

The magic of the crossing pulled at my energy and scraped across my skin. Archion touched down on the ground before lifting back up, pushing into the sky. Those portals weren't meant for dragons, since they weren't in the sky, unlike those of the Underworld. The other dragons flew in after us, and then the troops followed.

Nobody was waiting, but somehow that didn't reassure me.

WE TOOK AN accelerated path through the Realm, heading toward the castle. My heart beat a steady drum in my chest, my adrenaline pulsed low, and I did my best to stay calm.

Is it always this deserted? Archion asked as we flew over little huts and empty fields.

I shook my head slowly, looking for any signs of movement and seeing none. *I don't know, but I doubt it. They are either hiding, or getting ready to fight.*

The land didn't change much, unlike the constant changes in the Underworld. Always pretty. Always leaning toward fake. I hoped Romulus lived to spruce the place up a bit, turning the walkways into pleasant gardens and the trees into more convincing semblances of the same thing. This whole place was just stagnant, waiting for a breath of fresh air. It almost reminded me of the Mages' Guild just before we busted it open. It needed some new blood. New ideas.

It was too bad it would take a battle and bloodshed to achieve that result.

There.

I flicked my eyes up at Archion's thought. Cahal flew to one side of me, Penny and Emery on the other, and their gazes were turned in the same direction. Penny glanced at me with wide eyes.

The breath left my lungs.

A massive host had gathered in front of the elves' castle. Catapults were lined up on the golden pathway, carts teamed with crews waiting beside them. Troops stood before them in neat lines, armed to the teeth, with elves at the back and creatures like minotaurs, centaurs, and trolls pushing out in front. Because *of course* they were being pushed into danger first. Even as we watched, creatures pushed up off the ground and flew into the sky, all manner of flying creatures—faeries, griffins, hippogriffs, lamassu… Their host had to be two thousand or more strong. Holy shit.

Coming toward them, spread out across the land, the scenery being stripped bare of its enchantments as they moved, came my father's host. Demons of all shapes and sizes wore battle gear or just their own skin. Other demons flew overhead, their bodies gross and spindly. Some of the trolls from the Realm had joined them, and I noticed goblins as well as several other strange creatures I'd never seen before. They walked amongst the demons, not in front of them. Vampires walked to the right in the army, all in their monster forms, moving like graceful predators ready to kill.

Behind them pranced the damn unicorns, creamy white and gorgeous, shaking their heads and neighing like a horse might do.

My gaze tracked upward, and I sagged on Archion.

There are all of your friends, I thought, seeing the large beasts fill the sky. Lucifer didn't have as many fliers as the elves, but his were of a much better quality. Larger, deadlier.

At the front, flying low, Lucifer rode atop Tatsu, her jet-black scales soaking up the night.

My heart thudded in my chest. A strange feeling of being misplaced settled over me.

I should be beside him, I thought without meaning to.

You will be, Archion replied.

I shook my head, looking at the messy horde he had following him, tromping through the land and thirsty for blood. His host was larger than the elves, no question. More eager. Likely more violent. He would win this battle if we didn't stop him. He'd tear into the elves and everyone who stood with them. He would show no mercy.

The memory of the grimy walls of my prison, my broken legs, my askew fingers, and the constant thrust of pain as I lay on that dingy floor filtered through my mind. Rage kindled into a fire within me. Lucifer knew what the elves were capable of. He'd seen it firsthand, applied to his own flesh and blood.

But what was Lucifer capable of? He had great darkness within him. It balanced the light I'd seen. I had to ask myself again whether he was any better.

There was too much hate in the worlds, and not enough compassion.

Someone had to stand in the way. *We* had to stand in the way. We had to be the ringleaders for a different, better future.

Our people moved forward in orderly rows, the most vulnerable in the middle and the strongest taking the front, back, and sides. It was the opposite of the fae's usual strategy, but Roger wanted everyone to make it to the battle without falling behind.

It doesn't look like we have time to rest before battle, Archion thought as we continued forward, unrelenting.

We'd rested along the way a couple times, getting water and food for those who needed it. Donors gave the vampires blood—with more vampires accepting than probably needed to. Roger had forbidden any banging, though. He'd even agreed to give Marie blood (who had *definitely* not needed it, given her age), but would not allow her to touch him anywhere, save her mouth on his arm.

When her serum hit his bloodstream, I'd watched with glee as his entire body tensed, like he'd grabbed a live wire. His stern expression could not hide the rush of pleasure from her bite, and his lack of clothing was further testament to what he thought of the experience. Marie had pulled back with a blood-soaked smile, her eyes twinkling. The whole experience had probably been one of the worst of his life. He'd done it for the team, though. I'd given him a cookie right afterward. He'd needed one.

The plan had been to stop about here and get one last rest in before we shoved ourselves between the two brawling worlds and played the good guy, whatever that meant. It wasn't to be, though.

I leaned over Archion's side so I could look down at Roger in his wolf form. He was looking up. When we connected gazes, he looked straight ahead. Romulus, still beside him, nodded, and pointed toward the battle. Overkill, but whatever.

Prepare for battle, I thought, a sheen of sweat breaking over me. *It's time we decide the fate of the worlds.*

CHAPTER 17

I TURNED TO Cahal first, wondering if he'd see the directive. He was looking back at me. He nodded once.

With a deep breath, I turned to Penny next. I hadn't gotten her into this mess—not really. Emery was the one who'd showed up on her porch and dragged her into trouble. I really shouldn't be blamed for everything that had unfurled since. I hoped she saw it my way.

Her gaze was straight ahead, and I was surprised not to see any fear or trepidation. I saw only determination.

Pride and aggression swirled within me. Penny Bristol was finally, solidly ready for battle. That, I *did* take credit for.

Emery caught me looking and nudged her before pointing. Her gaze swung my way, her eyebrows lifting.

I gave her a thumbs-up, followed by a fist. Then, because I didn't know if she'd know what any of that meant, yelled, "We're going to battle now!"

"Strength and honor!" she yelled, and it was clear she'd been watching *Gladiator* to boost her courage.

When I glanced down again, our vampires had stalled and were now undressing. I felt a surge of love through the bond, Darius wishing me well.

"We'll have our future," I murmured, hardening myself. "We will have our future if I have to pull a miracle out of my ass."

Here we go, I thought, and leaned forward.

Archion put on a burst of speed. The dragons would get there first, but I knew Lucifer wouldn't order our deaths.

There is one question I still don't really understand the answer to, Archion thought as we hastened toward the scene.

Lucifer's forces ran at the elves in a messy mass. Roars and shouts of blood lust rang up as we neared the melee. The dragons and the flying demons kept pace above us, Lucifer clearly having some sort of plan and choosing this mess as his strategy.

What is that? I asked Archion as I stitched magic into the sky. I'd been working on this and only this for the last two days. I would not wait until the sky was ripped away to construct another. Instead, I'd stitch my magic into the foundation of this place to hold the existing sky in place. I'd root my illusion to the ground in a weave of fire and ice that, in our practice, even Penny had been hard-pressed to tear apart. I was a hybrid—godly lineage merged with the Underworld—

and it gave me uniqueness that I would use to our advantage. The elves and Lucifer might try to break through it, but without plenty of time and focus, they wouldn't get far.

That was the plan, anyway.

My heart throbbed. My pulse pounded in my ears, a steady, fast throb. Adrenaline fueled me, followed by excitement.

I loved running into battle. That was my jam. I didn't slink closer and strategize; I burst into the scene and kicked in teeth. The situation might've changed, but I hadn't.

We're going to get in their way so that they don't fight, but if they ignore us—which they will—we're supposed to apply force? he thought.

Yup.

So we are basically the smaller force fighting against two larger forces on either side of us?

Yup.

How is that a good idea?

I honestly have no idea.

Dragons didn't talk, but his low growl was close enough. This was, quite possibly, a suicide mission, but fuck it. If we didn't take a stand for what we believed in, who were we?

We reached the edge of the battle, and the elves' heads turned as they took notice of us for the first time.

The fliers in the sky, on both sides, fluttered a little in the air, surprised. My father turned his head slowly, a grin sliding up his face. He nodded.

I couldn't resist giving him an answering smile. We might not be on the same side, but damn it, this felt good. Stretching the legs of our violent rage.

Give 'em hell, Archion, I thought.

He flew down the center of the open space between the elves and the demons, roaring. Coppelia and Saphira joined us, their cacophony merging, reverberating through the grounds and echoing off the castle walls. We'd worked hard to control our reactions to the dragons' roars, but this one was amplified somehow. Much more intense. Fear blistered through my body and nearly stopped my heart.

We'd always thought that effect was a tall tale until we started to practice at the shifters' private estate, Archion thought, clearly happy with himself. *We had endless time to practice.*

It was two months. Give me a break. It wasn't endless.

The non-dragon fliers froze up. Several of them fell to the ground like dead weights. The smaller dragons careened into the troops below, fire erupting from some and scorching whoever was unlucky enough to be in the way. The larger dragons lost height, struggling against the blast.

Our three roared again, their sounds intermingling to create that heart-shaking boost.

Demons hovered off their dragons, including my father. His hands came out to stabilize Tatsu in the air.

Thanks for the warning, I thought to Archion.

Surprise.

I sent a tidal wave of fire and ice at the elves, a blast of air chased by flame. I flattened their first troops as the roars wore off. Archion veered toward them and opened fire. Romulus had said the elves depended on organized warfare—or at least they had once upon a time. Since the same leadership was still in effect, he'd figured they still would, and those orderly ranks suggested he was right. They also would've heard that we'd be here as attempted peacekeepers. Crushing part of their army might seem counterintuitive, but the goal now was to blow their minds, get them scrambling, and then prepare for the onslaught from my father, who would want to take advantage of the melee. And who also might think I'd joined his side.

Romulus seemed very good at strategy. We'd see if he was right.

Coppelia and Saphira came after us, blowing fire down on the scrambling troops below. The elves' fliers were slow to rise, and it was clear some had broken limbs or necks in the fall. I slammed down with air, not allowing them to climb back up.

A blistering spell zipped past the line of elves and to the castle beyond. It slammed against the (very new looking) closed front doors and exploded, like a bomb going off. The wood blew off the hinges and tumbled out of the way. Stone rained down from a pockmarked and scarred surface, as though someone had done that previously. Probably Lucifer's way of knocking when he'd come to collect me.

Another spell, just like the first, followed it, this time flying into the open crevice.

This wasn't part of the plan, I said, throwing my magic around before taking a moment to stitch this portion of the sky into the scenery.

This is probably part of Penny's plan, Archion said, turning away from the castle and setting fire to another catapult. *Saphira has said Penny has a lot of anger to work through.*

Now is not the time, though.

We may not get another one.

He had a point.

Change of plans.

Archion tilted his great wings before I even finished that thought. We followed Saphira closer to the castle.

I'd meant to send a swell of magic after hers. I'd meant to summon hellfire and cut at least part of that place down. I'd meant to do a lot of things.

But then I saw them. The king and queen, pushed

back from their people, standing on a dais with tele-scopes to either side of them in case they wanted to look more closely at a battle they had caused. While I led this force, and Lucifer led his people, these cowardly bastards had hung back to let someone else die for them. I was putting my neck on the line to save most of their people, and they couldn't even stand at the last row of their troops.

There, I said to Archion, my focus razor sharp, my vision tinged red. Being the bigger person was all well and good, and very adultlike, but it turned out I just couldn't get over it. I might not wipe out the whole damn force of elves, but I would at least kill those assholes. *Those two there.*

Are they the same person?

They certainly look like it. Head there.

Archion put on a burst of speed.

Get lower to the ground, I thought. *When you feel their magic—and you will—veer right into that field behind them. Once the magic lifts, we'll need to split up. Help the others with Romulus's plan. I'll take these dickheads down on my own.*

I won't leave you.

You will do our duty, since I am too much of an ass-hole to do it with you.

When you're done, hover high and I'll pick you up.

No need. I'll attack the rest from behind.

It seems my surprise won't be the only one they'll get today.

Correct.

A hard fist of magic wrapped around me and squeezed, sending shooting pain up through my middle and stabbing behind my eyes. Archion shuddered under me and let out a burst of fire as he lost altitude, doing as I'd said and veering toward the field, only he was going to miss the fluffy section of grass up ahead and land on the hard stone and packed dirt beyond it. At least, that was what the illusion made it look like.

I extended that fluffy bit toward his probable landing site, pulling it up over the dirt and then layering the design on top of the stone. It was coarse and unrefined and looked utterly ridiculous, but it should work. I tacked the magic down so it would hold under his crash landing and then threw myself from his back.

My *Glaciem* magic didn't catch right away, and I dropped like a stone. Pain stabbed through my head and felt like it was gouging my eyes. A hot spike drove up through my center, starting between my legs and pulsing out through the top of my head, as though I'd been impaled on a spike.

The shock of pain, and where it had originated, triggered a very female part of me. Shock and fear clawed at me. Tugging at my vulnerability. Urging me to run off to a dark corner to hide. Because everyone knew about the inexcusable things men did to women when conquering lands.

Whether the elves intended to stir those fears or not, they had.

Vulnerabilities made us stronger. My father had said that. You could not really hate unless you knew how to love. And you could not revel in rage if you didn't know great passion. You would never know your true strength unless you gave in to your greatest weaknesses.

They hadn't tapped into my greatest weakness, but they *had* triggered the kind of hot, consuming rage that took no prisoners.

I shoved back at their magic as I fell, catching myself in a hover for a brief moment before resuming the fall. I hit the ground and rolled, no stranger to being tossed around and rolling out of it. As soon as I found my feet, I charged straight at those bastards. Just like old times.

I dipped my hand into my pouch, lost a couple spells in the process, and found the one I wanted. I snapped the casing and threw, hitting the edge of their fancy little dais as they pushed together, shoulder to shoulder, and faced me, arms coming up.

This was going to hurt.

Their magic hit me like a fucking brick. It slammed through my middle and drove all my insides out through my back. They peeled my skin from my body and stole my vision. At least, that was what it felt like.

"Shit birds sucking on a crack pipe, what in the holy fuck?" I said, continuing to run. I pushed out my magic in front of me, like rolling a carpet under my feet, making sure I didn't trip on anything. I didn't stop. Probably should've, but I refused to give them the satisfaction. Fuck 'em.

I sliced through their magic, unraveling pieces of it, but they were both at my power level, working together, and I was outmatched.

My magic hit a bump, and then my foot did. My body kept going in total blackness, my vision still cut off, and flew. I threw out my hands, and good thing I did, or I would've hit one of them face-first. As it was, my palms hit a pair of boobs, and I latched on, angling my body to make a solid hit and take her down with me. We rammed into the dais, and I grappled instantly, so incredibly used to this sort of thing from years of bounty hunting and tackling marks. I wasn't the best at that job for no reason.

I landed three quick punches to her upper chest, then adjusted my aim and smashed her nose. Hot liquid sprayed across my face and my vision flickered back to life. I crashed my fist into her face again and then struck out with air, throwing my hand to the side to get her beau.

"Guards!" the other turd shouted, warding off my attack with a blast of magic. Not only were they way back here away from the battle, safe from most danger, but they apparently had guards, too.

"Come on, Gumby, let's fight fair and square." I pushed up a little and yanked my foot up, slamming some lady balls before hopping over her and repeatedly ramming my foot into her side. She tried to fling magic at me. Tried to push at my face with her hands. I just kept going, slashing and burning with my magic at the other one while I physically assaulted this one. They clearly were not used to animalistic close combat. Where was Roger when you needed him?

Stinging magic rolled over me, and hands grabbed my shoulder and ripped me back. Their help had arrived.

"Gotta kill you quick-like," I said, my vision still splotchy but good enough.

I threw back an elbow and connected with a sternum. The hands loosened and the guard's breath flowed over me, but he didn't let go. Someone else grabbed at my arm.

I swelled air to throw them off, but my attention was divided, and the king had an unimpeded shot at me. My vision flickered out again, and pain nearly doubled me over.

I felt a blast of magic rush by me. A hoarse cry

sounded before the pain ceased and my vision flickered back to good enough. The hands yanked at my shirt before disappearing entirely.

I spun with wild eyes in time to see Cahal's sword slice into one of the guards that had restrained me. Emery punched another before grabbing the dagger from her belt and stabbing her in the chest. He turned to another one, wild-eyed, and let loose a spell that tore the guard's chest wide open. Blood and guts spilled out. The guard tried to catch them in crimson hands as he sank to the ground.

Penny shot off another spell. The king barely managed to redirect it before falling off the other side of the dais.

She glanced over, and I felt relief so thick it was choking me. She met my eyes and nodded.

The queen had turned over and was crawling to the back of the dais, clearly not sure where she was going, just *away*. Marks did this too. Usually I'd step on their backs and demand answers, or just haul them up and take them in.

But she wasn't going anywhere. Neither of them were.

"I got the king," I said. "I've already primed the queen for you."

"Nah. I'll let Emery take that sack of monkey balls."

"You can't swear, even here?" I grinned, my rage

swelling, my magic swelling with it. "Still know how to do hellfire?"

"I can't without your dad's magic here too. I can light a bunch of guards on fire, though."

"Good. Don't go overboard. We don't want you losing yourself to rage and never coming back."

"My mom already warned me about that. I'm good. I'll let Emery handle it."

I nodded and stepped up onto the dais, ignoring the queen. Emery would handle that, as Penny had said, and we'd forgive him for his lack of decorum when he did.

"Fucking with us was a big mistake, your highness," I said as I stalked toward the king, shoving at his magic with gritted teeth. "Oops. Found your equal, did you?"

"You're trash," he snarled.

"If name calling helps you cope with this situation, by all means." I tangled with his power. It was volatile and unstable sometimes, and cool and smooth others. I had no idea what that meant, but I did know these suckers weren't great with their hands.

I gave a big push as I rounded the corner, shoving his magic right back at him. Then I physically rushed forward, jumped, and kicked. My heavy boot cracked him in the face, and he fell backward like a log. He shot his hand up, but I slashed with air, ridding him of that ability in the future.

"I have to ask…" I slashed down at him, my magic

skimming across his neck. He cried out, an inhuman sound, throwing everything he had at me.

I spared a bit of my magic and endured the pain. I worked around his gale of power.

"You're not banging your sister, right?" I stabbed, the thrust of air magic shoved aside but not enough, because it came down in his side. "Because that would be gross." My next slash was accompanied by another swell of magic. I cut through his middle this time.

He yelled, clutching the wound, and I swiped once more, silencing him for good. His head rolled away.

Archion now stood on the field he'd crashed into, my hasty grass illusion torn up in a couple places, but at least it had done the job. He appeared unhurt. The other two dragons dropped down as well, Coppelia huffing smoke.

Emery stood on the dais looking at the castle, his chest rising and falling. He'd dealt with the queen. He glanced my way, saw that I was good, and then found Penny shooting off spells into the much-reduced crowd of guards like a gunslinger. None of the other elves had come back to help. Not one. That spoke volumes.

Your people need help, Archion thought. *You will have to surprise the elves another time.*

I told Emery and the others what he'd said.

"Penny!" Emery shot out a spell, cutting down a guard who'd thrown some kind of nasty magic at her. Cahal lopped off one elf's arm, another's head, and then cut through a third's leg with cool economy, like he was dancing with his sword. It was vicious and vile, and I loved it.

"Let's go, show over," I yelled, waving my arm in the air.

He is worried about you, Archion said as we ran their way.

Who? I asked as I took a running leap and hovered onto his back.

"That's not fair," Penny called. "How can I get style points when I can't hover?"

"Not my problem," I yelled.

Lucifer, Archion said, lifting off. *The vampire. The shifter—take your pick. They are cutting the elves' forces down, trying to get to you.*

I grimaced. I'd totally get in trouble for this.

In fairness, they'd known something like this was liable to happen. I couldn't be trusted to follow a plan. Everyone knew that. In fact, hadn't most of my friends encouraged me to go rogue?

The others are working with Lucifer? I asked.

Not exactly. But they have a common cause right now.

I'd definitely get in trouble.

"Let's fight back the demons," I yelled at the others. "I doubt the elves think of us as friendlies after killing their monarchs, so don't get killed in the process."

CHAPTER 18

W E FLEW OVER the line of elves, now completely scattered. Fliers swarmed the sky now, healed from our efforts, beating back the demons as the rows of elves waved their hands in the air, using their magic to target the dragons and dragon riders. The front line clashed with shifters and demons alike as the vampires on our side tried to cut a path through the elves' army. Darius was trying to get to me, just as Archion had said.

Tatsu bellowed, the effect sliding off me, and pushed up higher into the sky. My father sat atop her, and he noticed me immediately, relief washing over his face. My heart glowed at this show of genuine emotion, but I pushed that away. I could feel affectionate toward him later. Right now, I had to beat him back.

I swelled my magic and *shoved* with air, putting everything into it. It shoved away demons and dragons, both on the ground and in the sky, creating some space. A few from the elves' side were caught up in the blast of air, but they'd just have to be collateral damage.

We dove down to the troops, and I layered the

friendlies with cold while Archion blew fire across the demon side in a smooth line. Some demons burned and writhed. Trolls caught fire or turned to run. A cluster of gross little goblins was caught in the blast. Those behind pushed back even more, scurrying away.

A lone wolf howl floated up to us. A big gray wolf—probably Roger, though I couldn't really tell from this height—turned from the elves. He ran forward, joined immediately by shifters and fae. Definitely Roger. Spells changed direction, once aimed at the elves and now swinging toward the demons.

But the elves didn't suddenly decide to stop fighting. They pushed forward, emboldened by our people's altered focus. Swords swung and magic blasted, yelps of pain and shouts erupting. The demons slammed into our forces on the other side, too, led by those most resistant to fire.

Tatsu flew over our people and went directly for the elves, raining down fire as Lucifer pummeled them with air spears. Other dragons blasted fire at our people, catching a shifter before I could cover them with protection. I threw down knives at the demons as Archion turned to go after Lucifer. Lucifer's team of dragons followed his lead, attacking the line of elves. Our dragons went to lend aid, the only fliers we had. We were severely outgunned in the air.

Flame went up behind me, and I turned to see a

demon spear a mage with it. I gritted my teeth, sending my own air spear to take it out. I hadn't been there in time for that mage, though, not to mention there was a whole sea of demons pushing forward with the same sort of magic. I wouldn't be able to protect everyone. I had to turn my attentions to where I could do the most good.

A thought curled through my mind, unbidden. *How does this end?*

It was a good question. Lucifer had thousands. We wouldn't be able to hold them off forever. They'd shove us forward until we were basically fighting side by side with the elves...except the elves would kill us right along with the demons. We'd be trapped in the middle, a position Lucifer had always known I'd end up in if I didn't join him. A position he planned to pull me from, leaving everyone else behind. Which wasn't going to happen, obviously.

There had to be another way, and Lucifer was the key. He could call this off. We'd taken out the monarchs—the elf leadership would be vulnerable. They'd be ready to compromise, they had to be, especially if they knew he'd take it all if they didn't.

To Lucifer, I thought, and Archion rushed forward. The way to make my father see reason was to force his hand, and everyone had always known that would be my job. I was the only one that could.

I blanketed the elf troops with protection as fire rained down over them, their magic doing a little something to provide their own brand of resistance. They worked their magic up at the dragons, making their wings flutter uncomfortably, and a couple came crashing down. I grimaced and lifted my spell enough to let those dragons right themselves before pushing them away. I wanted them to stop, not to get hurt.

Lucifer threw magic that materialized in a wide splash of air that sliced through flesh and bone. I slapped him back with my magic, knocking him to the side. His head snapped up as he clung to Tatsu, whose bleats had the dragons around her shifting and moving. Those on the outskirts turned toward us, and Archion tensed below me, preparing for battle. But they didn't attack.

The dragons flapped, crowding us, getting in the way. They were a deterrent. They wouldn't kill me, and I wouldn't kill them.

What a stupid kind of battle I'd found myself in. This wasn't my speed at all.

Keep trying, I thought to Archion before throwing my leg over and hopping off.

"Reagan," I heard as I fell before catching myself, seeing Penny and Emery looking around, probably wondering how they were going to follow. Of course they would; that was a certainty. Right or wrong, Penny would not risk allowing me to save her a third time.

I pulled them off their dragons, who would get their directives from Archion. Cahal jumped, of course, just as damn stubborn as the others. Near the ground, I caught them all, thankful the elves were more worried about Lucifer than us.

"What's the plan?" Emery yelled as they ran at me. He fired off a spell to take down a centaur, cutting out its legs, and Penny finished it off with some sort of bone-breaking thing. They'd clearly studied the best way to take those creatures down since we'd dealt with them the last time.

"Always with a plan, even though you're the one that told me to attack without one," I grumbled, throwing my hand wide and cutting down a row of goblins vying for space. What a very handy way to take down a bunch of things at once. *Thanks, Pop.* "We need to make Lucifer give up this fight," I yelled.

"Oh, only that?" Penny said. She shot a spell at a minotaur, catching it in the chest and flinging it back.

I didn't get to see what that did, too busy ripping at three enemies in front of me and blasting a fourth with fire. "Null his magic, and I'll shove with mine," I yelled. "Help Cahal…"

I let my words slip away as I felt Darius's presence throbbing through our bond. He was close and coming closer. Monsters burst through the crowd of bodies around us, claws ripping. A goblin went flying. Darius reached forward to grab another, but only took out its throat. The rest of the body slid to the ground.

What is the plan? Darius asked as the vampires seeped into the area, clearing out the enemy.

This time I could actually pretend I had one. I relayed it to him, throwing air at a minotaur trying to ram his way into our group from the elves' side.

"We're trying to bloody help you, you miserable shithead," I yelled, frustration eating at me. A pegasus flew overhead, its legs gyrating through the air as if it were running along solid ground. A winged horse reminded me of the unicorns. They hadn't engaged in the battle. I wondered why they'd even come. They hadn't seemed too keen on seeing action back on their island.

The pegasus neighed as it pulled up and kicked out with its back feet, its hooves cracking into a dragon's hide. The dragon turned to deliver retribution, but it must've been slapped with magic, because its wings tilted dramatically. The pegasus kicked again, and then again. The dragon crashed into the ground, disappearing behind a crush of bodies. Its roar cut off, and my heart jumped into my throat.

"Hurry," I said, shoving forward, pushing with air, cutting down anyone in my way. "We have to stop this now! Vampires, keep everyone off us. Cahal, you come too. Emery and Penny, null Lucifer's magic."

"I'll null the magic. I know how," Emery said. "Penny, cut out the elves' magic if you can."

"I'm not close enough to feel their magic," she said. "I don't know how to stop them unless I can."

"Then we have to get closer." I pushed Cahal to the side and blasted out with air and fire, pushing and killing at the same time, cutting a line to those elves so Penny could get close enough to do her thing. The vampires stepped up quickly, helping me. The front-line creatures fell away, surging around behind us. I doubted we'd be able to get out of this as easily as we were pushing in, but that was a problem for another time.

Fire scoured the ground around us, kept off us by my hastily thrown-up magic. Bodies writhed and creatures screamed. Blood splattered my face from the side. Still we pushed on, tearing a path forward. More dragons flew overhead now, intermingled with the elves' flying troops, trying to fight them back.

Tatsu, her back empty, opened her mighty jaws and crunched a sylph between her teeth. Faeries around them flittered away. I didn't know if they'd decided to battle someone else, or if they'd (wisely) decided they'd rather not give their lives for the elves.

"So why the hell am I?" I said as I spotted Lucifer in his demon form, hovering near the back of the elves. He was going for the most powerful of them. Other demons flew around him, creating a sort of circle. A protective ring, maybe? He likely knew tricks with which to combat the elves, and I had taken out his biggest threat.

Yeah, real great decision-making, dummy, I thought to myself as a sword made it past Darius and licked the side of my leg with blinding agony. I grunted and staggered, nearly falling. That one had sliced deeply. Dang it.

Darius stabbed through the chest of the enemy. The ugly creature with a flat face and protruding mouth shrieked and shuddered as he ripped it down and away from me.

Are you okay? he thought.

"Good." I wasn't—it hurt something awful. I had to pay more attention to keep moving.

Limping now, I felt Emery and Penny's spell float into the air like fog. It drifted slowly, aiming for Lucifer and his band of merry men.

"Still can't feel them," Penny yelled from behind me.

She meant the elves, who had to be just beyond this line of enemy.

Out of the corner of my eye, I saw a vampire hiss before dropping. He convulsed on the ground as the vampire behind him stepped forward, picking up where he'd left off.

A dragon flew overhead, bearing down with fire. I

covered us as two centaurs went down from Cahal and the vampires' combined efforts. I smashed a third with air, allowing the dragon's fire to help keep it down. Behind them, the roiling and surging group of elves focused on Lucifer and the dragons. Mostly undamaged, most standing, it was clear they were doing just fine at keeping my dad at bay. We had a chance at stopping him before he did the kind of thing he couldn't walk back from.

Someone hit me from behind. Penny shouted, and the burst of magic she'd been sending out shot wide. It hit a dragon and clamped its wings to its sides. The beautiful purple and black body crashed down to the ground.

"No! Oh no!" Penny surged that way, but a vampire stepped in her path. "Move, Marie," she shouted.

The dragon roared and fire blasted into the air. Wings beat and then the dragon tramped through the crowd, knocking people over as it tried to get back in the air.

Marie in monster form recoiled and dropped Penny, who was done with being saved or stopped and had clearly hit her with a spell. Once on the ground, Penny charged toward the dragon, cutting down the creatures who were trying to chop at it with weapons and stab its eyes.

"Follow her," I yelled, altering course, blinding agony vibrating up my thigh each time I stepped on that leg. *Heal already, leg.*

Emery caught up to Penny quickly, as did Cahal, detouring from my father to cleave a path toward the dragon.

"I didn't mean to, sorry," Penny yelled. The dragon stopped in its thrashing, its great head turning her way as she and Emery shot out rapid-fire spells at its attackers. I covered the far side in fire. A demon appeared at the dragon's rump, slinging air and also a weapon, not powerful enough to just use its magic. Another appeared beside it, and it was clear they'd followed us toward the elves. We were running out of time.

The dragon bellowed and flapped its wings, rising into the air, and demons surged into the hole it left behind. The dragon turned and blasted the area in front of Penny with fire, repaying her for her help.

I let my magic pulse as the demons rushed toward and around us, reaching into them as a group, thankful for their limited power level. They felt my magic and slowed their movement. They turned their gazes toward me in confusion. I willed them to slow further, to allow us to go first. They pushed against the directive, shaking with the effort. Lucifer must've already had his hooks in them.

"Damn it," I said, kicking a downed body. Pain coiled around me, hard to shake off. I winced and clutched the wound briefly, willing myself to heal faster. My leather pants bulged with the slit, and gooey wetness slid down my leg. That wasn't great. I wished I'd thought to bring duct tape so I could patch up holes in thighs.

Closer now, we moved into the throng of elves. The dragon Penny had hurt then helped blast the closest elves with fire, doing us a favor, and the demons fought in front of us, letting us surge in behind them.

"Got the elf magic," Penny said, magic welling around her. "Now, what do I do with it?"

Emery shot out another nulling spell, their earlier spell still drifting closer to Lucifer. Almost there. He was clearly trying to fill the gap in time until the original spell actually hit.

The recent spell hit one demon and splashed against another to its right. Clearly the fog was needed to get around the demons and to my father. The two affected demons looked at their hands, then glanced around wildly before their wings froze up, the Penny-borrowed elves' magic taking hold. They dropped to the ground in convulsions.

Dragons swooped in with fire, probably to keep the elves from attacking the fallen bodies. Lucifer looked at the hole I'd created. A moment later he dipped his gaze, seeing me on the ground. The fog reached him. Lights out went his magic.

He didn't look away from me, even as the demons

around him started to convulse. He tensed; I could see it. The pain of the elves' magic was digging into him, it must be, but he was ignoring it, resisting. Probably doing a much better job than I was at fighting the effects of this blasted leg.

The thing felt like it was leeching the heat out of me, taking my energy with it. My magic thrummed to compensate, fueling me, but it felt strangely heavy and cumbersome. I was a little woozy, probably from blood loss.

I took a deep breath and pushed on, determined. The pain would die down shortly. I'd survived worse.

The demons around Lucifer fell. His wings beat fast but shallow now, then faltered. The dragons bellowed as they tried to help the fallen among the surging elves, but their efforts weren't enough to save everyone. If Lucifer fell, they'd kill him. Shit.

"Penny, hit those elves with their own magic," I yelled, pushing at the demons rushing in front of me, throwing fire to either side of us, drawing the notice of the closest elves. I needed them to split their forces.

"On it!"

I needed to tear down Penny's spell and then shove Lucifer away before he could magically stop me.

I sent off fire at Penny's spell, layered it with air, and then started picking it apart. I was an old pro at it by now, but it still took a second. A second Lucifer might not have.

CHAPTER 19

Penny PUT EVERYTHING she had into the magic she'd shoplifted from the elves, sweeping it over them as Emery shot spells. Cahal's crimson-coated sword flashed, slicing into one elf after another, hacking them down. He jerked but then stepped forward, fighting their magic, it seemed.

That was when Penny felt it: a hot stab of agony ripping through her middle. Oh yeah, those dirty slug monkeys were coming at them now. If they'd just chill for a second, they'd figure out her group were actually here to help them. A fat lot of good it was doing at the moment.

Penny pushed through the pain as Reagan worked at her spell.

"Almost…" Reagan said, the words almost drowned out by the shouting and hissing around them. And then she took a step back and her face closed down in concentration. "That bastard is quick," she said through her teeth, staggering into Darius beside her. She cried out and reached down for her thigh.

Dawning understanding prickled Penny and then fear welled up. She let go of her magic, of the spells, and turned toward her friend. Reagan never admitted she was in pain. She never gave in to it, not without throwing out some horrible violence to compensate for it.

Darius couldn't help right her, too busy making mincemeat of an elf in front of them. Penny grabbed her upper arm to hold her steady and ducked around, slipping between her and one of the vampires to do it. She sucked in a breath.

Blood was seeping out of a nearly foot-long gash, gushing down her leg and pooling on the ground. She healed fast, but the wound was deep—with the exercise she was doing, she'd bleed too much before her body could close it up.

"I don't know how to heal," Penny said, looking around frantically. "You have to stop fighting, Reagan. Hover into the air. Hover out of here and get on Archion. Lucifer will let you. If you don't, you'll bleed out."

"I'll be fine," she said in a gruff tone, back on her feet, her hands moving through the air, one shining a deep crimson from where she'd grabbed her thigh. Her spine curved, her energy clearly drained.

"How bad?" Darius said, and though the words were jumbled through his big teeth, Penny understood him perfectly.

"Very. If she doesn't get help, she'll die," she said, desperation and terror clawing at her. "She will *die!*"

"I won't—"

Penny doused her in a nulling spell. The currents of Lucifer's magic hit Reagan like a punch in the face, snapping her head back. Clearly her father was taking a second out of his busy schedule to play a little game of chicken, one that would cost valuable lives on all sides. That dangling ball sac obviously didn't give a horse's dong about anyone but his fun.

Demons rushed around them, going straight for the elves. They didn't bother their crew, though, so right now Penny didn't care.

Using a spell to carry her words, she yelled to Lucifer, "She's hurt badly. If you are going to take her, take her now."

"No!" Reagan shoved Penny off, unraveling her spell. She'd gotten really quick at it, unfortunately. "I am not leaving. We'll finish this."

"You tried. You failed," Penny told her. "It was always a long shot."

"No." Reagan sent her magic at Lucifer. Three of the downed demons that had been flying with him rose into the sky. Dragons swooped down around them, lighting the world on fire. Demons rushed in, joining the fray. From the direction they were coming, they weren't going through the shifters, mages, and fae to get here—

they were going around. At least that would spare some people. It wouldn't spare the elves, though. That battle was clearly lost, and maybe the world with it. Penny wondered what that would mean for the Brink. Reagan had had the right idea—there needed to be balance, and Lucifer controlling two worlds probably wasn't it.

Not like they could do anything about it, though. Someone stronger would have to take up the fight.

"You're hurt, and if you don't get help, you'll die. Is that what you want?" Penny asked with tears in her eyes, nulling Reagan again. The demons shoved by them, apparently not realizing the heir was in the mix. Hate filled the magic in the air.

"Hurry," she yelled at Lucifer as Reagan threw off her arm again. "Stop fighting me, Reagan."

"I can't go," Reagan said. "I doubt he'll spare enough dragons to save very many people. I can probably take a couple of you, but what about the others? What about Roger and Callie and Dizzy? I will not leave this battlefield while they are still on it. I *will not* leave them to die without doing everything I can to save them."

Penny's heart broke. She knew the truth of those words. But damn it, Reagan had already risked so much to help them. The shifters, mages, and fae had a chance—they had powers and abilities of their own and might still walk away. Maybe Penny and Emery and the others, too, if the demons let them fight their way out. But if Reagan didn't go now, she wouldn't have a chance at all. Penny was no nurse, but that much was obvious. If Reagan didn't get help, she would very soon be beyond it.

Lucifer appeared above them, looking down. He reached a hand out, and Penny ripped her spell away so he could grab Reagan. He might have to wrestle her magically, but it seemed he was adept at that. He was more experienced. He'd get her out of there.

He'd save her.

"Go," Penny said, looking at her friend for what was maybe the last time. This time, though, Penny wouldn't have anything to regret. She wouldn't be the one looking back as she escaped. This time, she was the motherfucking savior.

CHAPTER 20

HORRIBLE FEAR DRENCHED Lucifer as he pulled his daughter up from the throng of people fighting with her. Fighting *for* her. Her face was incredibly pale and bloodless. Her energy had flagged, and while she was still fighting his hold and his magic with skill, her power had greatly diminished. Blood dripped from her leg in a nearly solid line as he pulled her up.

"What have you done?" he said, pushing higher with her, turning her so he could look at her leg. "Stop fighting my magic, Reagan. You're hurt."

"I'll live. Put me back."

Tatsu soared near them, looking on. A lick of pain crept up his spine. The miserable elves were not smart enough to know when they were beaten.

She is dying, Tatsu said, each syllable jackhammering into Lucifer. *I can feel the slide of her being toward the never. Her will is strong, and she is using her magic like a crutch, but her energy is all but sapped. Once that is gone, she'll lose the grip on her magic and fade with it. Did you not feel this when you were battling her?*

That sounded like an accusation, and Lucifer bit out a response before he could help it.

No, I didn't fucking notice! I am in the middle of a battle, being attacked from all angles.

But that wasn't totally true. He'd been too puffed up with pride in her to notice. She'd used her resources to strip away his protections and gain the upper hand. She could've killed him, most likely. He'd half wondered if she planned to try. But then she'd helped him recover.

His hands shook as he looked at her face, her eyes drooping and her pupils dilated.

The whole time, she had been mortally wounded. Even now, she did not want to leave her friends—her people—preferring dying beside them to escape.

But why hadn't she known she was this close?

"The vampire," he said softly, remembering how their kind bonded. They drained their intended nearly dry and then filled them up again. And if that huge gap in her thigh wasn't gushing blood, that might yet work. She had allowed herself to ignore the warning signs in order to stay with the battle, though. She'd ignored the pain, too, having survived worse.

He wondered if the human mages down on the battlefield, surrounded by the unicorns to keep them from harm, would have field dressings. He knew humans used such things in battle. Or maybe he could find someone who had a snake…

It would take too long to find any of those things with the battle raging.

Make sure her people are not touched, he told Tatsu. *Get Archion here. He needs to fly her to the Underworld. She'll be stronger there.*

She won't make it.

She will.

She won't be able to hold on, Lucifer. Feel her magic—it is seeping from her. Her light is going out. Have you forgotten the feeling of an immortal slipping into eternal darkness?

No...

His eyes stung, covered in moisture now. His heart ached in a way he'd never felt before. A way that dug down into the very middle of him and bled pain. He hadn't known her long, but she was his flesh and blood. His perfect heir. A joy to know and a pleasure to have around. In such a short time, he had grown to love her like no other heir before her. He'd grown to love her as his daughter. He could not lose her.

She needs to be healed immediately, Tatsu thought. *You know there is a way.*

Lucifer's jaw ached with how hard he was suddenly clenching it.

No, he thought. Anything but that. There was no way he'd go to those kinds of extremes. He'd promised himself he would *never* again ask for anything from them.

Then say goodbye, Tatsu thought with great sadness. It pulled at her, and him with her.

He screamed, pushing higher into the sky. Archion flew closer, seeing Reagan in his arms. The dragon roared, the sound cutting through Lucifer, filled with misery. Lucifer knew how he felt.

How could he have let this happen? How could he have let her so close to the battle—actually *into* the battle? He'd planned to keep her at arm's length, letting her get her feet wet in safety while he clinched their victory. He'd intended to compromise so she didn't resent him. But he'd let her go too far, and look what had happened now.

He'd done this. He had caused this. The blame could rest at no one else's feet.

Her breathing turned shallow, and her lips curved into a smile, her eyes mostly closed. "My bad. I think you might be right." She let out a small sigh. "Please save my friends. Please save their people. The worlds need balance, Dad. The Realm needs their own leadership, just like the Underworld needs you. That leadership needs to be expanded to include representation for all who live here, but the people who are of this place need to rule it. You know that is right. Please do what is right." She sucked in breath, one arm dangling lifelessly over his forearm. "Can you bring Darius up here, please? I'd like to say goodbye."

Misery tore through his chest and filled every inch of his person. She had planned to marry that vampire. Sire offspring, like a traditional sort of family. Lucifer had never had that sort of nuclear arrangement, but he'd be damned, again, before he let anyone take it from her.

He couldn't let this be the end. He would do what needed to be done, no matter what it cost him.

He tilted his head back and looked into the sky. Drawing on the age-old magic that he'd been born with, blessed with, he summoned *them*. The healers. The bringers of light and goodness.

The cursed angels.

CHAPTER 21

MAGIC SANG THROUGH my blood and crackled through my heavy limbs. Desperate cold crowded every inch of my being, warning me that death was right around the corner. I had ignored the signs, trying to struggle on, and I'd screwed myself. Whoops.

Light blossomed all around us, filling the burnt-orange sky. Glowing orbs, it seemed like, sifting down from above.

"Please, I'd like to see Darius," I said, my voice not much more than a whisper. "I need to say goodbye."

I swore I'd already asked that. I didn't think my dad would deny my last wish, would he?

"Hold on," Lucifer said, looking upward. "They're coming."

I meant to ask who, but my head was unbearably heavy.

Not to rain on your parade, I thought, since it was so much easier than talking, *but I don't have long. I screwed up with that wound.*

"I know. *Shh*," he said, and the glowing orbs grew

brighter and brighter, nearly hurting my eyes. Sound diminished until I could only hear Lucifer breathing. I'd already stopped. It took too much effort.

One of the orbs grew and grew as it came nearer. Only then did I realize it wasn't an orb at all, but a person with snow-white wings beating at the air.

I frowned and let my head loll that way, blinking against the ethereal glow emanating from the man's dewy-soft skin.

You've got to be kidding me, I thought. *Is that an angel? Like, for real? I've heard them talked about, obviously, but a part of me didn't believe it.*

"They spawned those horrific stories for the humans, yes," Lucifer said, his voice filled with annoyance and disdain.

"Lucifer," the being said, but not with his mouth. Also not in my head. It was very confusing. He smiled at me, a serene sort of expression that annoyed me for reasons I couldn't really understand. His face was the image of loveliness, as perfect as Vlad's but not obnoxiously so. His disposition was as polite and graceful as Romulus's, but in a more pleasing way.

"Michael," Lucifer said. "Thanks for coming." He didn't sound all that grateful. More like spiteful. They clearly didn't have a great relationship.

Michael's smile stayed in place, and he bent his head a little while spreading out his hands. He wore a flowing shirt and pants so wide they almost looked like a skirt, obviously not a fan of color, since everything was the same shade of cream.

"I was not expecting to hear from you," Michael said without speaking. "The last time I saw you, you were so adamant that we'd have no more interaction. When was that?" He tapped his chin in thought.

"You paid me a visit after your people spared and ruined the druid," Lucifer supplied.

"Ruined?" Michael's beautiful face turned quizzical. "Ah, with our magic, you mean. You detest it."

"*Your* magic. I remade mine."

"Yes, of course. How could I forget."

He'd clearly not forgotten, judging by his mocking tone.

"Your people altered the druid's magic," Lucifer said. "In their heavy-handedness, they disguised his ancestral magic, dooming him to walk the earth alone. You wouldn't know this, of course, because you abandoned him." Lucifer *tsk*ed. "Very bad form, dooming your favorites."

A lovely frown pulled at Michael's features.

"That's not why I call you, though," Lucifer said. "Some things are more important than my hatred of you." He looked down at me. "She is dying. She's in need of healing."

Michael looked down on me with compassion and

pity. "She has your magic, does she not? I cannot heal the likes of what you have become. A disastrous, disgusting sort of monster."

"Has it been so long that you've forgotten what your heritage feels like in the veins of mortals?" Lucifer asked, and I thought that was rich coming from him. He apparently hadn't recognized my mother's heritage, or he never would have taken up with her. "And *I* am the black sheep? At least I pay attention to a world other than my own."

Again the lovely frown, this glowing fellow very slow on the uptake.

"Godly magic," I whispered, too tired to put any oomph behind my words. The only good news was that time seemed to have stopped. That, or everyone below had gone totally still, and they were all looking on like a very polite audience. Given Lucifer's feelings regarding angels, I didn't think that was likely behavior for the demons, at least.

"Her mother is of your line," Lucifer said. "Well..." He paused. "Hopefully not *yours*. I'd hate to think there was a smug dick somewhere in her past."

"Such colorful language you have accrued." Michael pursed his lips and bent a little more, sniffing as though smelling me. He peeled back one of my eyelids, studying me with gorgeous, deep blue eyes. "Ah. It is true. How interesting." His smile stretched wide, his gaze returning to Lucifer. "You sought out a woman with magic from your past and married it with what you are now. How do you find the result? Better than the previous, I should think, if you are asking for my aid."

"Not your aid specifically," Lucifer said. "I would've given all the gold in my kingdom to keep you from coming."

"And yet all the gold in your kingdom wouldn't have been enough to save your daughter."

Smug dick was right. This guy might appear lovely and virtuous, what with the cream and gold and flawlessness, but his arrogance was pretty extreme.

"I didn't know what Amorette was," Lucifer admitted.

"Ah, but part of you must've. It drew you in, I would wager." Now Michael's smile was triumphant.

"Can you guys do this later?" I asked, letting my heavy lids fall again.

"Why should I do this for her?" Michael asked.

Not much for doing things out of the goodness of your heart, huh? I thought. *Your image is obviously a false advertisement.*

"She seems to have your wit. How truly unfortunate," the angel murmured, clearly also able to hear thoughts. I'd figured as much.

"She took a wound standing against me," Lucifer said. "Surely that is worth your good humor."

"Is that all? Even your friends want to do that more often than not."

Lucifer's arms tensed. "Unlike me, she has worthy intentions. She was tortured at the hands of the elves, badly mistreated, and even still, she showed up here, leading a party of loyal friends, to protect the creatures of the Realm from being overtaken by us. As she lay in my arms, waiting to die, she asked that I help the elves rebuild a more fair and just leadership in the Realm so the worlds would exist in balance, something you seem to have forgotten was important when you shut yourself away and turned your back on the humans who worship your kind. She is attempting to sacrifice herself for the greater good, Michael. Surely that is her mother's magic talking, not mine. She *is* worthy of your healing touch, as much as it pains me to admit. She is a child— *my child.* I must ask this of you."

Michael paused for what felt like ages. A cool hand landed on my forehead, blaring light behind my eyes.

"I see you are speaking the truth," he finally said to Lucifer. "I see the blackness of her soul and the purity of her heart. How intriguing."

That sounds like a great compliment, I thought, and would've smiled if it hadn't required so much effort. At least the pain in my leg was gone. Ordinarily that would be bad, meaning I was beyond feeling pain, but with this clown dragging things out, it was nice to have a break from that intense pounding.

"She has a friend graced with our magic," Michael went on.

"Your magic," Lucifer corrected him.

"Two mages, it seems. Connected." Michael turned to look below. "And Cahal Druer is her ally." He smiled. "I have never met him in person, but I've heard such great things. I should like to meet him. Sometimes the ladies can make an average man sound great—"

"Just in comparison to you," Lucifer muttered.

"—solely because of his appearance. I wonder if his soul matches the accounts I have heard."

"You wish to see the handiwork of your brethren? Fantastic. You can witness the haunting sorrow behind his eyes," Lucifer taunted him. "Regardless, that druid has taken a liking to her. He protects her. How much damned proof do you need that she is worthy?"

"Damned, yes." Michael studied Lucifer's face and then his body, black as night and demonic in appearance, his flying form. "It seems you have damned her and are looking to us for her salvation, correct?"

I felt Lucifer tighten again. "Whatever sucks your cock, Michael, sure."

"Good heavens," Michael said, and I did grin this time. If he'd had some pearls, he'd be clutching them.

Michael looked down at me again, his ethereal glow starting to stress out my eyes. "Release her," he said, holding up a palm.

Lucifer did so, pulling his arms away and stepping back. Although I didn't sink or fall through the air, I reached for him in a sudden, inexplicable gush of anxiety. I hadn't realized it, but while on the brink of a death that I had not seen coming (my bad), he'd been my security blanket. My comfort. I hadn't been afraid when in his protection.

On my own now, hovering in the air in front of a creature I did not know, I felt vulnerable and exposed.

"Why should you live?" Michael asked me.

"That's not for me to answer," I replied. "I don't make the rules regarding life and death."

His brow furrowed. He clearly had not expected that reply. "Would you like to live?"

"Of course."

"Why?"

I sighed and tried to get a view of the fields below me. My body tilted up to a somewhat standing position, although it was not controlled by me.

My impression earlier had been spot-on. Everything below us was frozen, as though someone had flipped a switch, turning off time. Angels floated above the highest of the fliers, looking down at the battlefield. Each of them had a sheen or an ethereal glow of varying brightness, the strength of which probably had something to do with their power.

Surprise flickered through me. Unicorns mostly surrounded the shifters, mages, and fae, not crowding them but keeping the demons or other creatures from getting to them. They were also keeping my people from getting out, cutting them off from the battle. The demons on Lucifer's side didn't push or look like they were trying to get through the line. They were instead going around them on both sides, pouring into the elves' forces, able to do so because of the small force we'd brought. We'd created an impediment to keep them from directly attacking.

My vision magnified as my gaze shifted to those within the unicorn barrier—some effect of magic, obviously, still not controlled by me.

I could just make out a collection of mages, Dizzy and Callie among them, their canvas satchels thrown open and their hands reaching in. They were ready to fight but unable or unwilling to harm the unicorns. Roger and Steve were within the protective barrier as well, trying to push through it to get to the action on the elf side. They'd clearly realized the demons weren't a threat to them specifically, and the battle had moved beyond them. Roger wasn't one to give up a fight when he was needed.

"You'd planned to protect my people all along," I whispered to Lucifer, finding Penny, Emery, Darius, and Cahal where I'd left them, each paused mid-action.

They'd continued the fight, pushing me to safety but not trying to follow. "Well...some of them."

"All of them," Lucifer said, following my gaze. "I'd planned to protect you all. The unicorns volunteered to push you out of the fight. They did want a crack at the elves, but they decided protecting your people in their time of need was more important."

A host of vampires, led by Vlad, had worked around to the elves and were closing in on them. Dragons hovered overhead, frozen as they looked down, some with fire streaming out of their mouths onto the cowering elves and creatures below. Demons pushed in from all sides, massed more in some areas than others. Various creatures dotted the landscape, in the process of fleeing. They did not plan to stay until the bitter end, or to give their lives for abandoning a cause that was not their own. With their intolerant leadership, the elves had sunk themselves. They'd never stood a chance. We hadn't made any difference, and nor could we have. My group had been a bunch of cowboys trying to do the right thing regardless of the odds, and in the face of logic.

Every one of us would do it again, though. We'd hoped to find a better solution for everyone, one that didn't cost so many lives, one that allowed the people of the Realm to continue ruling themselves. Maybe one day someone would be strong enough to make that happen.

"I don't really care if you save me," I said, suddenly tired. "I've only ever had a half-life, anyway. Only worried about myself. That's not really someone of moral fiber. If you're going to expend any effort, help the people down there. Help the people of the Realm. They've been in the shadow of tyrants for a long time, it seems like. Help them get set up for a better life, and please save the people who fought beside me down there. Take my life for theirs, if you have to, I don't care, but make sure they live. And flip Penny off as you do it. She'll be so pissed I got to be the hero again."

"I know what you want for yourself and these worlds," Michael said, his not-voice echoing through my brain. "I see it clearly."

"First, it's rude to go digging around someone's head without asking. Second, if you were going to do that, why bother asking?" I closed my eyes and leaned back. "You're exhausting."

"Like father, like daughter, it would seem," Michael murmured. "I am thankful you were born in the Brink so we didn't have a repeat of what happened with Lucifer."

I didn't know what that meant, so I didn't bother replying.

"You wish to live in the Brink still," Michael said. "Is that world to your liking, then? Unlike the Realm, it needs no improvement?"

Lucifer huffed out a laugh but didn't comment.

I had to agree with Lucifer. "It's my home. It's the home of my mother. It means something to me. Improvement, though? Yeah. I'll say. Non-magical humans are running amok. It's an utter shitshow at the moment."

"I'd be happy to step in," Lucifer said, and I could tell he was taunting Michael again. "Though I'm not sure what more I could do. They are already well versed in sex, war, hate, violence—"

"Yes, yes." Michael held up a hand, studying me but talking to my father. "I take your point. You are right, if I must admit it. We have been gone for too long. It is time we assert ourselves into their short little lives and see what can be done. Maybe strip away all that…color you seem to allow your subjects." His eyes cut to Lucifer, who returned the look with a wolfish grin.

"Just leave New Orleans alone," I said. "We like color. The louder the better."

Michael lifted his hand, and I rotated in the air, my eyes suddenly level with his sparkling baby blues.

"I will forget, for the moment, who your father is," Michael said, his gaze sharp. "You are not correct—I can see that you have lived more than a half-life, for most of it. You had a full heart when your mother lived. And a full heart with your vampire and your mage friends and your home within the...loud, colorful place you love so dearly. It was only in those dark years after you lost her that you wandered, and that, I think, is understandable. Now, here you are, thinking of others above yourself. Desiring peace and balance not only for yourself but for all the worlds. You are in tune with goodness, Miss Reagan Somerset, even if you do not always display it. The balance of your mother and your father has done you well, though it partially pains me to admit it. Your father is intolerable." He paused for a moment. "I will help. You desire someone stronger to keep your father in his lane. It is a job I will happily take up."

"That's not what she was asking," Lucifer drawled.

Michael's smile was slight. "Rest assured, Reagan. When you awake, all will be right. Thank you for the part you have played. We will do our due diligence from here on out."

I wasn't sure if I'd helped or hurt. But it was clear they wouldn't be able to push too much, since Lucifer would be here to push back.

My lids slid shut—still not my doing—and blackness overcame me.

CHAPTER 22

DEEP SHADOW DRAPED across the familiar surroundings of my bedroom when I opened my eyes. Darius sat in the corner with an ankle over his knee, his gaze focused on a romance novel he must've pulled from my shelf. Moonlight streamed in through the window, and I could just see a smattering of stars spread across the slice of sky in my view.

"Getting some pointers?" I asked, taking stock of my body.

He lowered the volume and allowed it to close around his thumb, holding his place. "No. This one is ridiculous. The supposed hero is a pushy ape who speaks in grunts. I'm expecting him to grab the heroine's hair and drag her back to a cave at any moment. If I were in the story, I would kill him instantly and take his prize without breaking a sweat. The heroine clearly does not know that if she would like to flirt with danger, there are better options at her disposal with a lot more charm and tact."

"Are you forgetting that it's fiction, or is there a sore

point in your past I'm not aware of?" I pushed to sitting and marveled that I didn't ache anywhere. Sliding back the covers, I saw that my leg was in tiptop shape, no marks or scars or pain whatsoever. My arms didn't have any bruises from fighting, and my energy was in full force.

He reopened the book and went back to reading without comment.

I laughed softly, stretching. No sore muscles. Better and better.

The last thing I remembered was Michael telling me he would help. Clearly he had healed me, and someone had brought me home.

I checked the time. Three o'clock.

"What day is it?" I asked, swinging my legs over the side of the bed. A tank top hugged my torso and only panties covered my lower half. Darius must've dressed me for bed, then. He knew this was my normal sleeping attire when I wasn't planning on getting lucky. Not that that would have stopped me.

He flipped a page. "Friday. You have been sleeping for nearly two days."

"And you?"

"I am on the second book in this accursed series, and I need to know how it ends."

"So you haven't slept, then?"

"No. Once you were healed, I took some of your

blood. I apologize for not asking, but Michael assured me that it would do you no harm, and I assumed you wouldn't want me to take from another."

"You assumed correctly," I muttered, thinking back to that pretty unbelievable scene in the sky.

"He is repulsed by me, by the way. He is not a fan of vampires in general. It did not trouble me in the slightest."

I laughed. I could definitely see that. It would probably make my father like vampires that much more.

"That really happened, huh?" I shook my head, gazing out the window but not seeing what lay beyond. "My father called down angels to help me. *Angels.*" I gave Darius a wide-eyed look he was too distracted to notice. "There is a fourth world—which I'd been told about, sure, but seeing is believing—and there are actual, real, honest-to-God angels living in it."

"Yes. And now they appear to want to take more of an interest in the worlds. I would hazard a guess that it is because Lucifer will be doing his own dabbling."

"The dislike is strong, yes."

Darius shut the book with a click and pushed it down to his lap.

"Aw…" I crossed the room, took the book, tossed it onto the bed, and then lowered into his lap. He put his arms around me. "You're tearing yourself away from the book to focus on me?"

He gazed up at my face. "I nearly failed you. If it hadn't been for Penny, you would've died on the battlefield. I felt your pain, but you didn't seem troubled by it. I'm sorry."

I rolled my eyes at him before grazing my lips against his. "I didn't realize it was as bad as it was. That didn't hurt as much as the torture."

"Those who torture aim to cause pain, and they can do that without blood loss. This was a different kind of wound."

"Oh, so you have twenty-twenty vision on past events, too? Amazing. I thought I was the only one."

His lips curled upward, and he ran them against my throat. "I feared I would lose you. I couldn't get up to you."

"I asked my dad to bring you up so I could say goodbye."

His arms constricted me, crushing me to his chest. He held me that way for a long moment, his chin resting on my head. Turbulent emotions rolled through the bond, but he didn't comment further.

I changed the subject. What happened was in the past. Might as well move on.

"How did the battle end?" I asked. "I saw the field but went lights out before the end."

"One moment we were in the battle, having just decided to force our way off the field, and the next we were coming out of a daze with angels flying above us. They have immense power...which Penny quickly circumvented when she panicked."

I felt a grin work up my face. "What'd she do?"

"She harnessed their magic and forced the nearest three from the sky. Just ceased their wings from beating. Then she blasted spells every which way, opened an avenue for escape, and tried to drag Emery out. It took Michael to subdue her by landing in her path and speaking reason. Though he got a blast of demonic fire for his efforts, followed by some sort of slicing spell that ruined his outfit with blood."

I was laughing so hard that Darius loosened his hold on me a bit. "Do not surprise Penny. Now everyone in the worlds knows it."

"The elves and their people were protected and moved away," Darius went on. "The angels struck down those they felt wanting."

"On the spot?"

"Yes. Half of them fell, right then and there. New leadership was chosen."

"Seriously? Literally right then and there?"

"Yes, though I have a feeling it took longer than the blink it felt like, as with what happened with you."

"Ah, got it. Yeah, probably. They take forever to get things done. Or, at least, they do when they're enjoying a good bicker with my father."

"And I'm sure they did. He had a hand in the end of the battle. He pulled all his people back, although the unicorns stayed with our group. It seems Lucifer—"

"I know. I saw all that from the sky."

He nodded. "New terms were drawn up. It seems…your desires were the blueprint used."

I crinkled my nose. "What does that mean? Half-naked cabana boys for everyone?"

His eyes narrowed. Apparently he didn't find that hilarious.

"Magical people will be free to come and go throughout the Realm, the Underworld, and the Brink," he said. "Lucifer had already opened up the Underworld, and it will be left that way. The Realm will allow demons within their borders, providing they follow the rules."

"Each world will have a set of rules?"

"Yes. Lucifer's code is well established, but the Realm, under new leadership that includes an ambassador from every race, will go into talks to nail theirs down. The fae, as in days of old, will uphold the new rules."

"Law and order," I said. He nodded. "Every race will have an ambassador?"

He nodded again, and his eyes sparkled with pride. "The angels agreed that it was a justified desire. Not just in the Realm, though."

"In the Brink as well?"

"Just so. There is a large magical community in the Brink, and it should be better organized. New rules will be established, and the shifters will do more to uphold them, relying on the Magical Law Enforcement offices when the magical community needs direct communication with human law enforcement."

"Similar to what it is now."

"Yes, though they are no longer under the elves' employ. They are an independent faction that will be paid by all three worlds. They'll have a separate Brink governing body, the leadership of which has not yet been defined."

I formed a duck bill with my lips. That made sense, and it wouldn't require the system to change too much—just who was funding it.

"Lucifer will not be immune to ambassadors," he said.

"He already communicates with the different sect leaders."

"If vampires will be living there, or trolls, they will need to have a voice."

My eyes widened. "And he went for that?"

"No, not as such. He will relent when the angels open their world and allow ambassadors as well. I wouldn't hold your breath for that to happen. But he did mention that he'll need someone to manage other races that choose to live in his kingdom—so he can hear their pleas and ensure they are following the rules."

"He has a bunch of demons to choose from."

"I think it is a half demon he had in mind. One with the power and bravery to assert her will. One with connections across all the worlds."

I could feel the color leave my face. *No thanks* was on the tip of my tongue, but I couldn't bring myself to say it.

Darius didn't push. He probably felt my rush of excitement through the bond.

"I'd like to go see him," I said.

"And you will. Just now, he is probably getting everyone settled from the battle, but once that is done…"

"What about Archion and the other dragons? How is Penny and everyone?"

"The dragons went down to the Underworld with their peers for now. They are allowed to travel freely between the magical worlds, though, so you can reconnect with Archion wherever you choose. Even in Roger's shifter commune, if you'd like, since it is a closed section of land with no worry of human eyes."

"I'll meet him in the Underworld and see what he wants to do."

Darius nodded. "Both dual-mage pairs are downstairs. They're eager to see you. Roger, Romulus, and Charity probably have their hands full right now, what with the changes to the Realm. They didn't lose nearly as many as they could have. The unicorns kept good watch over them. Maybe too good. Roger wasn't incredibly excited that he was kept away from the heart of the battle."

"Sucks to be ground-bound, I guess."

"Indeed. The Red Prophet has gone missing. Karen has signed on with Roger as a consultant."

"And the vampires?"

"Vlad is in the Underworld just now, scouting areas that we will entrench. The vampires' main lair will be moving, and each of the elders will recommend their choice of location. They are eager to hear what I have to say, but I'd like to speak with Lucifer first, if you would arrange it."

My stomach flipped, and a dopey grin lit up my face. "You're moving to the Underworld?"

"I will maintain my homes in the Brink, of course, and my network of spies in the Realm. I can live any-where and be content, Reagan. Anywhere you decide to stay, I will be there. It's time for me to realize my promise. It's time for us to put down roots and see what grows."

My stomach flipped again, and I kissed him deeply. "That isn't a very grand proposal…"

"How dare you assume that was a proposal." He scoffed. "If it were, I would be no better than the fool within those pages." He gestured at the book on the bed.

I laughed and stood, retrieving the book for him. "Here you go. See you downstairs when you finish. I'll go say hi to the mages." I dressed but paused in leaving. "Oh, and did you speak to Vlad about…his role in your past?"

He hesitated, looking at the outstretched book. With an annoyed sigh, he grabbed it and leafed open the pages. "No. I didn't want to leave you."

I nodded and left him to his book. I wouldn't tell him that the author planned to do a bait and switch, and he'd be much happier with the outcome than he thought.

A chorus of voices greeted me as I neared the kitchen. Inside, Penny and Emery sat on one side of the table, their faces closed down in anger. Dizzy sat across from them with a half-full glass of wine. Callie was cooking something at the stove.

"I definitely think he's more powerful, Emery," Penny said, pointing at some distant location. "He *froze* everyone, not to mention time, could rifle through people's heads, fly—"

"Lucifer can fly," Dizzy said.

"Lucifer can't rifle through people's heads," Penny responded.

"Reagan can hover," Dizzy intoned.

"Reagan can't rifle through people's heads either, or

see their memories. Lucifer cannot *freeze* freaking time, Emery, give me a break," Penny said, her face red with anger.

"All I'm saying is that everyone has different powers, and you have no idea how many angels were helping with all that," Emery replied. "It wasn't just Michael doing that—it couldn't have been. Lucifer is a fallen angel, clearly, and Michael's his brother, Penny. His *brother*. They have the same power scale, just different kinds of magic. Lucifer can fight godly—or angelic, I guess—magic. Remember?"

Michael was my uncle? Gross.

Penny scoffed. "You're being obtuse."

"Hey," I said, leaning against the doorframe. "Made it, huh?"

Penny and Emery's faces snapped up. A huge smile glowed on Penny's face, although it quickly crumpled into anger again.

"Are you stupid, Reagan Somerset?" she yelled, her voice so high that all the dogs in the neighborhood were probably barking. "You nearly died!"

"Whiskey or coffee?" Callie asked, turning from the stove.

"I'm surprised Darius didn't insist on making a meal," I said, sliding into a chair next to Emery. I didn't trust Penny not to throat-punch me.

"He was watching over you. Where is he?" Emery

asked.

"Reading." I pointed upstairs. "Coffee, please, Callie."

"Well…you brought about change." Penny sighed and sagged back into her chair. "You did it in the stupidest way possible, but you brought about change."

"The angels were clearly the big secret the Red Prophet was keeping," Callie said, handing over a mug. "And I have to say, it's good she didn't say anything, or it might have gone down very differently. Which would've gone all sorts of terrible."

"Because Reagan almost dying wasn't all sorts of terrible?" Emery asked with a crooked grin.

"You know what I mean."

"The Red Prophet has been involved in two decisions that nearly got us killed," I said, and sipped my brew. "I'm a nope on any more of her shenanigans. In fact, no more *Seers,* period. No offense, Penny, but I've had my fill."

"I get it." Penny held up her hands. "I'd like to take a break on battles for a while, too."

"Let's take that vacation," Emery said, reaching a hand over the table. She took it, and her expression softened. "We'll take a long honeymoon."

"Oh!" Dizzy beamed. "Did you two set a date? How exciting! I love weddings."

Emery's thumb slid over the top of Penny's hand.

"As soon as possible."

"Whatever happened to Ja?" I asked. "I forgot to ask Darius. She wasn't with his contingent of vampires. Was she with Vlad?"

"Nope." Callie turned back and put a fisted hand to her plain gray sweatpants. I wondered whether I should be worried. "From what I overheard Darius—"

"You shouldn't eavesdrop, hon," Dizzy said.

"Well, how else do you think we'll get information? He certainly doesn't ever come clean and just tell us," she replied. "Anyway, it seems she was found skulking through the Underworld by Lucifer himself. She was given a choice to help him or die. She chose to help him, obviously, which was why she called up those demons at the compound. The thing with Reagan's ex and Darius's past was just a little detour. The vampires can't find a trace of her, so Darius isn't sure where she went."

"He'll need to stay allied with Vlad," Emery said, "or they run the risk of her gaining too much power in their faction. She is…dangerous."

"Yeah, keep the hits coming, Emery." Penny pulled her hand back from his grip. "I didn't mean to wake her up or whatever, okay? That wasn't my fault. That was Darius's fault."

"Don't mind her," Dizzy told me. "She's awfully wound up."

"My ex," I said softly, having forgotten about that

issue. "What do I do about that?"

"Nothing." Callie moved a pan off the stove and turned the burner off. "That's a vampire issue. We can all give Darius credit for not killing him before now, but obviously that line has been crossed, and now you just need to look the other way while he sorts it out, Reagan. I mean, hello? That idiot vampire challenged an elder. How has he even made it this long? Reagan, honey, you ended up picking a good guy—for a vampire—but your choices in the past were less than exemplary."

"I wasn't in it for the conversations at the time," I said.

Dizzy patted my hand. "You can't have that sort of thing following you around like a fart. Callie is right: you'll just need to look the other way. It's just a vampire, after all, and quite a dumb one at that. No big loss."

I should've known what their stance would be on the issue. After all, they'd offered to kill Darius in the beginning.

"Well then." I wiped my hand over my face. I was still tired, but not just from surviving the battle. Ever since my mother had died, I'd been living from one day to the next, surviving. Sometimes I'd have to hide, and sometimes run headfirst into battle. My situation had gone from counting on one person to several, one home to possibly many, one world to a few. I had some big decisions to make.

A path to choose. A life to begin. A future to chase.

But all of that could wait until tomorrow. Right now, I would sit with my closest friends and give thanks that I had them in my life.

"What's for breakfast—or dinner? I'm famished."

CHAPTER 23

CAHAL SAT ON a stone bench in the park near the French Quarter in New Orleans. Shadows encircled him, shrouding him from view as a couple ambled by. Deep night waited around them, not masking the sounds from the cars and city in full swing.

Michael had requested a meeting. It was a week after the battle, and still the angel hung around.

The flutter of wings above brought back memories. A stone floor. Constant pain. Darkness all around. A groggy mind spent from torture.

Cahal had no idea how the angels had found him, locked down in the bowels of the Underworld and tortured by the one-time heir. He'd expected to die. Had been praying for it, actually. He hadn't seen another end to the situation, given he would not be broken.

Lucifer had blamed him for his son's ruin. Had thought he'd tried to kill Julius.

Cahal could see why, even at the time. The heir had been mentally weak, corrupted by power. Cahal had tried to talk him around, to stabilize him, but his efforts had only seemed to hasten the heir's downfall. Logic could not be spoken to a mind already bent and twisted. Julius had attacked him, and Cahal had lashed out to defend himself. He was stronger and faster. If it weren't for the other demons that had gotten in the way, he might've killed the heir in self-defense. As it was, he'd been thrown into the dungeon.

His attacker had become his torturer.

Lucifer, at his core, was a good father. He'd treated his various female companions well over his many long years of existence. There was decency in him; Cahal would never say otherwise.

There was also ruthless violence, of course. Rage, spurred on by pain.

He'd blamed Cahal, maybe to ease the blow of his son sliding into ruin, and Cahal had accepted it. He'd tried to ease the man's pain. At the time, he still hoped he'd one day have children of his own. He had decided he'd want someone to make it easier if he should ever feel the torment of witnessing his child's gradual demise.

And maybe it was that understanding, that sense of forgiveness, that had touched the heavens. That had brought the angels.

There had been two. Women, both, and as lovely as anything he'd ever looked upon. Pure wholesomeness and light—or that was what he'd thought at the time. His mind had been fevered and in turmoil, his death rattle not far away.

Their touch was like a whisper in a breeze, soft and nurturing. The healing light had flowed through him, filling up all his empty places and mending the broken ends. His body had felt like new.

His mind had turned foggy then. He didn't totally recall how long it had taken for him to be released. He knew Lucifer had done it, though. Disgusted. Frustrated. He'd sent Cahal away and desired never to see him again.

Joke was on him, it seemed. But this time, things had worked out as they should have. Cahal had done his part to keep Reagan whole. Her influence, in turn, had made the Underworld stronger and would continue to do so. He was eternally grateful for that—and for the thanks she had given. It had mended a sore spot he'd carried all these long years, no longer certain he'd done the right thing back in the day. Wondering if maybe Lucifer was right, and he was somehow to blame for the former heir's failures. Now, he could finally rest easy.

Michael dropped down in front of Cahal, no regard for whether he might be seen. Roger wouldn't be very impressed by that.

Power thrummed from the angel, and a soft glow enveloped his body.

"Cahal Druer, the druid," Michael said.

"Your grace." Cahal stood and bowed.

Michael motioned for Cahal to sit back down before joining him.

"I must apologize," Michael said after a short silence. "Those who gifted you with our magic did not realize they would make it impossible for you to find your one true mate. We ought to have checked in with you. We have left you to a trying fate, one you have borne with decorum."

"It's nothing, your grace."

"You are so quick to forgive, even now. It does you credit."

Cahal felt a rush within him. His senses momentarily dulled as the angelic magic was stripped away. Before he could miss it, a stronger rush of power filled him up, surging warmth to his limbs. The touch of godly magic he had possessed had been strengthened. His heart sank. It seemed he was destined to wander the earth alone forever.

"Do not despair," Michael said softly. "I have altered the gift. You should be able to meet your true mate now, assuming she walks the worlds at this moment. I cannot see the timing, but you have the ability to form an eternal bond with her, should you meet her."

A wave of relief made Cahal sigh. "Thank you, your grace. It is too much that you should take such an interest."

"Nonsense. It was our error. You have suffered. Tell me, is there anything else I can do for you? Name it."

Cahal considered it for a moment, but the angel had already informed him that he could not help him find a mate. Instead, he figured he could request the angel's assistance for someone else. He'd pay it forward in the hope the universe would one day find him worthy as well.

CHAPTER 24

P ENNY HAD MADE good on her promise to run to the altar with Emery the moment the battle ended. Well, not that exact moment—Darius had insisted we make more of an occasion of it—but it was no more than two months later that I waited beside Darius at the front of a massive, unreal, gorgeous church in Rome. Columns rose along the main floor, decorated with paintings and accented with stone statues and embellishments. The ceiling arched high overhead, the skylights glowing with light that shed on the floor far below—provided by my magic, of course. Rustic wooden pews filled the aisle in front of us, lined with fragrant baby-blue flowers and festooned with white satin ribbon.

It had been two months since the battle to reorganize the worlds—which was what people had taken to calling it. Not too much had happened, other than a lot of to-do lists. I still hadn't headed down to the Underworld. Although I knew I'd have to stop dragging my feet eventually, it was a big step, and it felt like I should let Penny take her big step with Emery before I took one of my own.

Courage in the face of monster life changes—it was a fleeting thing.

"We should probably take our places," Darius murmured to me, his fingers entwined with mine. He squeezed them and stepped away, closer to Emery, who waited nervously by the altar in a white tux with a blue bow tie and vest to match the flowers. His pants slightly squeezed his powerful legs and stopped a smidge short of his shiny black shoes.

He and Penny hadn't had a lot of time to get everything perfect. Ms. Bristol had very deep suspicions it was because there was a baby on the way.

She would be wrong, of course, but no one wanted to correct her.

The real reason was because Penny felt bad for Emery, who had no family to invite. No friends he didn't share with her. No aunts or uncles or cousins he'd kept in touch with. If the wedding had been organized in the usual way, with plenty of time and extensive preparations, his side of the church would be filled with strangers or no one at all, and that was something Penny would not allow.

Not to mention she still had so much on her plate with the Mages' Guild that she didn't care about having a big wedding. Or much of any wedding, really. She just wanted the man. And the break the honeymoon would provide.

So Darius had arranged for their ceremony to take place here, in one of the finest churches Rome had to offer. He'd chosen the flowers and the satin, Emery's tux, and all the transportation. The dinner afterward would be held at his private estate in the countryside, featuring a menu he'd chosen and a wine selection that included all of Penny's favorites. Penny might not like planning elegant affairs, and Emery was mostly terrible at even the concept, but Darius had been happy to pick up the slack.

I took my place beside Veronica, the other brides-maid. Like me, she was dressed in a blue dress to match all the other blue, something Darius assured us was both proper and elegant, holding a bouquet of cream, blue, and yellow flowers. She looked excited as she glanced down the large aisle, waiting for the bride.

Darius was Emery's best man. Even so, I didn't think Emery totally trusted him, a deep-seated issue that would likely never fully pass. Luckily, relationships were complex, and it was possible to both like and respect a person and think they were capable of stab-bing you in the back if the situation required it.

Roger sat in the first pew on Emery's side, and Ms. Bristol sat in the opposite pew in the pride of placement owed to the mother of the bride, a large, flowered hat thing adorning her freshly styled hair. Marie sat beside her, the picture of elegance in a demure light yellow gown, the cut beautiful and the color all kinds of hideous. Behind them sat Callie and Dizzy, though judging by their frequent glances at Roger, the only one on Emery's side, I wondered if they'd pull a runner and change sides. It was clear they didn't want Emery to feel bad.

He wouldn't have noticed. A bomb could go off and he wouldn't have noticed, because at that point, the string quartet changed their tune to the wedding march. The door at the end of the aisle slowly opened. Nothing happened for a beat, and then Penny stepped forward with her hand on Cahal's arm.

With Darius's help and excellent tailors, Cahal had cleaned up incredibly well. He wore a sharp black suit that fit his robust body, power and strength refined into dangerous grace. A cream tie was expertly tucked into his closed suit jacket. His hair had grown out a little from the close cut and was styled in an artfully messy do.

Penny practically pranced down the aisle beside him, her gaze focused on Emery. Happiness glowed in her eyes, and white satin flowed around her legs. She held a cream bouquet, and in her hair glittered a tiara, made from real diamonds because Darius was more than a little ridiculous.

Everyone stood as she came closer, the sound of wings reverberating above us. A feather floated down, twirling through the air. A moment later, in time with Penny walking down the aisle, Michael lowered from the ceiling from some portal or other that I didn't really understand. He wore a cream-colored gown cut through with blue and yellow, his person glowing with ethereal magic. If anyone had happened to walk by, they would've had a genuine religious experience, especially since this church had been fashioned in honor of Michael himself back in the day.

Cahal had asked for a favor, and since Michael was a bit of a turd (and also because Penny blasted him with magic at the end of the battle), he'd insisted on meeting Penny in person before he would consent to marry her and Emery. The angels now had another couple of favorites. Michael had immediately seen the goodness in Penny, and I guess he wasn't totally awful, because he felt for the turbulence poor Emery had endured before finding her.

I was still only mildly tolerated. My father had not been allowed to come to the wedding—not that he'd been invited.

"Oh my stars," Ms. Bristol uttered, her hand on her chest, looking up at the descending angel.

"Holy shi—Is that—What is that?" Veronica exclaimed.

They had been told of the existence of angels but…well, it really was a "see it to believe it" situation. Clearly.

Michael touched down as Penny met Emery, no veil blocking her face, something she'd insisted on, and Darius had grumpily let go. Emery reached out, and Penny gave him her hand, tears in her eyes and utter love and devotion in his.

"We are gathered here today…" Michael began, but I doubted Penny or Emery heard any of it. They continued to stare into each other's eyes, soul mates if ever there were any. They'd met by chance, a couple of times over, and their bond had grown until it had become the solid, enduring connection I witnessed now—endearing in a way that didn't annoy me.

I slowly blew out a breath and blinked my glassy eyes, sliding my gaze over to Darius. He was looking back at me, and love glowed through our bond.

I smiled a little, wishing I could be beside him, our hands linked. I thought back to when I'd stood in my rooms in the Underworld, looking out at the beautiful view spread beneath me. I'd wanted him to share that with me. I hoped I could still make that happen. At least there wouldn't be an arrogant, badly dressed angel there, I'd say that much.

"You may kiss the bride," Michael finished.

Emery stepped forward in a rush, connecting his lips with Penny's. She clutched him, her rock in any storm. Actually, yes, it *was* a little annoying how cute they were.

"My baby is all grown up," Ms. Bristol said, dabbing her eyes with a white handkerchief.

With a smile that could blot out stars, Penny took Emery's hand and turned to Michael. "Thank you for making this so special."

Suck-up.

He bowed. "May you both find peace. Guard our gift to you, and guard it well. It will serve you in dark times."

After hearing the story of how Penny had come by her angel magic, Michael had taken it away—and then given it again of his own free will. I was pretty sure he'd only done that so I could stop making fun of Penny for offing the Redcap. Killjoy.

Penny beamed at me before Emery walked her down the aisle, off to start their new life together. Or so the storybooks said. Really, they were just giving Ms. Bristol different things to gripe about. But whatever—at least they could say they'd been married by an arrogant angel. That had to count for something.

Veronica and the others followed, but I hung back with Darius. Roger slowed to keep pace with us.

"What's next for you, Roger?" I asked, finally taking Darius's hand.

"Same ole," he said, snazzy in his formfitting suit. The guy had glossed up like a new penny. He could be incredibly hot when he wanted to be, which was apparently not often. Not in the "I'm a millionaire" sort of way, at least. "We're still hammering out the particulars of the changes in the Brink." He cut his gaze to Darius. "There will be a lot fewer restrictions on what vampires are allowed to do, so long as you have willing partners."

Darius bowed his head. "I thank you for that. It takes a good leader to push back on popular opinion and judge the situation with a logical, unbiased mind."

"And I just barely managed." Roger chuckled, pausing near the door of the church. His dual-colored gaze hit mine. "Michael has all but promised to..." His lips tightened, and I knew he was struggling to figure out the best way to phrase it.

I helped him out: "Dabble in the lives of humans? Barge in and mess with all your crap? Swing his dick around and act like the greatest thing since sliced bread?"

He blinked a few times. "Help, is what I was going to say."

I grinned. "Sure. Help, yeah."

He centered his weight. Uh-oh, he planned to ask for something. He always got very aggressive when he was cornered into doing that.

"I wondered," he started, like pulling teeth. I could feel the mirth swirling through the bond with Darius as he watched this unfold. "You have pull with Lucifer, and Lucifer seems to be...comfortable pushing back with the angels."

"We've ascertained that they are brothers, after all, are they not?" Darius asked.

Roger ignored him. "I don't want any one world to have too much power in the Brink. We've been given the opportunity to create our own organization, and I'd like to keep the power in the hands of elected officials. Given the elves and the other representatives in the Realm are busy rebuilding their own lands, that leaves the Brink wide open for the angels to..."

"Help, I think you said," Darius supplied.

Roger cocked his head and somehow continued to ignore him. Kinda. "I wondered if you might take an interest in the Brink on behalf of the Underworld. You know it better than most, both the underbelly and the normal workings. You also have the power and the...wherewithal to push back on the angels where you see fit."

I would've gone with stubbornness, but wherewithal works, Darius thought.

It was my turn to ignore Darius.

"I haven't decided if I'm taking the—*a* role within the Underworld," I said carefully. "I need to head down and talk to my father. I just haven't had the time, what with Penny's wedding and everything..."

I blamed everything on Penny. What was one more thing?

"Well." Roger nodded to me. "We could use you. Most of the fae have been called to duty in the Realm. A small subset will remain with Charity and Devon's pack because of their schooling. We'll join forces if need be, but it'll largely be the job of the shifters to patrol the Brink again. Until the Realm is more stable, at any rate."

"You'll have much less to do," Darius said. "I'll be speaking with Vlad shortly. We'll keep our factions in line. We'll police our own, so to speak."

Shivers coated me. Whereas I had been dragging my feet about my father, Darius had been much more proactive with Vlad. He didn't say much, but I had a feeling he was worried about the outcome of their meeting. He had a sentimental attachment to Vlad, even if that attachment might not be shared. I didn't think he wanted to keep brawling with the other vampire. We'd find out soon, though. That was next on our to-do list. Followed by my biting the bullet and figuring out my future.

"That would be a help," Roger said, taking a step back. "We'll be in touch." His gaze slid to me before he left. "Don't be a stranger, whatever happens with the Underworld, okay? I've gotten used to you. I'd hate to have to work on a new normal."

"Aww." I winked at him. "You've grown to actually like me, haven't you? You can't live without me."

"Actually, I was just hoping you'd bring Penny

around. She's much nicer than you."

"Yes, she is, but you totally like me." I grinned as he headed for the doors. "We're going to be *beast*ies—get it? It's best friends between animals and their people familiars. I just made it up. I'll get matching necklaces. Want to do mood rings?" I called after him.

The door shut, leaving one presence behind us.

Darius kissed my temple. *I'll be outside. Don't make an enemy.*

I turned slowly as Darius left me alone with Michael.

The angel had a little smile on his handsome face. His robes hung straight, and I was glad they didn't magically ripple like an elf's would've. At least he had that going for him.

"So…" I said, suddenly not sure what to do with my hands. "Thanks for saving my life."

"Your journey has been an intriguing one, Reagan Somerset. It is not your bloodline that sets you apart from Lucifer's other heirs. That simply allows you to exist within Lucifer's corrosive magic without your soul bleeding out of you."

"Graphic."

"What sets you apart is within you." He touched his sternum. "Despite our grievances, I will admit that Lucifer has created a strong, balanced world. That is easier when it is closed off, however. Now creatures will be able to come and go once again. He will meet with other leaders and nobles. He will need help to keep the balance. I think you would be a welcome relief to him. You've brought about change. You should partake in the effects of it."

It was a very long-winded way of telling me to go work for the family business.

"Thanks again," I said, to cut it short. Honestly, what did this guy know? His world was still closed off, last I heard. They might come down to meddle, but it wasn't a two-way street. Not yet, anyway.

I wondered what my father would have to say about that.

"You are welcome." Michael bowed, and so I did the same. "We are family, in a way. Don't believe all the things your father tells you. If you have any questions, I'd be happy to answer."

I nodded because I didn't want to thank him again. I sounded like a broken record.

"Until next time." His wings snapped out, and he lifted into the sky.

What a crazy life I was living. Angels were real and I was the princess of the Underworld. What in the holy fuck??

Clearing my mind, I straightened my back and headed for the door. Freaking out could go on my to-do list.

EPILOGUE

T HE SHADOWS LENGTHENED across the cracked pavement and crawled up the walls of the cemetery. Smokey waited in his usual spot, watching the goings-on in the street. His gaze swung right, and he tensed. Confused, he looked at me.

The door opened in the house next door. Mikey stepped out and closed it behind him, his shirt freshly pressed, his jeans new, and a great-smelling aftershave wafting toward me. He glanced my way and scowled so hard I nearly warned him that his face would get stuck like that. Though I didn't want to give him ideas.

"When are you moving?" I asked as Smokey went back to watching something down the street.

"Fuck you," Mikey spat, leaning against his freshly replaced railing. A gold watch glittered on his wrist—a Rolex.

"Millionaires do not live in this neighborhood, Mikey. You're in the wrong place."

"You're a millionaire and you're still here," he said.

"No, my boyfriend is a millionaire. He doesn't live

here."

He pointed at me with perfectly clipped and buffed nails. "I'm still not talking to you. You're dead to me."

"Why are you blaming me? The Red Prophet told you to invest in those stocks, not me."

"I bet she told you I'd have the cops swarming all over me, didn't she?" He crossed his arms over his chest. "I bet she told you that I'd spend a month worried I'd go to prison for a white-collar crime. Do you know what they do to guys like me who get pinched for white-collar shit?"

"Nothing, because you'd beat them senseless if they tried."

He huffed and looked over at Smokey, who had taken the whole thing much better. He'd endured the investigation into insider trading with few words and a habitually pale face. But they'd made it, just as the Red Prophet had said they would, and now they were filthy rich. The guys who were actually guilty of insider trading were currently awaiting trial.

"Where'd she go, anyway?" Mikey asked. "She brought the heat on me and then disappeared, is that it?"

I shrugged, watching the quiet street. It had been three months now since the battle, but no one had heard from her. Romulus was still looking, as a matter of fact. He didn't like that she'd been missing for so long. Karen refused to use her *Sight* to track her down.

"It was hell, but…I guess I should at least say thanks, know what I'm saying?" He scratched his head. "I don't like talking about it, because it's nobody's business, but I heard Smokey tell you, so I'll just say it…" He rolled his shoulders. "I'm set for life. I don't never have to work again. If I have kids, they probably won't have to work, neither. Though they will, because they need to learn that life ain't easy. But still…" He turned his face away and then put his hands on his hips. "I should at least say thanks, you know?"

"If I ever see her, I'll tell her to stop by. If you're gone by then, I'll tell her for you, how's that?"

He nodded and leaned against the railing. "What's your plan?"

"I don't know." The words rode a sigh. "Probably go meet my dad tomorrow."

He pointed downward and lifted his eyebrows.

"Yeah," I said.

He nodded. "I liked that guy better than the fanged fuckers. He seemed more like one of us. More down to earth, you know?"

A slight figure sauntered into view, all hips and breasts, even with her dainty frame. I squinted at the sky, the last of the sun's rays finally disappearing. That was why Smokey was confused, most likely. A vampire, walking in the failing sun.

"Did you turn back into a human or something?" I asked Ja as she stopped in front of my house.

"At my age, the dying sun is merely an aggravation."

She was aiming for dramatics, then.

She was wasting her efforts on me.

"Fuck that." Mikey jogged down his stairs and started away. "See ya around, Reagan," he called.

I crossed a heavy boot over my leather-clad knee as Ja approached, not bothering to get up. "To what do I owe the annoyance?"

"You won, as I knew you would."

"I thought you were supposed to be on my side when that happened?"

"I was on your side. Delayed in the Underworld, but on your side."

"Hmm." I chuckled. "You tried to mess with Darius, then me, and you helped my father...but you were somehow on my side?"

She fixed her long blond hair, a change since I'd seen her last. "You know enough about vampire politics not to equate...my information gathering with sides. I helped your father contact you, that is all. I would've done more to protect you had I not been the subject of...scrutiny in the Underworld."

That had another meaning, but I didn't much care what it meant. "Fine. What do you want?"

"You will need strong allies when you take your

place within the Dark Kingdom. I am here to remind you that none are stronger than me." She held out her hands. "I have a long history in the Underworld. I would be an incredible asset."

"Maybe. And if my father gives me a job, my first order of business will be to make Darius an ambassador so that he can deal with you."

"Remember who helped you," she said softly.

I laughed. "Remember who helped *you*."

She opened her mouth to reply, but instead I tossed my hand. Air gathered and fire coalesced. In a moment, she went tumbling down the street in a ball of flame. It wouldn't kill her, but it would certainly ruin her day.

"How's that for dramatic?" I murmured as Smokey grinned and gave me a thumbs-up from across the street. Too bad he wasn't magical, or he could visit me in the Underworld.

I squinted at him and half wondered if he'd want to become a vampire. Or a shifter. Either could be arranged...

A lime-green Lamborghini revved as it rolled down the street, cutting into my thoughts. The timing of Ja's visit wasn't lost on me. Darius pulled up to the curb in front of my house and got out, his hair styled just so, his suit like a coat of paint, and his whole person incredibly mouth-watering. I smiled like a dummy as he fixed his cuff link and then closed the car door. He nodded a hello to Smokey before coming around the car.

"Hello, *mon ange*," he greeted me, walking up the steps. "How is your evening so far?"

"I got a visit from Ja a few moments ago. I sent her up the street in a ball of fire."

He glanced in the right direction before taking the seat next to me. "Dare I ask what she wanted?"

"A strong connection in the Underworld." I shared the gist of the conversation with him.

"She is disheveled, it would seem. Some things haven't gone her way. She's trying to gauge what options are available to her. This meeting with Vlad couldn't come at a better time."

A wave of butterflies overtook my stomach. "I won't let him hurt you, you know that."

"I am hoping it won't come to that. He has made no actions against me. He has kept his distance, like he did before all of this started."

"But, like…if it does come to that, I will not stand aside while you two brawl. He won't be allowed to hurt you."

Darius reached for my hand. "I understand."

A crummy older Honda puttered up the street. It pulled in front of Darius's car. The sound of an old handbrake being applied preceded Vlad exiting the car. He nodded to Smokey before coming around the hood to the sidewalk.

"You don't match," I called, still holding Darius's hand. "That incredibly expensive suit does *not* match that car."

Vlad didn't glance at his wheels, but instead stopped at the bottom of my porch steps. "May I come up?"

"Sure, yeah." I motioned him on.

"I like to blend into neighborhoods like this," he said, stopping near the banister. "It annoys me when I walk out to discover my car has been boosted."

"No one would steal your car in this neighborhood," I replied.

Vlad looked at me before turning to the rest of the street. "No, likely not."

I stood and opened the front door. I'd taken the ward down for this meeting.

Darius waited as I entered, gesturing Vlad in after me.

"Please," Vlad said, repeating the gesture. "I insist."

I took a seat at the kitchen table. Darius had mentioned beforehand that we'd keep this meeting casual. Vlad took the chair opposite me, and Darius set about collecting drinks.

"Congratulations," Vlad said to me, his perfect smile matching his perfect face. Though, unlike Michael, Vlad at least had a whole lot of menace just below the surface. "You achieved your goal. Your method was unorthodox, but the end result is all that matters."

"Yeah. Maybe I'll nearly die the next time I need something, too." I leaned back. "Sucks you didn't think of it."

"Indeed," Vlad said.

Darius delivered a cognac for himself and Vlad and then set a whiskey in front of me. He took his chair and then my hand.

"Ja visited us in the shifter compound. I'm sure you've heard," Darius started.

"A few times, it seems." Vlad took a sip of his beverage. "She is going to be a problem."

"Agreed. She filled me in on the part you played, regarding how I was made."

"Yes, I heard. I did not bring my pistols, sadly. How do you plan to settle this?"

Darius's eyes glittered. Vlad was clearly making a joke, but the sentiment didn't reach his cold, calculating eyes.

"Why did you never tell me?"

Vlad sat back, studying Darius. "You are a changed vampire since Reagan. Dare I say a changed man? You would not have treated the matter with such indifference back in the day. For a long time, that woman was a sticking point for you. You were not rational about it."

Darius slowly took a sip. "It is true, then? You orchestrated everything?"

"No, as a matter of fact. I did not plant her. My

driver would have run her over had I not stopped him. No offense, old friend, but she was a nobody."

Darius didn't comment.

"That was the first time you came to my notice," Vlad said. "Quite gallant. Large for the time, strong frame, ease of movement... I looked into you then. You know what I saw."

Darius inclined his head. Vlad would've seen his fortune, basically. His land. All of his assets. He also would've figured out that a man so adept in keeping his fortune had a keen business sense and intelligent mind.

"I did coax her toward you and seed her foolish notions about vampires, of course," Vlad said.

"Were you fucking her?" Darius asked, and a flash of cold washed through me. I wasn't even sure what had caused that emotion. I guess I just hadn't expected Darius to ask. Maybe I hadn't expected him to care?

Maybe I'd hoped he wouldn't...

As if hearing my thoughts, he stroked his thumb across my skin.

I merely want everything out in the open, he thought.

"No, I was not," Vlad said. "In those days, I would've tied blood with sex. I couldn't take her blood, for obvious reasons." Namely, it would have given her a different "vampire" to fear. "I doubt I could've seduced her, anyway. She was quite religious. Fanatically so."

"Of course," Darius said, his thumb still stroking

my skin. "Reagan was amazed you went through the effort."

Vlad slid his gaze to me. "Yes. Times have changed."

"That's what I told her. Have you experienced what the Underworld has to offer?"

"Will we race to sire a brood?" Vlad asked with the briefest of smiles.

Cold ran through me for a different reason, and then sparklers flared in my stomach. This time, Darius's grip on my hand tightened.

"No," Darius replied. "We are in no hurry. Reagan needs to decide what she'd like to do in the present before we look to the future."

"But it's in your plans?" Vlad asked.

Darius looked at me, his beautiful eyes soft and bright. "Yes, someday. If Reagan wishes it."

I did wish it, but…not yet. Darius had his finger on the pulse of the situation. I needed to settle down and live my own life for a while. Only when that was going steadily could I think of creating another. I was thankful he understood.

That didn't mean we needed to wait forever for…well, forever. Emery had wasted no time proposing, and he and Penny had wasted no time in tying the knot. I'd honestly expected Darius to ask when we were in Rome. It had been plenty romantic.

"Speaking of the present," Vlad said, thankfully changing the subject, "I hear Roger is a lot more amenable to vampire activities in the Brink." Just like that, I knew they'd put the issue about Darius's making behind them. It was a small thing, obviously, in the face of much bigger issues, like Ja and the changing of the worlds. I was happy it had proven so anticlimactic.

I did wonder why Darius had wanted to have their meeting here, though. That seemed odd.

"Yes. I'd hoped to get your help there." He turned to me. "Reagan, this will be vampire politics. You are welcome to stay if you want or—"

"Nope." I let go of his hand and pushed my chair back. "I'll make myself scarce."

Darius and Vlad both stood when I did, gentlemen from a different era. Vlad would keep up the manners even if he was plotting to kill me, I knew. Which I definitely doubted, given my new standing.

I tried not to smile. But honestly, it was seriously cool.

"I wondered, actually," Darius said before I could get away, "if you'd do me the honor of putting on one of the dresses upstairs and getting ready for dinner? I have a very important meeting to attend, and I'd hoped for your company."

I paused at the edge of the kitchen. It wasn't like him not to warn me about that kind of thing. Then again, he might've been worried this evening would go horribly wrong with Vlad. It was always hard to tell with him.

"Yeah, sure," I replied.

Reagan, Vlad thought, and I paused again. They couldn't have said all of this before I left the table? *I know if you'd asked, Lucifer would've delivered me to you. I can only assume that would've been to kill me, which we both know is in your power.*

I nodded, waiting for more.

He gave me a slight bow. *There was a time when you might've leaned on that power, out of spite. Maybe for a joke. There was a time Darius would've demanded it. I am in your debt. Darius will know what to do with that information, if you don't.*

I stared, wide-eyed and mute. I hadn't expected that admission, even if we both knew it was true. Since when were vampires so forthcoming in putting themselves at someone's mercy?

When that someone was connected to Lucifer, maybe. This was probably Vlad's way of sucking up.

I inclined my head instead of bowing, and headed upstairs.

Three dresses awaited me, although I had no idea when they'd been put there or by whom. Then again, I was getting used to that sort of thing.

"Hello—"

I sent a burst of air and slammed Marie to the wall. She grinned mischievously and waited for me to release her.

That explained how the dresses had gotten in here.

"So powerful," she purred, slinking closer. "Darius is a lucky vampire."

"What are you doing here?" I asked, turning back to the dresses.

She gave the answer I was expecting. "I will help you get ready. How are these selections? I have others in the car, if you'd prefer."

She must've snuck in the back while we were talking to Vlad. Darius was being very sneaky. This dinner had to have be important.

I shrugged and crossed the room to my chair. "Don't care."

She selected a frosty-blue number with sparkly strips across the neck that looked like diamonds. It had a plunging neckline and a swooping back. The bottom would hit the floor but not impede my steps. It would make me look graceful and gorgeous, glamorous and elegant.

It would also put my knockers on display. *You're welcome, Darius.*

Marie left the room and returned with a high chair and standing lights. I sat dutifully and let her work her magic on my face and hair. There was no point in resisting. Besides, I'd rather save myself the trouble.

That done, I undressed myself, because she could get handsy, and accepted barely there lingerie. The dress skimmed down my skin like a waterfall and clung to all the right places. She attempted to offer me very pointy shoes, and I pushed for flats instead. She relented because she probably knew my next suggestion would be boots. This wasn't our first rodeo.

Darius waited in the living room, another book in hand. Action adventure this time. He closed it when I walked in, his eyes taking me in.

"Beautiful," he said. He stood gracefully and dropped the book to the coffee table. "I love you."

"I love you too," I said, smiling. Vlad had clearly left.

His lips curved up at the corners as he drifted closer, his suit and poise and movements blending together to create an impression of elegance.

"Shall we?" He held out his arm, and I took it.

"Dare I ask where we're going?"

He opened the door when we reached it, stood aside for me to pass through, and then closed it behind him. Apparently Marie would see herself out.

"You can ask, if you'd like." He held out his arm again, and I noticed his Lamborghini was gone, replaced with a black sedan with a grumpy driver in the front.

"But you won't be filling me in." I waved to Smokey as Darius opened the door. "You are very predictable."

"I enjoy surprising you."

"Do I need to be on my best behavior?" I asked as I got in. He closed the door and crossed to the other side.

"No, not for this."

Moss's hard gaze appeared in the rearview mirror, trained on me, but his brows lowered when I noticed him. Without a word, he looked back down and we were on our way.

I expected to head downtown or to the airport. That was where Darius usually took me for one of these things. This time, though, Moss drove to the highway heading away from town.

"Why bring Moss if we're driving?" I asked. "I mean, don't get me wrong, his surly silence really complements any long and tedious car journey, but usually you take a faster mode of transportation."

"I met you through one of your bounty hunter contracts," Darius said, entwining his fingers with mine. "Do you remember? You nearly stole the mark right out from under me."

I furrowed my brow, digging through my hazy prebond memories. I wondered where he was going with this.

"Yeah, I remember. You needed to send a bunch of your vampires after me to get him back. I lost out on that contract because of you."

"Yes. You intrigued me, which does not happen easily. I've been alive for nearly a thousand years. I've seen all manner of creatures and learned to expect the unexpected. I did not think I could be surprised by a mere human, magical or otherwise. Most shifters are not even fast or strong enough to combat a vampire of my stature. Only Roger would give me pause, and I knew he wouldn't be able to get there in time."

He took a deep breath and glanced out the window.

"And then a beautiful, if somewhat disheveled, woman waltzed in and stole my prize right out from under me. I couldn't believe the audacity."

"I recall that you were quite arrogant back in the day, yes."

"Still am, actually. Just not with you." He smiled and then leaned over to kiss me. "Your speed took me by surprise. Your affinity for violence. The menace you oozed, as if it were a birthright." He shook his head, his smile growing. "Your smell enticed me. Your grace in battle. Your fire. I wanted you that night."

"You had a helluva way of showing it," I said with raised eyebrows. "You seemed incredibly put out by the whole thing."

"Of course I did. An elder vampire does not show reactions to trivial things."

There was that arrogance I remembered.

"I couldn't stop thinking about you after we parted. It hadn't happened in…a great many years. So many I can't think of the last time. I was unsettled, and so I cornered you into a meeting. When Vlad met you, he had a similar reaction."

"And so you cornered me into a new contract."

"Exactly," he said, and I knew for a fact he didn't feel even a little bit remorseful. He looked over at me, warmth seeping into me from our bond. "The surprises continued. How your magic was so incredible and unique. How the unicorns reacted to you. How you handled people, refusing to let them handle you." His gaze dipped to my lips. "How you pushed back when I tried to steer you or manipulate you." His pupils dilated. "How your blood called to me. When I think back on it, I realize the signs were always there. I started to fall for you that very first night. You have been on my mind ever since. I didn't know what it meant at first, but your influence on me was a constant pressure until I had no choice but to give in. I may have tried to trap you in the beginning, Reagan, but you were the one who really trapped me, and I'm glad for it."

He kissed me again, and I fell into it. His tongue claimed my mouth, deep and sensual, but all too soon he pulled back. He wasn't through with his confession.

"When I found out what you were, I was blindsided, to say the least. The first thought that would've gone through most elders' minds was the advantage of such an asset. They would immediately start thinking of ways to use you or leverage you for a better position. But I didn't think of that. Instead, my first thought was about protecting you—guarding you—against those who might seek to use you." He put his other hand over our joined hands. "What truly blindsided me wasn't what you were, but the way I reacted to it. The effect you had on me. In the days that followed, I became aware of the feelings I was developing for you. Feelings that vampires are said to be incapable of. But there they were, against all odds. And they were deep and true."

I blinked back moisture. It was official. He'd turned me into an incredible sap. Moss better not tell Penny, or she'd make fun of me.

"Moss is driving today in remembrance of how we met. He's driving to give homage to the start of our journey together."

"And if we could go back in time and pick literally anyone else…"

There came those dark eyes in the rearview mirror again. I grinned wickedly at Moss and tightened my hold on Darius's hand.

It was then I became aware of where we were. I'd been so engrossed in what Darius was saying that the scenery had passed by without my noticing.

A scowl creased my face as we turned off the main

road. I recognized the little red house on the corner, and the town was just as sleepy as I remembered. A couple of people ambled along the sidewalk, one with groceries and another with coffee.

I turned my head as we passed, watching them. A pit formed in my stomach, and sorrow rose to choke me. At this point, I expected the next turn, and the two that followed. I didn't utter a word as we took the long driveway deeper into the trees and then stopped in front of the tiny house I'd grown up in. That my mother had died in.

"Why are we here?" I asked in a wooden voice.

Moss turned off the car and pushed open the door, getting out. He shut the door after him and moved away from the car.

"I thought you might like to see it again," Darius murmured.

Tears clouded my vision, and I clenched my jaw, looking out through the window at the woods where I'd learned my magic. Half of my magic, anyway. Memories of my childhood flashed through my mind. Of playing hide-and-seek with her in those woods, and of my explosions of anger when I couldn't harness the power I knew was there.

I remembered the stack of bills on the kitchen table, none of which I could afford to pay after she passed. The slip of paper tied to the door, telling me to evacuate. The debt collector turning up with the cops and forcing me out.

"I tried to earn enough money to buy it back, but it had already been sold." I stared at the two-room paradise that held so many happy memories. Its dark windows served as an unneeded reminder of what it had been like at the end, when all I could feel was pain.

Pain that still reverberated through me.

"I never had a chance to buy it back. So I moved on. I have the memories—that's what counts."

"This house hasn't been lived in since you left," Darius said. "An investor bought it from the bank. He planned to tear it down and build a country club of sorts on the land. He envisioned it as a destination spot for city dwellers."

I snorted, leaning into him. "Out here? He's dreaming."

"Yes, he was. He had big ideas about what to do with his family money and ended up squandering most of it. He gave the property back to the bank. It's had no takers since."

"And you bought it so you can play savior."

I didn't mean to sound so bitter. This was just one thing I would have preferred for him to leave alone. He'd bought my house for me, fine. He'd remodeled it, okay. He'd bought out the person behind me so he could add space and started building upward—

whatever. I wasn't attached to that place like I was to this one.

This house had been my world, and I'd let it go. It had been my inheritance, and I hadn't been able to hold on to it. My mother had worked so hard to keep a roof over our heads, and I'd lost everything. To hear that Darius had just handed this to me, like he'd given me everything else… It was a tough pill to swallow.

Not that he could've known that. This wasn't his fault.

"Is there actually a dinner?" I asked, hating the emotion that clogged my throat. The car ride had been so amazing. I looked amazing; he looked amazing. I didn't want this situation—my past—to dampen the present.

"No, there's no dinner. Not just yet." He pushed open his door and got out.

I waited a moment, composing myself, reminding myself again that he meant well. Not many men would care this much about a girl's past. Not many men were sentimental. I was incredibly lucky to have him.

I took a deep breath and wiped my eyes.

"Big-girl pants, Reagan."

With another deep breath, I pushed away the confusing rush of pain and anger and got out of the car. Darius met me there and held out his hand. I took it and allowed him to lead me to the front door, which he unlocked with a wave of his hand.

It felt like the world came crashing down as we stepped inside. The dim interior showcased our heavily used gray couch, the color much darker than it had started. The coffee table was covered in dust, but it still had duct tape wrapped around the joint of one of its legs. I couldn't believe the vase of fake lilies still stood on the end table next to the secondhand armchair. Darius made a beeline for the books in the particle-board bookcase against the wall.

Dust motes swam through the air. The done-in wood floor hadn't gotten any nicer or fancier since I'd left.

"Wait," Darius said in a hush, barely interrupting the silence. He had a knack for reading the mood of a room.

I turned toward him as he stepped back from the bookcase. He gazed at me with intense eyes.

"Six of these books are in your shelves at home."

"Obviously. Everyone needs their own copies of the greats. *Jane Eyre, Pride and Prejudice, Wuthering Heights*—some books need constant re-reads."

"*Shadows?*"

I shrugged in embarrassment. "I was a member of John Saul's fan club back in the day. In my teens I probably read every book he ever put out. I loved fantasy-horror. I found that one at a thrift shop, signed.

You don't throw away signed books by your favorite author."

"Yes, of course." He looked back at the bookshelf. *I will read every one of these books,* he thought, and I knew it wasn't a comment for me. He just wasn't shielding the thought.

I rolled my eyes and couldn't help a soft smile, my heart glowing despite the circumstances. He'd do it because he wanted to learn more about my past in a way he knew I loved. And I'd read along with him to share the moment.

"I hate you," I said, just because it was a nice change from saying, *I love you.*

"Ditto," he replied, coming my way, playing along.

He gave me a poignant look as he took my hand.

Here we go, I thought, and made sure to keep a very tight lockdown on my emotions. He was blameless. He deserved none of my ill mood.

I pushed through the door-less frame into the teeny tiny kitchen, the countertops a relic from the sixties, the cupboards not big enough to hold half the food Darius's people brought to my current house. Everything looked as I'd left it, except for the badly worn circular table.

My mouth dropped open.

A stack of gold bricks covered the four-person table, arranged in the form of a pyramid, reaching up toward the ceiling. I could still see dirt clinging to their edges.

The sliding glass doors leading out to the garden were covered with heavy drapes, and the kitchen window barely let any light past the hanging sheet that we'd meant to replace with actual shades for years. I couldn't tell if it was real gold.

"I'll explain that in a moment," Darius whispered into the hush. He tried to pull me toward the sliding glass door.

"Is that...gold?" I asked, trying to get closer and peer through the gloom.

"Yes. Please, let me explain in a moment."

I let him pull me along, craning my head to stare at the table.

"Who... Did *you* put that there?" I asked softly. "Was that left by the guy that was going to tear this place down?"

"Neither." He waved his hand and then reached into the drapery and pulled open the sliding glass door. Fresh air fluttered the fabric, washing across my face. "Come."

I frowned and followed him out. This was not like him. He might subtly stuff my bank account with funds or leave money out where he knew I'd find and likely steal it, but he did not leave stacks of precious commodities out for me to deal with. He'd think it lazy. If he wanted to give me gold, he'd establish a safety deposit box or something, furnish me with the key, directions to it, and probably a market report on the price of gold.

Actually, come to think of it, nothing about this was his normal way of doing things. I wasn't surprised he'd kept the old furniture—he'd understand my sentimental need for it to be the same—but it wasn't like him to leave it dirty.

Perplexed by his behavior and his choice to leave the drapes closed, I nonetheless stepped through with him. A face full of dust and a musty smell that broke my heart later, we stepped onto the creaky back porch. The boards should've been changed out years ago. Years and years ago. It was a safety hazard at this point, not that it mattered.

A thatch of gnarled bushes rose just beyond the porch, choking the backyard. They looked unchanged, other than their size. This had never been the part of the yard my mother had cared about.

He sauntered with me to the edge of the porch, apparently not worried that one wrong footfall might send him plummeting through the boards. The stairs at the side had crumbled away, leaving gaping holes of jagged wooden teeth hellbent on breaking an ankle.

"Get us down?" Darius asked.

"Why are we here?" I asked again, hovering us to the weed-covered dirt.

He didn't answer as we strolled along the little path

toward the tree line. A million memories pushed to the forefront of my mind, jockeying for position. My mother and I strolling down this very path, similar to what Darius and I were doing. Sometimes bickering about what was going wrong with my magic. Me running and tripping, skinning my knee and crying. Mom hadn't kissed it better and cooed—she'd made me walk into the bathroom and then sit still while she applied stinging antiseptic.

"She never coddled me," I said as we wound along the path. It seemed strange that the overgrown bushes hadn't impinged on the path and crowded our progress. "She never babied me. As far back as I can remember, she was mostly indifferent to my cuts and scrapes. She patched them up like a doctor and marshaled me on."

"She probably knew you'd need to be tough for the life ahead of you."

A lump formed in my throat. Hindsight, as they said. Even while hiding me, she'd been training me for the life that she knew I was bound to walk into. I wondered if she'd known how special my magic would be. Or that I would be adaptable to the Underworld.

Maybe she'd prepared me *just in case*. She'd been a planner—genes that had skipped me.

We turned a corner in the brush, right before the trees, and an explosion of emotion stopped me short.

The unruly brush cleared away, and a scene plucked

from my memories rose before me. The garden was so similar to the one I'd seen in the Underworld, only this one was perfect. The white lattice, a little worse for wear because of the weather, arched high above us, crawling with fragrant, blooming roses. It extended over the pathway, blue sky peeking through the tops even though it wasn't day.

"How…"

Managed but still unruly plants lined the sides of the path and a swarm of flowers blanketed the grounds. Beautiful chaos, enhanced to make the biggest possible impact.

The emotion welled up into small sobs.

Romulus had been here.

I couldn't pinpoint the proof, but wasn't that proof in itself?

The little gaps in my mind had been filled in with the kind of beautiful details only achievable by a master. I remembered all the colors, for example. The scents. But I didn't remember exactly which flowers he'd used. My father had filled in the details, and it had been similar to what I remembered—a mess of color.

This wasn't a mess. Although the flowers were everywhere, they gave the impression of a sort of soft, beautiful design leading the eye along until it ended at the repainted and repaired gazebo beyond. The bushes on the sides were natural, not magical or altered, but healthy enough that their vibrant colors showed through. They had been trimmed, I saw now, but not groomed. Not at all. The branches still stuck out in all directions, shaggy and shabby, but of a height that lent a certain youth to the garden. A freshness. It looked like it would've in my childhood, not like a place that had been abandoned to years of neglect.

I couldn't speak. This wasn't like in the Underworld, where Lucifer's garden had made me steep in memories of my mother and pushed me toward Cahal. This time love thrummed through me, coloring everything I saw and stripping away the pain of her passing.

"This is perfect," I croaked out, clutching Darius. My eyes moved over those beautiful flowers, an explosion of color and fragrance. An environment where plants could proliferate and thrive without rules or restrictions. This was probably what she'd been trying for.

"Romulus nailed it," I said, bowing with emotion. "My mother would've absolutely loved this. She would've lost her mind over it. I wish she could see it."

"Ah. You've ferreted me out. I should also mention that we are trespassing."

"You didn't buy it?"

"No. I didn't know how you'd feel about that."

Tears dripped off my jaw line. "How the fuck do you always manage to be so perfect?"

"I'm a vicious beast that exists because of stealing blood from mortals. I hardly think perfection is one of my attributes."

"I'm not mortal."

"Are we sure about that?"

"Yes. I overheard a conversation between Lucifer and Tatsu and pieced together the gist. I was dying like an immortal."

He flinched. "Please don't mention that again. My guilt is hard to bear."

We wound around to the gazebo.

"You did all this, but didn't buy it? Why the restraint?"

We stepped up into the enclosed space and looked out at the flowers for a moment, the beauty arresting me. He turned me to him, his hazel eyes like liquid gold. He slowly lowered to one knee.

"Reagan Somerset, you are my everything. I cannot contemplate an existence without you in it." He pulled a black velvet box from his pocket and opened it. Two bands twinkled up at me, one inlaid with rubies alternating with diamonds, and the other with sapphires. He was paying homage to the two halves of my magic in a way that would allow me to punch someone in the face without worrying about ruining the settings. "Would you do me the honor of marrying me?"

I smiled and maybe cried a little and possibly tried

to sink to his level. He stood so that I would too.

"Yes," I said, allowing him to take my hand and slip the rings over my finger. They fit perfectly. Of course they did.

"I love you," he said, and kissed me so deeply it dried up all the air in my lungs.

Sometime later, we sat on the gazebo bench and looked out over the flowers. "When I was in the Underworld, I wished you could be there with me to experience the garden Lucifer had made. It was nothing like this. Close as far as the overall layout, but Romulus gave it something that..." I shook my head, tears swimming in my eyes once again.

"I'll explain that gold now. I'm from a different time than you—"

"Understatement."

"During my time, marriages were typically arranged, but when they weren't, it was customary for a man to ask permission from the father of his intended."

I pulled back and studied his face, seeing nothing but love, a sentiment mirrored through our bond. "You asked Lucifer for permission to marry me? The same guy who suggested I sex you away the day before he planned to go kill you?"

A smile tilted his lips. "I asked for his blessing, not his permission. If he had said no, I wouldn't have mentioned it."

I blinked at him for a moment. That was a lot to unpack. "You asked Lucifer, the man that was going to kill you—"

"That seems to be a sticking point with you."

"And he said yes?"

His smile was flawless and my heart was going too quickly.

"He did. He also refused my plans to furnish you with a bank account solely in your name that you can manage yourself. Instead, he thought it fitting that you should have the stones he stole from the path leading to the elf castle. He'd planned to give them to you anyway. He was laughing when he said it. He thought this was a good occasion, whether you said yes or no to me."

"Perfect," I said, laughing. Maybe still crying. Today was starting to be too much.

"Yes. As soon as he said it, I knew that it was the perfect solution." He took my hands. "I want you to be independent of me. If you need to leave at a moment's notice, or if something should happen to me, I want you to have enough assets to help you disappear. I do not want you to rely on me for money. I don't want anyone to be able to corner you into taking a job, or something else you don't want to do. I will help you set up that gold to ensure it is so. In addition, once we are married, I'll put your name on my solid assets—the ones that are sure bets. The less...solid issues will come when you are either up to speed with them or they stop being risky."

"What kind of risky?"

"'Someone showing up and wanting compensation for a deal gone wrong' kind of risky. Or 'the government putting a lien on your assets' kind of risky. I am not always…by the book in my endeavors."

"Heard. Just the gold is fine."

"No." His eyes took on a severe cast. "I want you to be a part of me in every definition of the word. You will take half of my assets or more. You will be the mistress of all my holdings and estates, provided they won't come back and bite you on the ass."

I just nodded. We could fight about that later.

"I probably don't have to tell you so, but with that gold, you can buy this house from the bank. You can do with it as you wish."

I nodded again, needing to process that and wanting to store it away for later.

He nodded back, as though catching that thought, before standing. "Would you like to see what comes next?"

"There's more?" I asked, a little afraid to stand with him.

"Yes."

WE ENTERED THE Underworld at a different place than before, this section actually quite orderly. No walls separated the creatures from one another, and the stalls for trading and commerce were open, the energy calm. I was a little disappointed.

The steps lit up as we started down, and Darius stopped a few steps in, looking back at me.

"What?" I asked.

"You aren't skulking this time. You aren't hiding. You're coming home."

I scanned his expectant face and felt a grin bud.

I dug into the magic around us, deciding to have a bit of fun. The area strobed, disco-style, a couple of times before the stairs lit in flame. I ensured the flame was low heat but high volume, just to look cool.

Darius and I descended hand in hand, like royalty, and I felt like a douche. Still, appearances were important. I needed to put on some sort of show to get a buzz going about my arrival. Or at least to let them know that I had enough arrogance to match Darius. Nearly.

At the bottom, the various creatures gawked before bending. If they didn't bend? I made them. Because I could.

The smile grew on my face.

I knew this. I was comfortable with this. Forcing my hand. Being an ass. I could do this in my sleep and, moreover, it was damn fun. Way more fun than chasing shifters.

Well… Okay, it was fun in a different way. I missed chasing shifters. I wanted another go at Cole. That were-yeti was so fun to infuriate.

The beach before the river was mostly the same, just newer. A few embellishments from when Lucifer or whoever had had to rebuild after our crew's last visit. One exception, though: rose petals littered the ground in a path leading away right.

"Please." Darius gestured me that way, taking my hand again.

We followed the path, and I legit felt like a princess. I'd never much wanted to be a princess, but right then, with Darius by my side, doting on me and enjoying my reactions to each thing he'd obviously planned, I couldn't imagine feeling more special. I felt treasured.

The roses led to a dock, also covered in petals. Within, the boatman was wearing a rose wreath, devoid of thorns. It was very odd, but I didn't comment.

"Hello, your heinous," it said to me, and I wondered who had reprogramed this sucker. "Hello, Darius, most treasured and welcomed guest."

I frowned at Darius.

"Lucifer is making it clear that my station will only be elevated through your good humor," he told me.

"But aren't you guys moving your lair down here?"

"Yes. The details haven't been arranged."

"Ah."

The river journey was just as awful as I remembered, with flat-looking water and little bumps and whorls that signified it was a lie. At least there hadn't been any random splats of water on my head. I didn't know if that had been fixed or I'd gotten lucky.

When we disembarked, Archion was waiting on the other side of the river.

"Hey!" I ran a hand along his leg. "Good to see you again."

Did you say yes? he asked as I hovered Darius and I onto his back.

I did.

Good. That vampire is good in a bind. He'll protect you when I can't.

Why is everyone suddenly worried about protecting me?

It gives us something to do. Otherwise it's just females doing all the work.

I laughed as he lifted into the sky.

"I wonder if vampires can find dragon companions," Darius said as we flew over the kingdom.

I looked down with pleasure, having missed this place. Wanting to get more familiar with it. Wanting to be part of it. What a change from all of the time I'd spent hiding, trying to avoid coming down here.

I passed the question on to Archion.

I have never heard of a vampire bonding a dragon,

but I'm young. I don't see why not. They are tamer than some of the demons that develop a bond.

They are probably more conniving than those demons though, I replied.

I'll speak to Tatsu. She'll know how to go about it.

I probably should've excluded Darius in that comment about vamps, in the spirit of openness, but…it was still true.

Archion landed in front of the castle, and Tits McGee walked out to greet us, followed by a host of attendants.

"Good…time, your heinous," Tits said, its boobs as ridiculous as ever, its voice deep and sonorous. The huge beard was a nice touch, equipped with insects.

Good time? Darius thought.

"Slang is tough for them, but…that one I'm not sure of." I looked at the dawning sky, lighting gradually.

"I was going to say good morning," Tits said, "but I wasn't sure what time it was where you came from. I didn't want to confuse the heinous."

"Ah. Well, I think we're in about the same time zone."

Tits nodded and turned, walking up the steps at a measured pace. I glanced at Darius, and he jerked his chin. I was supposed to follow.

The way through the castle was the same. My floor was the same. The doors to my rooms stood closed and locked with such an intricate weave of fire and ice that it could only have been done by my father. Only the two of us could break it, which meant he'd kept this place for me.

I might've smiled. Or laughed. Maybe cried again. It was really hard to understand the happiness that was drowning me. It was making me very unpredictable.

With some work, I pulled down the spell and kicked in the doors. They slammed against the sides. I grabbed Darius's hand and yanked him in after me, heading to that one window. That view.

Once in front of it, I stopped, winding our fingers together. His shoulder grazed mine.

I took a deep breath and let my gaze roam the beautiful scene.

"This is very you," Darius said softly, once again reading the moment. "There's air now, too."

"I did that when I was here last. My dad obviously chose to leave it."

"Hoping you would return."

"Yes," Lucifer said, and although his voice made me jump a little, his entrance didn't surprise me.

I turned to him, keeping hold of Darius's hand.

"Hey, Pop," I said.

"Hello, Reagan." His gaze dipped to my joined hands with Darius. "You said yes, then?"

"What was your first clue?"

"Hm, him still being alive pretty much cemented it." His gaze cut to Darius. "And that loose thread? Is he still alive?"

"Her previous vampire lover has been extinguished," Darius answered. "By demons, it would seem."

Lucifer tilted back and laughed. "Guilty. My informant"—he put his hand to the side of his mouth—"Ja, obviously… She told me about that whole situation. She's not half as good at intrigue as she seems to think. My new hobby will be fucking with her. Vampires can be horribly arrogant, present company occasionally excluded." He winked at me. "That ex-lover vampire seemed like a sticking point with you, and for no reason, really. I figured I'd just take care of it. What's one more infraction against me, right?"

I couldn't help but chuckle and shake my head. "Yeah, I guess."

"So." Lucifer came to stand beside me, encouraging me to turn and look out at the view. "What's next?"

I took a deep breath and felt utterly confident in what I was about to say.

"I learn how to rule a kingdom, and we make this the best damned kingdom in all the worlds."

Lucifer nodded and then laughed. "Welcome, daughter. Welcome home."

I felt a mix of contentment and excitement wash

over me.

Home. That's exactly what it was. It had taken me a very long journey to find my home, which wasn't a place—it was a feeling. It was *me*. I would buy my family home and fix it up in a way that my mother would've loved, I'd keep my NOLA home for when I wanted a place to crash in my favorite city in the Brink, and I'd learn this new role. This new purpose. I'd find balance, and with Darius and my father on my side, we would indeed make this place the best place to live in all the worlds.

The angels could suck it.

The End.

About the Author

K.F. Breene is a Wall Street Journal, USA Today, Washington Post, Amazon Most Sold Charts and #1 Kindle Store bestselling author of paranormal romance, urban fantasy and fantasy novels. With over four million books sold, when she's not penning stories about magic and what goes bump in the night, she's sipping wine and planning shenanigans. She lives in Northern California with her husband, two children, and out of work treadmill.

Sign up for her newsletter to hear about the latest news and receive free bonus content.

www.kfbreene.com

CPSIA information can be obtained
at www.ICGtesting.com
Printed in the USA
LVHW041645131121
703252LV00004B/143